More deaths than one
FIC BERTRAM

2251?6

39204000020607

Bertram, Pat
Gilpin County Public Library

DATE DUE

FEB 0 2 2010	
FEB 2 5 2010	

Also from Dagger Books
by Pat Bertram

A Spark of Heavenly Fire

More Deaths Than One

By

Pat Bertram

Dagger Books
Published by Second Wind Publishing
Kernersville

Dagger Books
Second Wind Publishing, LLC
931-B South Main Street, Box 145
Kernersville, NC 27284

First Dagger Books edition published December, 2008.
Dagger Books, Running Angel, and all production design are
trademarks of Second Wind Publishing, used under license.

For information regarding bulk purchases of this book,
digital purchase and special discounts, please contact the
publisher at www.secondwindpublishing.com

Cover design by Pat Bertram

Manufactured in the United States of America

ISBN 978-1-935171-25-6

For Jeff

He helped, he listened, he cared.

1.

"What do you think of a guy who embezzles from his own business?"

Bob Stark recognized the voice of the graveyard shift waitress, the attractive one with the black hair. He glanced up from his contemplation of the scars on the laminated plastic table and saw her standing by his booth, gazing at him, her eyebrows quirked. She seemed to expect a response, but he had no idea what to say. And why would she ask him such a question? Though he'd been coming to Rimrock Coffee Shop for four weeks now, she'd never deviated from her standard lines of "What'll you have?" and "Here you go."

He took a surreptitious look around. Except for the two drunks arguing in a corner booth and a cook cleaning the grill in the kitchen, he and the waitress were the only two people in the twenty-four-hour coffee shop.

Beneath the overly long bangs, her dark eyes gleamed, giving him the impression of laughter. "Yes, I am talking to you."

"I'll have hot chocolate," he said, adhering to the unwritten script.

With a flip of her wrist, she brushed the hair off her face. Her skirt flounced as she whirled away from the table, and Bob noticed that she had nicely muscled thighs. Good calves, too. Not wanting her to catch him staring, he picked up a newspaper someone had left behind and leafed through it.

The waitress returned with his beverage. "What would you do if you were a girl who just found out her boyfriend is embezzling from himself?"

Bob stirred his hot chocolate, trying to think of

the right response, but nothing came to mind.

"Men!" she said, hurrying off to answer the ringing telephone.

Later, after the drunks had stumbled out into the night, she came back to Bob's table carrying a cup of coffee for her and another cup of hot chocolate for him.

He raised his palms. "I didn't order this."

She sat across from him. "Let's not quibble over details." She sipped her coffee, eyes laughing at him over the rim of the cup, then set the empty cup aside.

Folding her arms on the table, she leaned forward and stared into his face. "What do you have to say for yourself? And who are you? You've been coming in here every night, real late, and you never talk except to order hot chocolate."

She leaned back. "I bet you can't sleep. That's why you come, isn't it? What's the problem? Bad dreams?"

Bob felt a shudder go through him. He came here to get away from the nightmares, not remember them. He took a gulp of chocolate, grateful for the warmth sliding down his throat.

"You're a shy one," she said. "And you never did answer my question."

He lifted one shoulder in a disinterested shrug. "You asked a lot of questions."

"The one about the girl finding out that her boyfriend is embezzling from himself."

"Depends on their relationship. Is she involved in the business?"

"She helped him start it, works in the office during the day, and waits tables at night to pay the rent."

"Then he's embezzling from her, too."

She flicked the hair out of her eyes. "You're

right. God, what a fool I've been. Ever since I found out he's been cheating on his business, I've been wondering if he's been cheating on me. That son of a rabid dog. He promised we'd get a house together as soon as the business did well enough, and it turns out we could have been living in our own place for several months now."

"Even if he's not cheating on you physically," Bob said, "he's cheating on you morally."

"I want someone who's honest and true to himself, someone who likes and respects himself so he can like and respect me. Is that too much to ask?"

The door opened. A young couple entered. Mouths locked together, they slid into a booth and groped beneath each other's clothes.

The waitress stood. "I better go remind them this isn't a motel."

Grateful to be alone, Bob sipped his hot chocolate and read the newspaper.

The Broncos still reeled from their humiliation at the previous Super Bowl, having lost to the Redskins forty-two to ten.

Two youths found a man's decomposing body in a culvert off the South Platte River. The man had been tortured; the work of a gang, the police surmised.

Silverado faced insolvency, having squandered one hundred million dollars on bad loans.

And Lydia Loretta Stark was dead. Again.

"I brought you another hot chocolate. It's on the house." The young woman sat and peered at Bob. "Is something wrong? You don't look so good all of a sudden."

He tried to ignore the ache inching up the back of his head. "What would you do if you were reading today's paper and came across the obituary of your mother who's been buried for twenty-two years?"

She laughed. "Go to the funeral, of course." She must have realized Bob hadn't meant to be funny, because the mirth faded from her eyes. "You're serious?"

"Dead serious." He showed her the notice.

She read it aloud. "'Lydia Loretta Stark, sixty-six, of Denver, passed away August twenty-ninth, nineteen eighty-eight, at four p.m. Preceded in death by husband Edward Jackson. Survived by sons Edward Jackson, Jr. and Robert; six grandchildren. Services and interment Friday, ten a.m., at Mountain View Cemetery.'" She looked at him. "Are you Edward or Robert?"

"Robert. My brother is Edward, but he goes by the name of Jackson."

"What name do you go by?"

"Bob."

"I'm Kerry. Kerry Casillas." She eyed the obituary. "How many of those children are yours?

Bob massaged the back of his neck. "None."

"Jackson's been a busy boy."

"Seems like it."

"You don't know?"

"I haven't seen him since my mother's funeral—the first one, I mean. We never got along."

She pushed back her hair. "So this is really your mother's obituary?"

"Could be. She died in nineteen sixty-six at the age of forty-four and had no grandchildren at the time, but everything else matches."

"If it's not a coincidence, it must be a hoax."

Bob shook his head, stopping abruptly when pain shot to the top of his skull. "Why would anyone go through all the trouble of putting a fake obituary in the paper? And who's being hoaxed? It can't be me. No one knows I'm in Denver."

On Friday, Bob made the trip to Mountain View Cemetery. He wandered around the lush expanse, skirting formal flower gardens and stepping over white gravestones lying flush with the ground. The place seemed deserted, but as he topped a small rise, he saw a funeral party spread out before him like a stage play.

He paused beside a large clump of lilac bushes and scanned the small crowd encircling the brass-trimmed casket.

Everyone wore black except one young woman, scarcely out of her teens, who had pasted on a skimpy red dress that left no part of her voluptuous figure to the imagination. A much older man had an arm draped around her, his hand cupping her buttocks.

Bob recognized the man: his brother. Jackson had been a good-looking boy, having inherited his father's athletic build and his mother's blond beauty. He still looked good, though Bob could see that too many years of hard living or hard drinking had left their mark.

Bob's headache returned in full force. He closed his eyes and massaged his temples while breathing deeply. When the pain abated, he glanced at the crowd again and noticed two men with the tensed posture of police officers on duty standing off to one side. They seemed familiar, but he couldn't place them. As if becoming aware of his scrutiny, they turned in his direction.

He stepped closer to the lilac bush, out of their line of vision.

Clustered with their backs to him stood a man, a

woman, and six children ranging in age from about two years old to about sixteen. The obituary had mentioned six grandchildren, Bob recalled. Were these six his brother's offspring, by an ex-wife, perhaps?

One of the children, a pudgy little boy, reached out and yanked the pigtails of the taller, skinnier girl slouching next to him. She slapped him. The next moment they were rolling around on the ground and pummeling each other.

The woman turned around. "Stop it, you two."

Bob sucked in his breath. Lorena Jones, his college girlfriend? What was she doing here? How did she know these people? He certainly hadn't introduced her to them.

Feeling dizzy, he studied her while she scolded the children. Deep lines and red splotches marred her once satiny smooth face, and her body appeared bloated, as if she had not bothered to lose the extra weight from her last pregnancy or two. Despite those changes, she looked remarkably like her college picture he still carried in his wallet along with the Dear John letter that had ended their relationship.

Lorena nudged the man next to her. "Robert Stark, don't just stand there. Do something."

The man she called Robert Stark turned around to admonish the children.

Bob stared. The other Robert Stark seemed to have aged a bit faster than he, seemed more used, but the resemblance could not be denied. He was looking at himself.

Head aching so much he could scarcely breathe, he stood like stone. Not even his eyes moved as he watched the rest of the ceremony.

When everyone left, he approached the casket. He gazed at it, then turned to walk away. A flash of white caught his attention—the headstone, lying discreetly off to the side, ready to be inset: Lydia Loretta Stark, cherished wife, beloved mother; adored grandmother; born March 10, 1922; died August 29, 1988.

"What the hell is going on?" he asked aloud.

The mild expletive hung in the air until a sudden breeze blew it away.

2.

Bob set his easel in the backyard and let his fingers decide what to paint. His brain seemed to have disconnected itself from the rest of him while it sorted out the preposterous information it had received that morning at the funeral. Synapses fired as the data hurtled around the neural network of his cerebrum, and he could almost see the sparks of electricity they generated, but he found no answer to the conundrum.

The sound of a gasp brought him out of his trance. He turned around, palette in one hand, brush in the other, and bumped into Ella Barnes, his landlady.

Twisting the skirt of her prim shirtwaist dress in knobby fingers, she stared at the painting, then at him. She disentangled her hands from her skirt, clutched her chest, and hobbled across the yard.

Watching her disappear into the house, he wondered why he frightened her. He shrugged and stepped back to inspect his painting. It looked exactly as he had dreamed it: impenetrable jungle, serene yet menacing, so real he could almost smell the decay and feel the suffocating heat. He shivered. Perhaps the painting radiated too much vileness, but at least he'd transferred the image from his head to the canvas where it could no longer torment him.

When the light faded, he packed his materials, took them inside, and set out for Rimrock Coffee Shop on Colfax Avenue. As he drifted along the street with the rest of the strays, feeling as if he were one more nonentity with only fading memories to show he had ever been real, he saw a man wearing a homemade aluminum foil helmet.

The man accosted one pedestrian after another, but they all dodged him and his shrill proclamation of doom. "Why won't anyone listen to me? Sissy's going to get you. No one is safe. They can get you like they got me."

The man sidled up to Bob. "They're going to get you, too."

Bob nodded. "I think they already have."

Slanting a wide-eyed glance at Bob, the man scuttled away.

At the coffee shop, Bob discovered that Kerry's shift didn't begin until eleven. He ducked out the door and crossed the street to the Golden Pagoda where he'd been taking most of his meals. Picking at his firecracker chicken, he tried to figure out what to tell her. He'd promised to let her know what happened at the funeral, but how could he explain what he didn't understand?

"So?" she said, bringing him his hot chocolate. "Did you go? What did you find out?" She plopped down in the booth and gazed expectantly at him.

After all his careful deliberation, he heard himself blurting it out, like ripping off a bandage.

"I went. According to the headstone, they did bury my mother. My brother attended, and so did I."

She brushed the hair out of her eyes with a quick, impatient gesture. "I know. You told me you went."

He shook his head. "You don't understand. I saw another me there. Another Robert Stark. He looked like me and he seemed to be married to my college girlfriend."

Her eyes sparkled. "Another you? Wow, how did it feel talking to yourself?"

"We didn't talk."

"You didn't talk? Why not? I would have charged up to him and demanded to know why he wore my face."

Bob almost smiled. She probably would have, too. "I didn't have time," he said. He knew the excuse sounded lame, but he didn't want to talk about the headache that had paralyzed him. Unable to think, unable to act, he had watched Robert herd his family away from the gravesite. Then the headache loosened its grip, allowing him to return home and find serenity the way he always did: by painting.

Kerry flicked the hair away from her face again.

"Why do you do that?" Bob asked. "If you don't like your bangs in your eyes, why don't you trim them?"

She lifted a hand as though to touch her hair, then let it drop. "I'd like to, but I can't."

"Do what I do. Get a pair of scissors and whack them off."

"You don't get it. My boss wants me to cut my bangs or wear them pulled back with a barrette. He nags at me all the time about it, so I can't. Don't you see? And anyway, we're supposed to be talking about you and your other self." Her eyes gleamed. "Maybe it's like a story I once read where this guy kept winding up in alternate universes and seeing different versions of himself. Or maybe you're twins separated at birth and adopted out to people with the same last name."

Bob gave her a sour look. "These are not answers."

She folded her arms across her chest. "If you don't like my explanations, what are yours? What do you think is going on?"

"I have absolutely no idea."

"Then we better find out."

He drew back. "We?"

"Sure. I get off at seven, but sometimes I don't

finish my side-work until seven-thirty. How about if I come get you a little before eight?"

"I thought you worked for your boyfriend during the day."

"Not on Saturdays. Where do you live?"

He shook his head, not wanting her help, then decided the idea had merit. Although she wore him out, she had a car and he didn't. If worse came to worst, he could pretend she was another annoying cab driver.

After giving her the address, he said, "Come in through the gate off the alley, and knock on the French doors. The old woman who owns the boardinghouse is nosy, and it's best to try to avoid her."

Her eyes laughed at him. "No one lives in a boardinghouse anymore."

"Well, I do. I'm not going to be in Denver long enough to get an apartment, and I hate hotels."

Yawning, he stood and tossed a couple of dollars on the table. "I've had a rough day. Maybe tonight I can actually sleep for a change."

Bob stepped inside the door and froze. Someone waited for him in the darkness. He couldn't hear a sound, but he had the skin-crawling sensation of being watched.

Thinking Ella was poking among his things again, he sniffed but caught no lingering odor of the cheap perfume she doused herself with.

"Who's there?" he called out.

Getting no response, he flipped on the light. He didn't see anyone, but he could still feel the eyes on him. He looked under the bed, behind the chair, in the closet. No one.

He stood in the center of the room and pivoted slowly.

His gaze fell on the still-drying painting propped on a chair. He sucked in his breath and stared. Someone or something hidden in the fetid jungle looked out at him. He shifted position, thinking it a trick of the light, but the eyes still followed him. Unable to bear the feeling of those eyes on him, he thrust the painting behind the chair with all the others, and crawled into bed.

But not to sleep.

At seven-fifteen in the morning, Bob heard a knock. He hurriedly rinsed off the shaving cream he'd lathered on his face, pulled on a shirt, and went to answer the door.

Kerry smiled at him, looking as bright-eyed as if she'd spent the night sleeping instead of working. She'd changed out of her pink uniform into a white oxford-style shirt over blue jeans.

"You're early," Bob said.

"I know. I got my side-work done before my shift ended, so I came to look around. I've never seen a boardinghouse before. Can I come in? Of course I can."

Bob waited a beat, then stepped aside.

Kerry prowled around his spacious room, stopping to test the easy chair and hassock upholstered in a blue and yellow floral fabric that matched the drapes and bedspread.

She nodded her head. "Nice. Too feminine for my taste, but nice. I especially like the way the French doors lead right out to that big yard."

Bob glanced outside. The tree-shaded yard, with its manicured lawn, pruned rosebushes, neatly trimmed hedges, and tubs overflowing with pink and purple petunias, contrasted sharply with the untamed exuberance of his garden in Bangkok, but it had a sedate serenity he found appealing.

"I like it, too," he said. "It's the main reason I took this place."

Jiggling her keys, she moved toward the door. "I've seen enough. Ready to go?"

"I haven't finished getting cleaned up."

She made shooing motions with her hands. "Go on. Hurry."

When Bob came out of the bathroom, face tingling from his after-shave lotion, he found Kerry sorting through the paintings he had stashed behind the chair.

"What are you doing?"

She glanced up with a saucy smile, apparently not at all put off by his curt tone. "Looking at these paintings. They're very good. Why aren't they hanging on the walls where you can enjoy them?" She pulled out a two-by-three-foot canvas and propped it on the chair where last night the jungle scene had lurked.

Bob peeked at the canvas. The painting depicted a pond with no ripples, surrounded by forest.

"This is lovely." Kerry swayed as she focused on the picture. "Very serene."

All of a sudden, she stiffened and stepped back. She blinked rapidly, then bent forward and peered at the painting. A visible shudder went through her.

"Jeez," she said. "Whoever painted this is either an artistic genius or a very disturbed individual." She reached out as if to touch the painting, but jerked her hand away before it made contact. "You can almost see the monstrous thing that lives in the slime deep at the bottom of the pool."

Bob studied the forest scene. Feeling disquiet creep over him, he averted his gaze.

"Who painted it?" Kerry asked.

He hesitated. "I did."

She whipped her head around and stared at him. "Jeez, Bob. What the hell were you thinking?"

Stealing a look at his creation, Bob shivered.

"I tried to paint what's in here," he said, tapping his chest with a fist. He gestured to the picture. "I don't know how that happened."

"Are you a famous artist or something? I think I've seen a picture like this before. In a magazine, maybe."

Bob shrugged.

"Well, are you?" she asked.

"I don't know."

Putting her hands on her hips, she narrowed her eyes at him.

"It's the truth." He strode to the bedside table, retrieved a letter he had received before he left Thailand, and read aloud. "'Dear Mr. Stark: Mr. Ling Hsiang-li has informed us he will no longer be acting as your agent and that we must now deal directly with you. There is a growing regard for your work. We are interested in enough paintings for a showing, which would include an evening with the artist. Please contact us at your earliest convenience.'"

Bob set aside the letter. "It's from a New York art gallery. Now you know as much as I do."

"So what's the deal?" she asked. "Who's Ling Hsiang-li?"

"My mentor. A man who was more than a father to me."

"But you didn't know he sold your paintings?"

"Not really. I once mentioned that I painted one picture over another because nothing I did was any good, and he said, 'You're just an artist. How would you know what's good? Bring them to me and let me be

the judge.' When I protested that they all had a terrible
flaw, a hidden evil, he responded, 'That flaw, as you
call it, is what makes you an artist.'"

"He's right," Kerry said.

Bob hunched his shoulders. "Maybe so, but I
don't have to like it." He forced himself to relax.
"Occasionally, Hsiang-li would hand me a wad of cash
and announce he had sold another painting, but until I
got that letter, I never knew if in fact he'd sold a
painting or if the money was his way of encouraging
me."

Seeing more questions forming in Kerry's eyes
and on her lips, Bob said quickly, "We should go."

"Go? Oh, right. I can't believe I forgot about the
other you."

"It looks like a park," Kerry said, pulling up to
the gates of Mountain View Cemetery. She got out of
her blue Toyota Corolla. "Where's your mother
buried?"

Bob led the way to the newly sodded gravesite.
The headstone read the same today as it had yesterday.

Kerry bent and traced the grooves of the date.
"Don't you think it's strange that the headstone is in
place? When my grandmother died, we didn't get the
stone for months."

"Knowing my mother, she probably picked it
out herself years ago and had all the engraving done
except for the date. She always prided herself on her
foresight and preparations. Like buying side-by-side
plots for her and my father."

Kerry stepped over to the next stone and gazed
at it. "It must be terrible losing both parents."

"I've had plenty of time to come to terms with
their deaths." Twenty-four years before, he had stood in

this very spot with his mother, his brother, and a whole phalanx of cops, attending his father's funeral. His mother hadn't abandoned her grief when she had died of cancer and been buried next to her husband. Whether that death had occurred twenty-two years ago or recently, she was definitely dead now.

Bob turned away and made for the car. Kerry hurried after him.

They found Robert Stark's address in the phone book. Kerry drove to the house on Ironton Street off Eleventh Avenue in Aurora and parked across from the faded yellow bungalow.

"Now what?" she asked.

"You tell me," Bob said. "This was your idea."

She fixed her laughing eyes on him, apparently amused by his touch of asperity. "We go talk to him."

"And say what? That he stole my life?" A shaft of pain stabbed Bob behind the eyes. He stifled a gasp. "Maybe another time. Let's keep watch for now. See what we can learn." The headache diminished. He opened his window and listened to the sounds emanating from Robert's house. Doors slamming. Feet thudding. The television squawking. Children shouting, laughing, whining, sobbing. Lorena yelling.

"My God," Kerry said. "It is you."

Then Bob saw him—an unimpressive man dressed in a dingy white short-sleeved shirt, a mud-colored tie, and gray gabardine pants, trudging down his toy-strewn driveway to the ancient, wood-sided station wagon parked in front of the house.

The man, Robert, climbed into the vehicle and took off. With a screech of tires, Kerry made a U-turn and hurtled after him, braking abruptly when she caught up to the slow-moving station wagon.

They followed the station wagon along Havana Street to a shopping mall called Buckingham Square where Robert entered a computer store. He went through a door at the back, came out a minute later and half-heartedly cleaned the counter and straightened merchandise on the shelves.

A young, expensively dressed woman, who looked about Kerry's age—twenty-six or twenty-seven—marched into the store.

Bob, standing outside the door, pretending to chat with Kerry, heard Robert ask diffidently, "May I help you?"

The woman moved away from him. "Just looking."

Robert made no effort to follow her.

A young man immediately approached the woman. He was dressed like Robert, but his shirt was snowy white, his pants sharply creased, his tie bright. Seemingly unconcerned by the woman's lack of interest in his patter, the young man continued to pursue her.

An older couple hesitantly entered the store, and Robert went to wait on them.

Bob drifted away from the door.

Kerry trailed him. "I thought this would be fun."

"It never is."

She blinked. "You've done this before?"

"Yes."

A brief silence, then, "You feel no need to explain that remark?"

"No."

As Bob continued to watch his other self, he could feel Kerry's eyes on him.

"Do you know why you interest me?" she said at last.

He glanced at her, wondering if she were setting

him up for a joke. "I haven't a clue."

"I'd like to say it's because you have hidden depths, but your depths aren't hidden, they're obvious." She chuckled. "Maybe you have hidden shallows."

The corners of his mouth twitched.

She drew back in mock surprise. "Is that a smile I see?"

A few minutes later, she yawned. "Jeez, I'm tired."

"You should go home and get some sleep," Bob said, "but if you don't mind, I'd like to make a call first."

She swept her arm out in a magnanimous gesture. "Go ahead. I'll keep watch."

He found a pay phone and called the computer store. A woman answered.

"How late does Robert Stark work today?" he asked.

"Six o'clock."

"Thanks."

When Bob returned to his post, he noted with amusement that Kerry had situated herself so she could see both the computer store and a dress shop.

She pointed to the window displaying new fall fashions. "Which is my color, blue or red?"

"Deep rose," he said without hesitation.

She wrinkled her nose. "Pink?"

"Not pink. Deep rose. Bold, direct, courageous, but without the strident aggressiveness of red."

Her eyes sparkled, but for once they were not laughing as she regarded him.

Then the laughter returned. "It appears that your hidden shallows have hidden shallows of their own."

A tall, skinny man with a receding hairline and a prominent Adam's apple approached Bob. "Hey, Hank, how've you been? I haven't seen you for a long time. You living in Denver now?"

Bob nodded.

The man moved away, walking backward. He shot both index fingers at Bob. "Call me. I'm in the book. We'll get together."

Bob glanced at Kerry. She stared back at him, open-mouthed.

"That man called you Hank." She whacked herself on the forehead with the palm of her right hand. "God, I'm so stupid when it comes to men. This whole thing has been one big set-up, hasn't it? You've been messing with me."

"No, I haven't," Bob said quietly. "He mistook me for someone else. That's always happening to me, and it's easier to go along than to explain that I'm Robert Stark."

The angry flush faded from her cheeks. "You do have one of those faces. Even I thought you might be somebody I knew when I first saw you."

A huge yawn overtook her. Knuckling her eyes, she said, "You're right, I do need to get some sleep."

"I'll be here until six. Do you want to pick me up, or should I call a cab?"

"I'll come back." She smiled happily, but Bob could not tell if the tacit permission to leave pleased her, or the invitation to return.

That evening when Bob saw Kerry stop in front of the computer store and look around, he stepped out from behind a group of people.

Her eyes widened. "Hey, cool. You're good at this stuff. I never even saw you."

Bob continued to watch Robert. Kerry chattered about everyone who passed by, seemingly unconcerned that she carried on a one-sided conversation.

Promptly at six o'clock, Robert limped out of the store.

"Why is he limping?" Kerry asked. "You don't limp."

"Maybe he's tired."

They followed Robert back to his house. From where they were parked a few car lengths back, Bob could hear someone inside the house call out, "Daddy's home."

The front door burst open, and Robert's children came tumbling out to greet him. Beaming, Robert picked up one small, giggling girl and planted a big kiss on her chubby cheek. A shy little boy slipped a hand into his father's and gazed at him as if he were every super hero rolled into one. Even though all the children talked at once, Robert seemed to have no trouble keeping track of everything they said, and answered each in turn.

"I thought of another explanation," Kerry announced. "You could be doppelgangers. A doppelganger is the ghost of a living person."

"If we are," Bob said, watching the other Robert Stark, "then which of us is the living person, and which of us is the ghost?"

3.

The gingerbread-trimmed boardinghouse stood second from the corner on a quiet side street off Seventeenth Avenue. While waiting for a bus after a quick breakfast of granola and orange juice prepared in the communal kitchen, Bob looked across Seventeenth Avenue at City Park. The sun shone. The warm air smelled of mowed grass. Perhaps he should walk to his childhood home on Twenty-Second Avenue.

No. Better to save his energy for exploring the old neighborhood.

Two hours later Bob made the return trip on foot, tired, breathless, feeling out of place and out of time.

Very little of what he had observed seemed familiar. The wide empty streets where he had once played appeared narrow and inhospitable. Like spectators at a parade, parked cars lined both sides of the street while a steady stream of traffic made its way between them. The red brick house where he grew up had been painted white and looked smaller than he remembered. He did have a vague recollection of the four large pillars supporting the flat roof of the porch, but he did not remember the ornate carvings encircling them. Nor could he recall which room had been his, which window Jackson had broken and blamed on him, which tree he had climbed to escape his father's wrath.

How could he have forgotten so much? Maybe because he hadn't given a single thought to his childhood during the past eighteen years?

He trudged through City Park, which he did remember, and tried not to listen to the voice in the back of his head suggesting that perhaps all parks bore a decided similarity.

A flash of yellow on a bird's wing caught his gaze. Stopping to watch the bird until it flew out of sight, he became aware of the day's blinding brightness. The grass shimmered in the sun like green fire. The sky reflected a blue so deep it looked purple: the color of infinity, he thought.

All of a sudden, a sharp pain exploded behind his eyes. The sky turned black. He stumbled, fell to his knees. Cradling his head in his hands, he rocked back and forth. He tried to suck in air, but his lungs seemed to have forgotten how to work.

Over the sound of the blood throbbing against his eardrums, he heard the voice of a little girl.

"Mommy, what's wrong with that man?"

A loud sniff. "Probably drunk or stoned. Come on, let's get away from here."

Gradually Bob's vision cleared and his lungs started to function again. He took several shallow breaths, then deeper ones. The pain receded to the back of his head.

He struggled to his feet and dragged himself back to the boarding house. Collapsing on his bed, he waited for the oblivion of sleep.

But with sleep came the nightmares.

The next morning Bob took a cab to the Veterans Administration Hospital in Aurora. After an enormous amount of red tape and hours of waiting, he found himself in a room containing both an examining table and a small metal desk with a computer. Convenience? Bob wondered. Or a chronic shortage of space?

The doctor, a gray-haired man in his late fifties, marched in thirty minutes later.

"Dr. Albion," he said with a curt nod.

Although Dr. Albion had the barking voice and commanding presence of a general, he did not have the posture; his shoulders sagged as if all the ineptitude throughout all his years of service weighed them down.

Dr. Albion seated himself at the desk, shuffled through some papers, then glanced at Bob. "Robert Stark?"

"Yes."

The doctor steepled his hands and tapped the tips of his fingers together. "What seems to be the problem?"

"Headaches, nightmares, disorientation."

"When did you first notice these symptoms?"

"Vietnam. I had a mishap with a mine." Bob paused, remembering how he'd awakened in a hospital in the Philippines, feeling much as he did now, and being told he'd been unconscious for five days. That had been disorienting, but nowhere near as disorienting as discovering a twice-dead mother and another self. Realizing the doctor had impatiently cleared his throat, Bob said, "The symptoms mostly disappeared until about three weeks ago."

"Did you experience any change in your circumstances at that time?"

"I returned to the United States. I've been gone for eighteen years, two in Vietnam, the other sixteen in Thailand."

"You never came home for a visit?"

"No."

Dr. Albion consulted the form Bob had filled out in the admitting room, punched up something on the computer screen, and glanced at it.

He rose to his feet. "Let's take a look at you."

He listened to Bob's heart, then gestured toward

the scars crisscrossing his chest. "The mine?"

"A hunting accident when I was young."

The doctor finished his cursory examination and returned to the computer. After a moment, he looked from the screen to Bob's feet.

"This is strange. It says here you lost your left foot and now use a prosthesis. I couldn't have missed that, could I?"

"No," Bob said absently, his mind on the other Robert Stark who limped when he got tired. Could Kerry's preposterous notion about alternate universes be correct? Could the explosion have created a divergence, causing him to travel two different but simultaneous paths of probability? The thought made his headache flare.

Dr. Albion turned back to the computer. "There's no mention here of a head trauma, or of the cicatrices on your chest." Heaving a sigh, he pushed away from the computer and leaned back. "These records have your name, serial number, and social security number on them, but apparently they're mixed with someone else's. Unfortunately, that does happen. We'll be doing tests—blood, urine, and so on—and the results should be here in a week, but you never know. As usual, we're short-staffed and overworked. Hopefully, your medical record situation will be straightened out by then." His expression clearly said he doubted it.

"I can prescribe a moderate painkiller for your headaches, but I need to find out more about your head trauma before I decide on a course of treatment. Meantime, you might want to check in with some of the Vietnam vet support groups in the area." He reached into a drawer, pulled out a list, and handed it to Bob. "It's entirely possible your symptoms are due to something called Post-Traumatic Stress Syndrome. You've heard of that?"

"Yes," Bob said. "But it's been sixteen years since I got out of the army. Why would I get it now?"

"I'm thinking it could have something to do with your belated return home, combined with culture shock, possibly complicated by the high altitude."

Scanning the list, Bob noticed he had a choice of groups on any given day. He felt too tired to go to one tonight, but perhaps tomorrow evening he might drop in on the group that met in the basement of a church not far from the boardinghouse.

Bob stood in the open doorway, surprised to see so few men in the group: not quite a dozen. They all seemed to be in their late thirties to early forties, and most of them looked prosperous.

"My wife's an archeologist," a large man with a thin mustache said. "She's never forgiven me for blowing up the Mi Son tower."

A man with deep crinkles around his eyes spoke in what sounded like an Australian accent. "Didn't you explain to her that the NVA used it as an arms dump and a radio tower?"

"Of course I did, many times, but she refuses to see reason. She says that except for some minor damage at Angkor in Cambodia, no other archeological monument ever sustained war damage. She thinks blowing up the tower was the worst atrocity of Vietnam."

"Doesn't even rank in the top ten," exclaimed a dark-skinned man who looked like an athlete past his prime. "The massacre at Hue was by far the . . ."

Bob turned to leave. The painkillers didn't seem to be working, and it felt as if a ball bearing caromed around in his head. Before he could escape, a pleasant-faced man with thinning auburn hair approached him. Like Bob, he wore chinos and a white shirt.

He smiled at Bob as if they were old friends, and extended a hand. His grasp felt firm but without challenge.

"I'm Scott Mulligan."

Bob hesitated. When he realized Scott had not mistaken him for someone else, but simply acted open and friendly, he introduced himself.

"Nice to meet you," Scott said, sounding as if he meant it. "This group can seem a bit intimidating at first. Over the years it's evolved into something of a little boys club for history buffs." He cocked his head and raised his eyebrows. "What do you say, Bob? Since you're already here, why don't you come in for a few minutes? Have a cup of coffee. It's good coffee. I promise. I made it myself."

Bob let himself be drawn forward. To his relief, Scott did not make an issue of his presence, but poured him a thick white mug of coffee and ushered him to a chair slightly behind the haphazardly formed circle.

Hands wrapped around the mug, soaking in the warmth, Bob shot covert glances at the group. Combat veterans like these had begun making pilgrimages to Thailand where many had gone for R&R. Although strangers, the veterans always seemed to recognize one another, as if their sojourn in country had left a readily identifiable brand on each of their foreheads. They drank together and often discussed experiences they had never been able to talk about before.

Bob had mostly avoided those discussions. Despite his injury, he had not seen combat. He had been stationed in relatively safe Saigon until he received orders to accompany a convoy of supply trucks headed for Qui Nhon. En route, his truck hit a mine.

Listening to the discussion lapping against him, Bob felt a sudden twinge of unbelonging. Only Scott's encouraging smile kept him in his seat.

A high voice rose even higher in anger. "My kid came home from school the other day and told me we lost the war in Vietnam because the American military did not know jungle warfare."

"Horseshit," the archeologist's husband said. "We didn't lose. We left. And it wasn't a war. We were supposed to be there, a presence, until the people who make those kinds of decisions got what they wanted. Like in Korea."

The man with the high voice made balloons of his cheeks, then blew out the air. "I tried telling that to my kid, but he wouldn't believe me. I hate to think what other crap they're teaching him."

Bob set his still full cup of coffee on the chair and left the building. He stood in the shadow of the old stone church, breathing deeply. The cooling air had an earthy smell, like mushrooms.

Scott joined him. "Are you all right? You look green around the gills."

"I'm fine."

Scott gave him a dubious glance, then gestured toward the door they'd exited. "I guess you didn't expect that. If you want, I can put you in touch with other groups that are more into healing than history, ones that will actually let you air your problems."

Bob watched a single brown leaf falling from a nearby oak tree. "I'm not much of a joiner."

"Well, if you ever need anyone to talk to, I'd be willing to listen. I'm in the phone book, or you can check here at the church."

"Are you a minister?"

Scott laughed. "No. I help when I can—mow the grass, supervise various activities, whatever needs doing. I believe belonging to a church extends beyond Sunday attendance." He peered at Bob. "You don't look very good. Maybe you should come back inside."

Bob felt himself warming to this genial man, but he didn't want to hear any more talk of the war. As he tried to pluck polite words of refusal out of his aching head, he heard the sound of voices coming nearer and the clump of many pairs of shoes.

"The meeting must be ending early," Scott said. "My family will be pleased. They're waiting for me. This is Monopoly night. What about you? Do you have family?"

Bob shook his head. He hadn't considered Jackson family for a long time now, and he doubted the other Robert Stark qualified.

"Friends?" Scott queried.

"Not here in Denver."

"Are you new to the area?"

"Yes and no." To his surprise, Bob found himself explaining he'd grown up in Denver, but had spent the past eighteen years in Southeast Asia.

"Welcome home, Bob," Scott said with a smile. "Tell you what. Why don't you come to my house for dinner tomorrow evening. Say, six o'clock? You'll like my family. They're nice people."

Bob shifted his weight to one foot, preparing to leave. "I wouldn't want to impose."

"No imposition. We'd love to have you. My wife enjoys fussing over company. Besides, you'd be doing me a favor. My children have never met anyone who's lived in Thailand. It would be good to broaden their horizons."

Bob finally agreed. Tucking Scott's address into

his pocket, he headed for the car he had purchased earlier that day, and drove to the Golden Pagoda for dinner.

Bob dreamed he wandered in the jungle. A numb, helpless feeling permeated his body as he pushed against foliage too dense to allow passage. He could feel menace all around him, but it was nebulous, without form or reason. He let out a wordless cry. No one heard.

When he awoke, his heart pounded, his lungs heaved, his head throbbed. He stared wildly about him.

Wide-awake now, he remembered who he was, where he was. He sat up and buried his face in his hands until his heartbeat slowed and his breathing returned to normal.

He rose from the bed, pulled on his clothes, and slipped out into the predawn world.

"Do I know you?"

Bob glanced at Kerry, wondering what game she played now. "I'm the hot chocolate."

Her eyes brightened. "That's what I thought, but I didn't know for sure if you were you or your other self."

She hurried off in answer to the imperial summons of a business-suited woman with a pinched face, but returned a few minutes later with Bob's drink.

Setting the cup in front of him, she asked, "What have I missed?"

"Nothing. I've been busy and haven't been able to check on the other Robert Stark, and anyway, it's hard to tail someone if your transportation is buses and cabs. But I bought a car, so we'll see."

"What color?"

"Originally? Blue. Now it's so faded it looks gray."

Laughter sparked in her eyes. "You bought a junker. Why am I not surprised? What kind?"

"A 1969 Volkswagen bug. It runs well and cost three hundred dollars." Since he hadn't driven for many years, he'd had a hard time finding his rhythm, but he saw no reason to mention that.

She flicked back her hair. "You're not big on commitment, are you? You won't even commit to an apartment or a real car."

A ragged old man smelling of whiskey and urine entered the restaurant, sat on a stool, and carefully laid a few coins on the counter. Kerry poured him a cup of coffee, refilled the woman's cup, then paused by Bob's table, still clutching the pot.

"What about you and the cheat?" he asked.

She smoothed her apron with her free hand. "I have some more thinking to do on that, so for now I'm still peddling porches."

He gave her a quizzical glance.

"Didn't I tell you? I guess not. He owns a construction company that builds porches and decks. Calls it Pete's Porches."

She left, refilled the cups of the three or four other customers, made a new pot of coffee, then stopped at Bob's table once more.

The pressure in his head started to build. He rubbed his throbbing temples with two fingers of each hand.

"Headache?" she asked sympathetically. "Do you want an aspirin?"

"No, that's all right. It comes and goes."

She chewed on her lower lip, watching him with narrow-eyed concentration. "A couple of times I've seen you leaving the Chinese restaurant across the street. Do you eat over there a lot?"

"Most days."

"Well, no wonder you have a headache. All that MSG."

Bob blinked. "I'd forgotten about that. A long time ago, Robert Dunbar told me he loved Chinese food but could never eat it stateside because of all the additives, which gave him a headache. He said that since we made the food at The Lotus Room from scratch, using fresh and natural ingredients, he could indulge himself. I guess I need to cook my own meals. Where can I find Chinatown?"

She shot him a perplexed look. "You mean like in San Francisco?"

"I mean here in Denver. Don't all major cities have a Chinatown?"

"Not us. The Asians here have been mostly assimilated into the community, but there is a shopping center over on Alameda where you can find all sorts of special Chinese products. Why the insistence on Chinese food?"

"It's what I'm used to."

She laughed. "Why, are you from China?"

"Close. Thailand. I've been living in Bangkok awhile."

She gaped at him, then broke out into a smile, her eyes dancing. "Your shallows seem to be growing ever deeper. What's it like living in a foreign country? What's The Lotus Room? Is that where you worked? And who's Robert Dunbar?"

Bob deliberated a moment and answered the last question first. "Dunbar is an electronics engineer who works for Data Management Systems, a corporation based here in Colorado. He has the same fake chummy manner as the salesman at Lemons R Us where I bought my car, and he makes much of the fact that we share the same first name."

"As if that means anything," Kerry said. "There must be millions of Bobs in the world. Where did you meet him?"

"At The Lotus Room shortly after I started working there. He always tried to get me to go golfing with him at Bangphra on the Gulf of Siam. According to him, it has one of the longest, most beautiful, and most challenging golf courses in the world. You'd think he owned stock in the place the way he rhapsodized about it."

"Did you ever go?"

"No. I'm not fond of golfing." Nor of Dunbar, he almost added, but caught himself in time. He'd have to be careful around this young woman; she had a way of disarming him so that he imparted more than he intended.

"I don't like golf either. Not enough action. But I don't think I'd mind it so much if I could play somewhere exotic like Thailand." She flipped her hair out of her eyes. "I never associated Thailand with golf. I've only heard about it in relation to sex and sin."

"For the most part, Bangkok is a city of devout Buddhists. Patpong Road, the infamous red light district, is two and a half blocks long, but more than eight hundred ornate wats—temple/monastery compounds dedicated to Buddha and the study of his teachings—dominate the city. I used to go running early during the cool time, and sometimes it seemed as if no one but the saffron-robed monks with their shaved heads and bare feet shared the dawn with me."

She gazed at him, a rapt expression on her face. "I always wanted to travel. I come from Chalcedony, a small town on the western slope. It's a decent place, and I had a happy childhood, but I need more than Chalcedony can provide." She smiled ruefully. "I wanted the world, the whole broad picture, and I got Denver and Pete's Porches."

She fell silent. For a moment she left her face unguarded, and Bob could see how her problems with Pete ate at her. Then the eagerness returned to her eyes.

"What did you do at The Lotus Room?"

"I acted as manager, but I never had a title. I did everything from purchasing supplies to waiting tables and tending bar. Sometimes I cooked, if you could call it that. My awkward attempts at stir-frying afforded Wu Shih-kai great amusement."

"Was Wu Shih-kai the owner?"

"Hsiang-li owned the place. Wu Shih-kai was the cook, a wrinkled and withered ancient who appeared frail and unsteady until he went into the kitchen, and then he became a wizard, moving from pot to pot, refining his magic potions."

"It sounds like you loved Thailand," Kerry said wistfully.

"I did. Beneath the veneer of congested traffic and commerce is a city of great splendor. I felt at peace there."

"Why did you leave?"

Bob pressed his lips together and turned away. After a moment he said, "I lost my work visa."

"I'm sorry you had to leave Thailand, but I'm glad I got to meet you. You're different."

"So I've been told."

She laughed. "You have to admit, not many people have another self running around. I read something yesterday that made me think of you. It's from a poem by Oscar Wilde. 'And the wild regrets and the bloody sweats,/ None knew so well as I:/ For he who lives more lives than one/ More deaths than one must die.'"

Bob felt a shiver creep up his spine, but he tried to keep his tone light. "Dying more than once seems to run in my family."

4.

Kerry left to seat a party of boisterous drunks. Bob huddled in the booth with the Oscar Wilde poem hanging over him like his own personal storm cloud. When she turned and tossed him a sunny smile, the cloud dissipated, but he regarded her warily. What was she up to now? It seemed as if every time she went off to serve someone else, she got another of her notions.

Finished waiting on the drunks, she plopped down opposite Bob. "I get off work at eight. Meet me here."

"Why?"

"So we can go check on your other self. On your own, you don't seem to be able to get anything done. You're like a compass without a pointer. You lack direction."

"And you're going to be the pointer?"

She beamed at him. "Exactly."

At eight-thirty, they parked across the street from Robert Stark's house. Kerry sat behind the wheel of Bob's ancient VW, though he had no clear idea how that happened.

"Your talents are certainly being wasted in the diner," he said. "You should be in a boardroom somewhere keeping the other board members in line."

Her eyes lit up but darkened immediately. "We missed him. The station wagon's not here. Now what?"

"We wait."

"I don't believe in waiting."

He didn't remind her that she had invited herself, but merely said, "Waiting and patience are a big part of surveillance."

"So how long do we have to wait?"

"I don't know. We just got here."

"Look, there it is."

Bob turned to follow her finger. The station wagon raced down the street to the Stark house. It pulled into the driveway without any discernable lessening of speed, and stopped abruptly. Lorena jumped out. She wore a shapeless sweat suit and bunny slippers, and her hair looked uncombed.

"Is that Lorena?" Kerry asked, craning her neck.

"Yes. Probably took the kids to school."

He saw nothing else of interest until Robert came out an hour and a half later, climbed into the vehicle, and drove to Buckingham Square.

After watching him work for an hour, Kerry sighed. "He's not going anywhere. Since we're at the mall, I'd like to do some shopping. Coming?"

Bob glanced once more at Robert, who fiddled with a computer by himself, then followed her to a drugstore.

"Look!" she exclaimed, grabbing a paperback off a display by the counter. "A new novel by William Henry Harrison. Are you familiar with him?"

"Yes."

"I've read all his books. I didn't think there would ever be another one. This is great." She thrust the book into his hands, then darted down a nearby aisle and grabbed two boxes of hair dye.

When he caught up to her, she said, "I need a change." She raised first one box to her face, then the other, and looked at him expectantly. "Would you like me better as a redhead or a blond?"

It seemed a strangely intimate moment, as if they were husband and wife, or at least friends of long standing, and he found himself unable to speak.

"Well?" she said.

"It's never been established I like you at all."

"Of course you do." She laughed. "You find me annoying, but you still like me."

"If you say so." And he did like her. Somehow she made his bizarre plight seem normal, as if having a duplicate self were simply an interesting personality quirk.

"Ouch. I bet that hurt."

He wondered what she meant, then realized he was smiling.

"So which?" she asked. "Blonde or red?"

"Neither." He reached out to touch her hair. Remembering that she had a boyfriend, he let his hand drop. "I like your natural color. Sometimes it's a true black, but other times you have red highlights, as if your banked inner fires are glowing through."

She stared at him for a second, then slowly replaced the boxes.

"Do you mind if we go?" Kerry asked at four o'clock. "We aren't learning anything, and Pete and I have plans for this evening."

Not yet ready to leave, Bob decided to call a cab for her but changed his mind when he remembered Scott's invitation to dinner. It would be rude to cancel now, especially if the man's wife had gone to a lot of trouble. Besides, Kerry spoke the truth; they weren't learning anything.

"Okay, let's go." As they walked to the car, laden with Kerry's purchases, he said, "You did a good job today."

She rewarded him with a pleased but tired smile.

Scott Mulligan welcomed Bob warmly and

ushered him into a homey living room filled with well-worn furniture and floor to ceiling bookshelves, where a woman, a boy, and a girl waited. Like Scott, they were nice looking with open faces and they dressed modestly.

Scott gestured to the woman. "This is my beautiful wife, Rose."

Rose blushed becomingly, and for a second she did look beautiful. Her best feature was her shiny dark brown hair.

Scott gestured to the girl. About eleven years old, she looked like a younger version of her mother. "This is my gorgeous daughter, Beth."

Beth giggled. "Oh, Daddy."

"And that's Jimmy." Scott pointed to the sturdy, bright-eyed boy, who appeared to be about two years older than his sister. Both father and son had square, blunt-nosed faces, and unruly auburn cowlicks.

Rose held out a hand. "Please sit."

Bob perched on the edge of a dark green upholstered chair.

"We're glad you came," Rose said. "Scott mentioned you've recently returned home. I don't imagine there's a lot you remember. Denver's changed so much in the past eighteen years."

Bob shifted his weight. "I've noticed."

"At least we've been having nice weather, all these dry, sunny days, but then maybe you prefer rain?"

"I don't know if I prefer it so much as I'm used to it."

Rose nodded. "A person can get used to anything, I suppose, but I think it would be difficult to learn to live in an entirely different environment. Was it your experiences in Vietnam that prevented you from coming home?"

Bob glanced from Rose's sympathetic face to Scott's interested one and wondered if he had made a mistake in coming here. They seemed pleasant, and he'd sensed an affinity with Scott, but he didn't enjoy talking about himself, especially not to strangers.

He gave a mental shrug. It was a trivial matter after all. "No, nothing like that. Someone offered me a job, and . . . well, the years passed."

Scott spread his arms along the back of the green couch, which did not match the upholstered chair, and stretched out his legs. "What's your line of work, Bob?"

"The restaurant business."

"Ah, the food service industry." A calculating look crossed Scott's face. "Let me know if you have any free time. My church runs a soup kitchen. We can always use the help."

"Don't let him bulldoze you, Bob," Rose said. "He's as sweet as can be until he gets his mind set on something, then watch out."

Scott laughed. "I don't know what's worse, being misunderstood or being understood."

Rose smiled at him then turned to Bob. "Excuse us. We have to set the table." Gathering her children, she herded them into the dining room.

Bob leaned back in the chair and listened to the domestic sounds of children laughing and utensils clinking. "I've heard that Vietnam vets had a rough time of it when they returned home."

"Many did. We'd all been raised on World War Two movies, and somehow we got it into our heads we'd get the same reception as the soldiers in the movies did, but everyone treated us like pariahs. Now that they're making Vietnam movies, we're becoming part of the country's mythology, so people aren't treating us with quite so much disdain, but we had it rough for a while. I was lucky. I have Rose, I have my children, and I have my work."

"What do you do?"

"I'm an administrator of a literary foundation that runs a private bookmobile service for shut-ins and supplies books for nursing homes, hospitals, and hospices."

Rose reentered the room. "And every weekend he finds time to read to the elderly who can no longer read to themselves."

Scott made a dismissive gesture. "Well, so do you and Beth and Jimmy."

"Are you ready to eat?" Rose asked. "Dinner's on the table."

After everyone gathered at the table, said grace, and passed the food around, Rose asked about Thailand. She listened so intently that Bob found himself talking about his fascination with Bangkok, a city with no downtown, no neighborhoods, just a sprawling conglomeration of buildings with architectural marvels tucked in the most unexpected places. He told about the gibbons, the family pet of choice, about the weekend market at the beautiful tree-lined Phramane Grounds, and about the Thai kickboxing matches he had attended.

"Did you find much difference between Vietnam and Thailand?" Scott asked.

"I didn't see many similarities except perhaps for the weather at certain times of the year. Vietnam had a strong French influence. Many of the places seemed like they belonged more on the French Riviera than in a country at war. Thailand, on the other hand, is unique. During most of its history, the Thais were left alone to develop their own culture without outside influences. Thai architecture, for example, has no equal. It is stunningly beautiful—a perfect balance between simple, harmonious lines and intricate ornamentation."

"You speak like an artist," Rose said.

Bob took a bite of food and chewed it slowly.

Rose gasped. "How terrible of us. We've kept you talking so much we haven't given you a chance to eat."

While Bob finished his delicious dinner of roast beef, stuffed baked potatoes, mixed vegetables, and made-from-scratch dinner rolls, Beth and Jimmy tried to top each other with family stories that seemed to have been told and retold so many times they sounded folkloric: how Scott had fallen into City Park Lake, how Beth had dyed herself blue, how Jimmy had gotten sick from eating poisonous berries.

After Beth and Jimmy cleared off the table, Rose brought in a heaping plateful of homemade oatmeal raisin cookies, along with tea for the adults and lemonade for the children.

Stuffing a cookie in his mouth, Jimmy announced, "We're building a greenhouse in the back-yard."

"Don't talk with your mouth full," Rose said, but it seemed an automatic response. Bob heard no censure in her voice.

"So we can have a garden all year," Beth explained.

Scott took a sip of his tea. "I wanted a project the whole family could get involved with, and a greenhouse seemed as good as anything."

Jimmy grabbed another cookie. "Better. When it's done we can grow strawberries and tomatoes and corn."

"And toads," Beth added.

"You don't grow toads in a garden, silly," Jimmy said.

"Do too."

"And anyway, girls aren't supposed to like toads."

"I do. Toads and lizards and snakes."

When everyone finished eating, Scott complimented his wife on the meal and stood. Beth and Jimmy jumped to their feet and took off running, as if a school dismissal bell had been rung.

"Don't forget you still have the dishes to do," Rose called after them. "And homework."

Scott led the way into the living room.

"You have nice children," Bob commented.

Rose inclined her head. "Thank you."

"They grow so quickly," Scott said with a catch in his voice. "Before we know it, they'll have families of their own." He opened a photograph album and showed Bob pictures of his family.

As Scott turned the pages, Bob could see the young ones growing from babyhood to toddlerhood to childhood, and Rose growing more settled and serene. He wondered what it would be like to be part of a loving family such as theirs; then it occurred to him that if he had returned to Denver after Vietnam, perhaps he would have been the one to marry Lorena, and he would know.

But who would he be—Robert the computer salesperson, Bob the artist, or an entirely different Robert Stark altogether?

5.

The ample-bodied woman sitting behind the admitting desk at the VA hospital scowled at Bob. "How many times do I have to tell you? You cannot see Dr. Albion. Take a seat, and Dr. Montgomery will be with you as soon as he is able."

"But I need to talk to Dr. Albion," Bob said.

The woman pointed a stubby finger at him. "If you don't do as you're told, you won't be talking to anyone."

Bob waited. When the woman became involved with another hapless individual, he stepped from the crowd at the desk to a cluster of nurses and patients passing into the hallway. He remained with them for a minute, then veered off into another corridor and proceeded to Dr. Albion's office. He hoped to corner the doctor and ask him what he'd found out; he himself had learned nothing about his situation despite his continued observation of Robert.

Seeing a group of nurses huddled outside the doctor's office, he slowed his pace, but kept on walking.

"He was such a nice man," a sniveling older woman said. "Always so courteous and charming, with a kind word for everyone."

A buxom young nurse wiped away the tears streaming down her face. "I'll miss him. Why did it have to happen?"

A redheaded nurse shook her head. "I don't believe it."

The older woman wiped her nose with a lace-edged handkerchief. "We're all having a hard time believing he's dead."

"I'm not in denial. What I mean is I don't believe he drove while intoxicated. He never drank."

"Maybe he had problems and stopped to have a few drinks on the way home," a motherly looking nurse said in a soft voice. "Even non-drinkers drink occasionally."

The redhead crossed her arms beneath her bosom. "Not Dr. Albion. He couldn't drink—some sort of allergy to alcohol."

"What are you saying?" the older woman asked. "That someone killed Dr. Albion?"

"Of course not," the redhead answered. "We all know he died in a car accident. It's . . . oh, never mind. I have to go back to work."

The women dispersed. Bob left by way of a side door and wound his way through the grounds to his car.

Bob parked down the block from the boarding house, then spent the morning walking and thinking, trying to make sense of his situation. He could feel the anger and fear work their way up from deep inside him, and he missed the serenity he'd once had.

He returned from his walk by way of the alley. To avoid attracting his landlady's attention, he opened the gate wide enough to slide through, closed it soundlessly and skirted the yard, staying in the shadow of the hedge. As he neared the house, he caught a flicker of movement through his French doors.

He winced. Ella must be nosing around his room.

From inside the room came the rumbling of a voice too deep to belong to the old woman, and the answering growl of an even deeper voice.

Bob stopped short. Not Ella, then. Two men.

With barely perceptible movements, Bob edged closer to the house. Then he stopped, stilled his thoughts, stood like stone.

He watched.

Listened.

The crickets ceased chirping. A few amber leaves fell, sounding like raindrops in the silence. The men's voices seemed to grow louder.

"At least we finally found him," the man with the deep voice said.

"We didn't find him, shit-for-brains," the baritone responded. "The computer geeks found him." The baritone climbed to a falsetto. "We can find anyone, anywhere, anytime." It dropped back to its normal register. "Assholes."

Subdued sounds of a search floated out into the garden.

"Fuck it," Baritone said. "The papers aren't here."

"Mr. Evans is going to be pissed. He wants those papers and he wants Stark."

"Well, fuck Evans, too."

"What do we do now?"

"Wait until Stark gets back. I can hardly wait to get my hands on him after all the trouble he's caused us."

"I still can't believe he's been eluding us for a month. He must be very good."

"He's not. Just lucky. According to Evans, he's a nothing."

"Could be, but he was smart enough to have given us the slip at the airport and again at the VA."

"I thought for sure the funeral would have flushed him out."

"Maybe he didn't see the obituary."

"We've got him now," Baritone said with great satisfaction. "All we have to do is wait for him to show."

"You think so?" Deep Voice sounded dubious. He paced the room, but paused briefly to glance out the French doors, giving Bob a good look at his face. "If you want to know what I think—"

"I don't," Baritone interrupted.

Bob stood in the shadows of the hedge for another five minutes. He heard nothing more than the small, restless sounds of men bored with waiting, but he did catch fleeting glimpses of them as they moved about the room.

Very slowly, he inched backward. When he finally left the yard, he sauntered down the alley and around the block to where he'd parked his car. He'd almost reached the vehicle when it occurred to him that the VW could be under surveillance. Not wanting to remain in the area long enough to find out, he kept walking toward Colfax.

His brain churned. How had they traced him? Through the car? His traveler's checks? The taxicab company? What did it matter; in this age of computers, there is no privacy. As the man had said, they could find anyone, anywhere, anytime.

Striding along Colfax, Bob passed a small cinema that showed full-length skin flicks twenty-four hours a day. He backtracked and entered the theater. A few other dispossessed souls dotted the expanse of empty seats, and in the flickering light of ten-foot-tall tits, he caught a glimpse of gleaming silver—the man with the aluminum foil headgear.

Who was the foil man? Another refugee from an alternate universe? A time traveler from another galaxy, one with less harsh cosmic rays?

It did not seem peculiar to Bob that these thoughts should be coursing through his mind. They were no stranger than the fact that two men had been searching for him ever since he had landed in Denver. They had even staked out his mother's funeral; he had seen them—the men standing off to the side. Apparently they had not noticed him hidden in the shadows of the lilac bushes. No wonder they had seemed familiar to him at the time; he had also seen them at the airport scrutinizing everyone who got off the plane. How had they missed him?

Then he recalled the young woman who'd been struggling with a baby, a toddler, an oversized purse, and a huge diaper bag. When the toddler dropped his teddy bear, Bob picked it up and handed it to the boy, who promptly dropped it again. Bob retrieved the bear. Holding on to it, he asked the woman if she'd like some help. She looked at him for a moment, then nodded, and handed him the diaper bag. He draped the strap of the bag over his shoulder and entered the terminal with the woman by his side and the boy tugging at his pants, demanding the return of his Binky.

If Baritone and Deep Voice had been looking for a man alone, no wonder they missed him, but why did they want him? What papers were they searching for? Who was Evans?

Bob sighed wearily. Too many unanswerable questions. He closed his eyes and dropped his chin to his chest.

He awoke to find two bright blue eyes inches from his face. The foil man darted away, but after a moment he moved close again.

"I thought Sissy got you," he said in a loud, sibilant whisper. "Do you want a ray deflector? I can show you how to make one."

Bob gave the suggestion a moment's consideration. In a way, it would be a great disguise since no one ever looked closely at the foil man; on the other hand, the foil itself attracted attention.

"No thank you," he said, propelling himself out of his seat. He stretched, not at all refreshed by his nap, and left the theater. The foil man followed along behind.

Bob turned to look at him. "What's your name?"

The man stared wide-eyed at him for a few seconds, then bolted down the street.

A bus pulled to the curb. Bob climbed aboard, thinking prey such as he should keep on the move.

He gazed out the window, watching the world pass by. Toward the end of the line, he got off the bus and walked to a nearby motel.

He asked for a room at the back.

The blowsy, bleached-blond clerk glanced at the name on his registration card and handed him a key. "You're in luck, Mr. Blake. We still have one vacancy on that side. Room two-thirty-two."

Bob sat on the bed in the bland but clean room and stared at the ecru walls. He'd heard something today that kept poking at him, demanding to be acknowledged.

Then it came to him. Baritone had said, "I thought for sure the funeral would have flushed him out."

Had the obituary been a hoax after all? If so, it certainly had been an elaborate one, involving, as it did, a real burial.

Or at least the appearance of one.

Bob ordered dinner at the restaurant attached to the motel. Hunger made his stomach growl, but he ate slowly, savoring every mouthful of chicken-fried steak smothered in brown gravy, mashed potatoes, corn, and cherry pie.

"Can I get you anything else, honey?"

Bob looked at the waitress, a hefty, tired-looking woman about his own age.

"I'm fine," he answered.

She fluffed her short, curly brown hair, and smiled flirtatiously. "I get off at ten."

Bob studied her with interest, contemplating her offer. Although she wasn't his type, she seemed pleasant, if sad and lonely. Besides, he hadn't been with a woman since he left Thailand.

"I'm staying at the motel," he said non-committally, in case he misread the situation.

"What room?"

"Two-thirty-two."

"I'll meet you there when I get off work." She turned to walk away, then glanced back at him, frowning as if she already regretted her proposition.

At five after ten, she knocked on Bob's motel door. As soon as he let her in, she unbuttoned her uniform. She displayed no hint of the flirtatiousness she had shown in the restaurant, no smile, no small talk. She finished undressing with an air of dogged determination and slid between the sheets.

When he lay beside her, she took him in her arms, still exhibiting no amorous expectancy. Her manner seemed to be that of a person who had decided on a course of action and now wanted to get it over with as quickly as possible.

He wondered if she was punishing someone. Husband? Boyfriend? Herself? Had she picked him, thinking he'd deliver the retribution swiftly? If so, she had picked the wrong man. Neither his own urgency, nor her lack of it would hurry him.

He explored her body, luxuriating in the feel of her heavy breasts, the soft mound of her belly, her padded hips.

When he finally entered her, he felt his body melt into hers, and he lay on top of her for a few moments without stirring to prolong the sensation.

He moved in her, slowly, steadily. He caught the scent of frangipani in her perfume. All at once sixteen years disappeared, and he was back in Thailand, the first time he'd gone to Madame Butterfly's.

Madame Butterfly smiled at him, a tiny knowing smile, and ushered him down the hall of her brothel to a small room, where she left him alone.

The room looked nice enough, but compared to the sumptuously ornate reception area, it seemed simple. The walls had been painted a very pale gold, and a darker gold carpet lay on the floor. An ordinary bed made up with white cotton sheets, two pillows, and a red and gold spread jutted out from one wall. Next to the head of the bed stood a small red lacquer table with a fringed Chinese lamp on it, and at the foot of the bed reposed a matching red lacquer bench. A decorative folding screen partitioned off one corner.

A Chinese woman stepped out from behind the screen. She dressed like the other girls in a silk cheongsam, but she was older, angular—no soft feminine curves at all—and exceedingly plain.

The woman came to him, took his hand, and led him behind the screen to a plant-filled bathroom containing a shower stall and a tub filled with steaming water redolent of frangipani and sandalwood.

She undressed him slowly and methodically, and hung his clothes on a rack. Then she turned on the water in the shower and gestured for him to rinse himself off.

Afterward, she took his hand again and led him to the tub. Feeling his control slipping, he got into the fragrant water and lay back. The woman stepped out of her dress, knelt by the tub, picked up a bar of strange-smelling soap, and washed him. All her movements were brisk and unsensual. Still, by the time she had finished, he tingled with desire from head to toe, and he had an immense erection.

When she helped him out of the tub and began to dry him vigorously, he grabbed her and pulled her toward him. Instead of putting her arms around him, she reached down, cupped his balls, and jabbed the tip of her finger into a pressure point at the base of his scrotum. He sucked in his breath. The immediacy of his need drained away, but his erection grew even harder.

She laid him on the bed and proceeded to massage his head, his scalp, behind his ears. Slowly she worked her way almost to his groin, then she skipped to his toes and worked her way up his legs.

By the time she reached the top of his thighs, he was gasping for breath, desperately in need of release, but again she jabbed him with a finger, and again the immediacy passed.

She played with his nipples, soft bites and gentle scratches, acting as if she had all the time in the world. She turned her attention to his belly and finally to his crotch.

He lay there passively while she stoked his desire to a red-hot electric glow, igniting erogenous zones he didn't even know existed.

After one more painful poke, she climbed on top of him. She rode him steadily until he exploded with an orgasm so great he felt as if he had shattered into a million pieces.

Through it all, the woman never stopped moving. Still sensitized, he could feel himself grow hard again immediately.

He fell asleep for a few moments while she rode him, and he had the most wonderful dream of everlasting sex. His orgasm awakened him. This time it didn't come as a shattering explosion, but like surf crashing on the shore—warm, sweet waves of bliss that she managed to keep ebbing and flowing for so long he finally passed out from sheer exhaustion.

When he awoke, he gazed at the angular Chinese woman lying next to him. She smiled at him, not erotically as would be expected from such an accomplished courtesan, but innocently, almost mischievously, like a young girl. Looking at her, he could not believe that for even a second he had considered her plain—she was beautiful, perhaps the most beautiful woman he had ever seen.

The sudden scream from the Denver woman bucking wildly beneath Bob brought him out of his trance. He erupted; the woman screamed once more. They collapsed and lay still.

Later they came together again and yet again before they arose in the morning. While she dressed, she kept staring at him. She opened her mouth as if to speak, then closed it.

She left without saying anything.

6.

Bob looked at the address he had written on a scrap of paper, then at the group of buildings. Sperling Plaza, the sign said.

His brother lived in a downtown office complex? He checked the address again. According to the phone book, his brother did live here somewhere.

As he ambled about the plaza looking for his brother's building, he came across the sales office with publicity stills of the sales representatives in the window. Although the men and women all looked alike—smug, arrogant, prosperous—one face jumped out at him. The nameplate under the photograph confirmed it was his brother.

He went inside. The receptionist talking on the phone didn't look up as he strode past her. He saw an office door with Jackson's name on it, but found it locked.

When Bob left the building, he heard a man's overloud laugh. He turned his head to see his brother talking to a well-dressed couple in their thirties.

"You're going to love it here," Jackson said, clapping the man on the back and winking at the woman. "I myself live in one of the condos, and I couldn't be happier. Close proximity to great restaurants, theaters, museums, and shopping, to say nothing of the fabulous views—what more could a successful young couple like you want?"

Bob shook his head, thinking his brother still acted like a charmer—a snake charmer. He wondered if the prospective customers were aware of the cool calculating look in Jackson's eyes, or if they only noticed the wide smile, the bright teeth, the too effusive personality.

As if he heard Bob's thoughts, Jackson absently glanced his way, but didn't seem to notice him.

"I thought you left town," Kerry said, bringing Bob his hot chocolate. "I haven't seen you in here for a few days." Putting her hands on her hips, she frowned at him. "You look different."

Bob stirred his drink, watching the swirls of whipped cream disappear into the chocolate.

Kerry sat across from him, folded her arms on the table, and leaned forward. "You've discovered something."

"Maybe." He told her about going to the VA, and how his records indicated that he had no left foot.

"Robert limped," she said, eyes bright. "Those must be his records."

"Could be, or perhaps my name ended up on another person's file. According to Dr. Albion, such things are not uncommon in the military."

While he sipped from his cup, he could feel Kerry's gaze focused on him.

"There's something you're not telling me," she said at last. "I've never known anyone who talks as little as you do."

His head came up. "It seems as if lately that's all I do."

Light dancing in her eyes, she shook a finger at him. "You're evading."

He sighed. "It's too bizarre. I feel as if I've stepped into a maze of mirrors, and I can't tell if what's reflected back at me is real or not."

He busied himself with his chocolate, but she leaned forward and stared at him until he finally gave in.

"When I came home from a walk yesterday, I

found two men searching my room for papers. Apparently, they've been looking for me and those papers ever since I arrived in Denver." Spoken aloud, it sounded paranoid even to him.

She straightened. "What men? What papers? Why you?"

"I've been asking myself those very questions."

"What did you do?"

"I left, of course. Spent the night in a motel. I went back to the boardinghouse this morning and discovered a couple of men staking my place out. They're still there. I checked before I came here."

"What's that?" Kerry asked, indicating the shopping bag on the seat next to him.

"I bought some clothes and toiletries since it doesn't look like I'm going to be able to get into my room for a while."

She gave him a considering look. "Does this have anything to do with your other self?"

"I don't see how, though two completely different strangenesses centered on a single individual are a bit much to swallow."

"Could the obituary have been a hoax after all? To lure you in?"

He wanted to smile at the way their minds seemed to be working in concert, but his face wouldn't cooperate. It felt rigid, as if made of brick.

He worked his jaw. "I've been playing the funeral over in my mind, and it sure seemed real. I also went downtown today to the offices of the newspaper the obituary was in and found out the notice was paid for by Jackson. I located him, but I walked away without saying anything. Then it occurred to me that maybe the other obituary held the key."

"The first one," she breathed.

He nodded. "I checked both the News and the Post, going through a month's worth of obituaries—two weeks before my mother died the first time and two weeks afterward—and I didn't find a funeral notice." He stole a look at her. "You probably think I'm as delusional as the rest of the denizens of Colfax."

Laughter gleamed in her eyes. "I can adjust." Then, "What are you going to do now?"

"Find a motel for the night."

"You can stay with me." She seemed as surprised by the words as he did.

"I don't imagine Pete's Porches would appreciate that," he said.

The light in her eyes fractured into a whole galaxy of stars. "I didn't get a chance to tell you. I left the cheater. I'm staying with a friend, and she's out of town for a couple of days, so no one will know you're there. Maybe together we can figure this out."

Bob felt the hollowness in his chest ease.

She slid out of the booth. "I'll be right back. I need to make a phone call."

Returning, she announced, "I got someone to cover for me tonight. She'll be here in an hour or two." When the door opened to admit several customers, she added, "It looks like I'll be busy until then. Oh, no! What's he doing here? He's been eighty-sixed."

Catching sight of the foil-helmeted man loping toward him, Bob held out a hand to Kerry. "Let him stay. He can keep me company while you work."

She gave him a dubious glance. "You know him?"

"Not really. But on some level we seem to connect."

She pushed back her hair. "Okay, but if he bothers anyone, *you* have to get rid of him."

"All right. When you get a chance, will you bring two meatloaf specials? Also a cup of coffee for him?"

She nodded. Writing the order, she hurried off.

The man in the foil helmet neared and shoved something toward Bob's face.

Bob's hand shot out reflexively and he grabbed the object.

The man jumped back. He looked at Bob for a second before sliding his gaze away. "Sissy will get you. Sissy gets everyone in the end."

"Probably," Bob said, gesturing for the man to sit.

The man furiously shook his head no.

"Why not?"

The eyes darted back and forth. "They don't like me here."

"Tonight it's okay."

The foil man hesitated, then lowered himself onto the seat as if he were afraid it would blister him. He gripped the edge of the table, trembling with the effort to hold himself in check.

Bob examined the object the man had given him: a red nametag about the size of a credit card, with a nickel alligator clip attached to it. At first glance, the card seemed imprinted with only the name Herbert J. Townsend, a barcode, and a photograph bearing a vague resemblance to the foil man, but when Bob slanted the card, he saw the words Information Services, Incorporated encircling a holographic eagle with the letters ISI inscribed on it.

The last time Bob had seen the man he had asked for his name. Showing the nametag seemed more than Herbert's way of responding; he seemed to want Bob to know he had once had a real life, been a real person.

When Herbert's hand inched its way across the table, Bob gave him back the card. As Herbert carefully stowed it in his shirt pocket, it suddenly dawned on Bob the man didn't harangue about a girl named Sissy, but about ISI, which he pronounced Issy.

Kerry paused by the booth long enough to place a cup of coffee on the table and give Bob a look that clearly said, "I hope you know what you're doing," then she moved on to the next customer.

"Are you Herbert Townsend?" Bob asked.

The foil man gave a start as if it had been a long time since he'd heard the sound of his own name. He hunched over his coffee, shoulders curved forward. After a long moment, he bowed his head in a tiny nod.

"You worked for Information Services, Incorporated?"

Again that barely perceptible nod.

Bob studied him for a minute. The photograph had shown a man with slicked hair, a fleshy face, and a cocky smile, while the man sitting across from him, noisily gulping from the cup he held in both hands, was gaunt, almost skeletal, as though his mission consumed him physically as well as mentally. He dressed in threadbare jeans and a torn tee shirt, and despite the nippy weather, he wore no jacket.

Townsend looked down at himself then up at Bob, a slight deprecating smile smoothing away his usual glower, and Bob caught a glimpse of the man he must have once been.

"What happened?" Bob asked softly.

Townsend shrugged and drained the rest of his coffee. Bob noticed he seemed less twitchy with the caffeine in him.

By the time Townsend had worked his way

through meatloaf, whipped potatoes with gravy, salad, a chocolate sundae, and copious cups of coffee, he acted subdued. Bob remembered coffee used to have a reverse effect on his father, too. Edward had always guzzled several cups of coffee before going to bed, claiming it helped him sleep.

After Kerry had taken away the dishes and refilled the coffee cup, Townsend gave Bob a sidelong glance and whispered, "They put a microchip in my brain."

"Who did?" Bob asked.

"Smeary people."

"Smeary people? You mean they looked blurry?"

A nod.

"Were you drugged?"

Townsend seemed to give this some thought. "Must have been," he said at last.

"Why did they put the chip in your brain?"

"So they can control what I'm thinking." Townsend touched the aluminum foil helmet. "This protects me so I don't have to believe what they want me to believe."

Bob stared at him, not knowing what to make of the words. They sounded crazy, but said in that quiet, apathetic voice, they were also chilling.

"What do they want you to believe?"

"They said I saw aliens, but I didn't."

"Why would they want you to think you saw aliens?"

"I don't know." Townsend looked at Bob in surprise, as if he'd never asked himself that question. "Why would they?

"I don't know either," Bob replied.

Townsend's gaze wandered, and all of a sudden

his eyes grew round. He scrambled out of the booth.

Bob held out a hand. "Don't go."

"I have to. It's the mean one. She yells at me."

Looking around, Bob saw a frizzy-haired, dark-skinned woman in a waitress uniform, scowling at the fleeing Townsend.

"What was he doing here?" she demanded of Kerry.

"I let him," Kerry responded. "This once."

The scowl faded, but the voice remained hard. "If he comes in here again, I'm calling the cops."

The porch was old, solid, made of stone like the house. Its waist-high wall lined with potted plants hid a wooden swing from passers-by. Forsythia flanked the stone steps.

"Pete didn't build this porch," Kerry commented as she unlocked the front door of the house. A mocking smile glimmered in her eyes. "As old as it is, I bet it will outlast anything he makes."

"What does your friend do?" Bob asked, taking note of the expensive-looking décor in the living room. Except for the brass lamps and the touches of turquoise, rust and black in the throw pillows and in the abstracts hanging on the walls, he saw only tints of ecru.

"She's a property manager for a multi-national corporation based in Germany." Kerry tossed her keys and purse on the blonde wood coffee table. "We met in an accounting class at Community College where I went to learn how to do the books for Pete. Neither of us has a college degree, but she has a great job and travels all over. She also owns this house, stock in the company she works for, and a BMW. All I have are a few boxes of clothes and books, plus my car, which I'm still paying off. Life is strange at times, don't you think? God, what am I saying. Of course you think life is strange."

She took Bob on a quick tour of the house, explaining that she used the guestroom, but that he could stay in her friend's room.

"You look exhausted," she said. "Why don't you get some sleep? If you need me, I'll be right next door, changing out of my uniform."

Bob stood in the center of the gray-furnished room. The heavy musk perfume in the air made him feel claustrophobic, and he decided he'd rather sleep on the couch in the living room. As he left, he caught a glimpse of himself in the mirror over the dressing table. He moved closer to study his mirrored reflection and was reassured to see the same lean body, the same unimpassioned brown eyes, the same unremarkable, unsmiling face framed by shaggy brown hair in need of a trim.

He tried to superimpose the other Robert's image over his own. Was the resemblance as remarkable as he had first thought? The shape of their face, nose, chin seemed to match, as did their height and eye color, but there were differences, most notably weight, posture, skin tone.

He sat on the couch in the living room and got out his wallet—the same wallet he had carried with him ever since college. He left his money untouched, but one by one laid the rest of the contents on the coffee table. A 1970 Colorado driver's license. An ancient Denver Public Library card. A yellowed social security card. Lorena's picture. Her Dear John letter written on tissue-thin paper. Dunbar's business cards.

"I thought you went to bed," Kerry said, buttoning her shirt as she entered the room. She perched beside him. "What's this?"

"All I have to prove that I am myself."

She picked up Lorena's picture. "This is Robert's wife."

"And my college girlfriend."

"What was she like?"

"Kind, gentle, unable to say no. Whenever anybody needed help, they went to her. I remember once we planned to go to the mountains for the weekend. We both looked forward to it, but she cancelled out at the last minute because a friend had a crisis with his mother."

Kerry took one final look at the picture, set it aside, and reached for the letter. "'Dear Bob,'" she read aloud. "'I know I promised to wait for you, but our being apart has given me time to think about what I want out of life. I now realize you're not the kind of man I want. I've found someone else. By the time you receive this, we will already be married. I'm sure you understand that things are different now. This is the last letter I will ever write you. Don't contact me. Sincerely, Lorena.'" Kerry turned her head toward Bob. "She doesn't sound kind and gentle to me or like someone who can't say no."

Bob took the letter from her and reread it, though he didn't need to; he remembered every word.

"You're right," he said. "I never noticed that before."

Kerry gave a little laugh. "No wonder you have headaches. Thinking about how she broke up with you to marry another you makes my head pound." Her voice grew soft. "Did she hurt you?"

"I don't remember."

"How can you not remember?"

"Right after I got the letter, I had an encounter with a landmine. Some of my memories from that time are fuzzy."

He could feel the alarm radiating from her suddenly still body. "You were blown up?"

"I sustained no major injuries. My brain got a bit jostled is all. The doctor said I shouldn't have any problems, but there might be some minor memory loss."

"And was there?"

He shrugged. "I don't think so, but if I can't remember, how would I ever know?"

She nodded. "Good point." Turning her attention back to the contents of Bob's wallet, she grabbed Dunbar's business cards and flipped through them.

"Who's Robert Dunbar? Oh, right. The golfer. Why do you have so many of his cards?"

"Every so often he'd hand me a card, tell me if I'm ever in Denver to call him and we'd go to one of the golf courses around here. I always stuck the card in my wallet. I didn't realize I had so many."

"Are you going to call him?"

"No. He makes me uncomfortable. Golf wasn't the only pleasure he found in Thailand. He often boasted of threesomes and sexual exploits involving pain—not his own, of course. I never met his wife, but I felt sorry for her."

"He sounds like the kind of guy who thinks his infidelities don't count in a foreign country." She set Dunbar's cards aside, then studied the driver's license, library card, social security card. When she finished, she turned sideways, pulled her legs onto the couch, and sat cross-legged, facing Bob.

"Forgetting about the obituary that didn't appear in the paper around the time of your mother's first death, it does seem as if you're the real Bob Stark. Or one of them. But I don't see what that has to do with people hunting you. If they were at the airport waiting for you when you got to Denver, it means you had to come to their attention before you got back to the United States. What were you involved with in Thailand?"

Bob gathered his papers and replaced them in his wallet. "Nothing. I lived a very quiet, serene life."

Laughter sparkled in her eyes. "Serenity is a big thing with you, isn't it?"

"Yes. It's something Hsiang-li and I had in common."

"How did you two meet? If he's as uncommunicative as you, how did you ever get to know each other?"

"I went to The Lotus Room one day, attracted by its architecture. It was white and had a gold tiled roof with curled eaves, like a one-tiered pagoda. When I stepped inside, I found boisterous college students on spring break. Before I could leave, I noticed a door leading to an enclosed courtyard, and I went out to investigate. Eight-feet-tall, one-foot-thick walls muted the incessant noise of the traffic. Enormous flowerpots containing bushes, small trees laden with fruit, and an incredible array of flowers obscured the walls.

"In the center of the courtyard I saw a round pool laid with tiles shading from pale sea green at the rim to dark forest green at the bottom, making it appear fathomless. Pink and white lotus floated on the surface of the pool, and iridescent fish darted among them. Tables and chairs ringed the pool, but no one sat at them.

"Hsiang-li came out, wearing rich green pajama-like pants and a thigh-length tunic decorated with gold metallic braiding. He said, 'You like beautiful things,' with an inflection that made it not quite a question nor yet a statement. I agreed, and the two of us contemplated the pool in silence for a long time. Then Hsiang-li nodded at me, saying, 'Enough said,' and went back to work."

Bob stopped. "How do you do that?"

Kerry's eyes widened. "Do what?"

"Get me to talking. I don't like to talk, especially not about myself, yet when I'm with you I chitter like a cricket."

She laughed. "Maybe, but you still haven't told me what you did in Thailand."

"Nothing much. I worked for Hsiang-li. I painted. I explored the city. I went for long runs. Sometimes I had drinks with a friend. I led a very quiet life."

"People don't hunt down others for no reason. You must have been done something."

She propped her elbows on her knees, put her fists to her cheeks, and stared at him.

He tried to picture his life from the outside in, the way she would see it, rather than from the inside out the way he saw it. After a while his lips quirked in the faintest of smiles.

"Well, there was that one thing."

7.

Kerry's eyes danced. "With you there's always that one thing. 'My mother passed away, and oh, yes, she's already dead.' 'I went to the funeral, and oh, hey, I was already there.' 'I'm a mousy little fellow who's led an uneventful life, but oh, gee, someone's out to get me.'"

Bob's lips twitched.

"Aha!" She held up four fingers. "Smile number four. Before you know it, you might even laugh. Or not." The levity disappeared from her voice. "I guess you don't have much to laugh about. So, what's this one thing?"

"It's a long story."

"I have all night."

Bob drew in a breath. "Shortly after I met Hsiang-li, he mentioned that his restaurant used to be a quiet place, but a couple of years previously all these loud young people started to congregate there. When he said he didn't know why, I told him a guidebook called *A Pauper's Guide to Thailand* listed The Lotus Room as one of the cheapest places to eat. He got very still. Then, in a quiet voice, he told me that in China an Old Master Cook is a national treasure. His father had been an Old Master Cook and so had his father, and before he left China, Hsiang-li had been on his way to becoming one, too. He couldn't believe people came to his restaurant for the cheap prices and not for the great food."

"Why did he leave China?" Kerry asked.

"He was on Mao's list of people to be purged." Seeing her mouth forming the question, he said, "I don't know why. Neither did he. But that's another story. I suggested he triple or even quadruple his prices.

People who appreciated good food would still come, and the others would find another cheap place to eat. I also suggested fixed rates to attract businesspeople who were too busy to haggle over prices but couldn't stand the idea of anyone paying less than they did. He didn't say anything, but after that his prices crept up until his became one of the most expensive restaurants in Thailand."

Kerry laughed. "When you said long story, you meant long story."

"Perhaps I should stop."

"No, don't. I was teasing you."

"All right. When I finished eating that day, Hsiang-li asked if I would do a favor for him. He had a delivery to make at the Sheraton Hotel across the street, but he couldn't leave right then and had no one else he could trust. I agreed. He reached under the bar for a parcel about the size of a brick, wrapped in brown paper and tied with a string."

"Oh," Kerry said, her voice flat. "I bet I know what was in the package."

"I thought I did too," Bob admitted.

"And you took it anyway?"

"I trusted him, so I gave him the benefit of the doubt. A week later, he asked me to make another delivery, which I did, but the third time I asked if the packages contained drugs. 'No drugs,' he assured me. 'Then what?' I asked. 'Stolen merchandise?' He smiled at me and said, 'In a way.' 'In what way?' I asked. I told him I'd been in the army for two years and had no intention of spending any more time in mandatory confinement, especially not in a Thai prison. He smiled at me again and said, 'I am glad to hear you say that. Come, I have something to show you.'"

"What?" Kerry asked when Bob paused. "What

did he show you? Was it stolen merchandise?"

Bob held up a finger. "Hsiang-li unlocked a door behind the bar. It led into a cool storeroom containing his back stock of liquor, beer, and wine. He turned on the light, stepped aside to let me enter, and locked the door behind us. A few steps took him to a rack half-filled with dusty wine bottles. He pressed a spot on the wall next to the wine rack at about knee height. The entire rack swung out to reveal a solid metal door with a combination lock on it, like the door to a bank vault. He fiddled with the lock for a few seconds, then opened the door."

Seeing the rapt expression on Kerry's face, Bob feigned a yawn. "I'm tired. I think I'll go to bed now."

"You can't stop now," she exclaimed. "That's not fair." Then her mouth dropped open. She threw a pillow at him. "You're teasing me."

"A little."

She grinned impishly. "It's those hidden shallows again. I never know when they're going to ooze to the surface and amaze me. So, what was in the room?"

"Antiques. Old pottery, Thai bronzes, woodcarvings, porcelain figurines, jade Buddhas, heavy gold jewelry. One display case contained several small, very old, highly glazed figurines. All were the same color—pale tan with sepia accents—and all looked as if the same long-forgotten artist had made them. A few were realistic depictions of animals, like the ornate elephant in full regalia, while others were fanciful creatures such as unicorns, griffins, winged dragons pulling chariots, and eagles with peacock feathers."

"They sound beautiful," Kerry said.

"They were. I wanted to ask Hsiang-li about them, but he stared into the case with such a look of sorrow on his face that I couldn't intrude."

"Did you ever find out about them?"

Bob nodded. "But not then. Hsiang-li roused himself, and pointed out various porcelain bowls. Bencharong, Sawank'alok, celadon."

Kerry tilted her head. "Celadon? Isn't that a pale green cracked glaze? I've seen it in import shops."

"You probably saw Thai celadon, a reproduction made by following the original Chinese method of glazing with natural wood ash and firing it in a white heat kiln, so it looks exactly the same as the ancient Chinese celadon. Hsiang-li's celadon bowls, however, were some of the original pieces made in China. They were more than two thousand years old."

"You never answered my question," Kerry said.

"Which question?"

"Was it stolen merchandise?"

"No. All of it had been legally purchased from legitimate dealers and people who needed money so desperately they had to sell their family heirlooms."

"So what did Hsiang-li mean when he said that in a way it was stolen?"

"Because the people who bought it thought it had been."

An uncertain look crossed Kerry's face. "They thought it was stolen, and they still bought it?"

Bob nodded. "Hsiang-li told me people go to Thailand expecting to buy cheap antiquities. One way to get them to pay what the objects are worth is to make them believe they're stolen. People are willing to pay a lot of money for stolen merchandise, perhaps because they feel they are getting away with something."

Kerry spread her hands. "I don't get it. How did he make people believe the stuff was stolen?"

"Bribery, mostly. Periodically he paid cops to arrest him on charges of selling stolen antiquities. They always dropped the charges, of course, but word got around. Secret meetings, hushed phone calls, surreptitious hand-offs, and other clandestine activities also helped get the point across."

"That hidden room probably helped, too."

"He didn't bring customers there. He told me he'd never take the chance of showing the place to anyone who seemed willing to break the law."

"Was pretending to sell stolen property worth it?" Kerry asked.

"Hsiang-li thought so. Mao Tse-tung killed off perhaps sixty million Chinese and forced millions of others to flee their homeland. All they had left were the few treasures they managed to take with them, and Hsiang-li wanted to make sure they got the true worth of their heirlooms. He also bought antiques from dealers, added a hefty profit for himself, and sold them to rich people who still paid less than if they got them through one of the big international auction houses."

Kerry's brows drew together. "So what does all this have to do with the guys who are after you?"

"Maybe nothing. You're the one who wanted to know what I did in Thailand. But I haven't reached the end of the story."

Kerry uncrossed her legs, and stretched them. Then, curling up again, she said grandly, "You can continue now."

"About three months ago, when I passed the door to Hsiang-li's office, I heard voices inside. Since I understand a little Chinese, I knew someone was threatening Hsiang-li. I stepped into the office. Two Chinese men of average size with calm demeanors and very cold eyes leaned toward Hsiang-li. Their hands hung loosely by their sides, but their postures seemed menacing. They didn't look like typical bruisers. They wore expensive business suits and appeared well bred, educated. They glanced at me. One said, 'Oh, the *kwai lo*.' Then they turned their backs on me. Hsiang-li hunched in defeat, and I knew something dangerous was going on."

Kerry gave him a questioning glance. "How did you know?"

"*Kwai lo* is the Chinese name for barbarian, an insult of the highest order. To keep the back turned is a sign of disrespect. In this case, the insult seemed to be directed not so much at me but at Hsiang-li as my mentor. They spoke awhile longer in Chinese, then they started to leave. One man looked back and said, in English, 'As we have explained, we're consolidating the antiques business. We want you to join us or get out. We have excellent sources for new antiquities, and we don't want or need the competition. If you do as we say, your American dog will be safe.'"

Kerry shot bolt upright. "What? They threatened you? Yet when I asked what happened in Thailand, you said, 'Nothing.' How can that be nothing?"

"Because Hsiang-li did what they wanted."

"He closed his antiques business to protect you?"

"I told Hsiang-li he didn't need to give in on my account. If I left he would be safe, but he said he had other reasons for closing."

"Who were the men? Triads?"

"Maybe. Hsiang-li called them thugs in business suits. When I reminded him that he'd dealt with people like that before, he said, 'No, these men are different. Their power is far reaching.' When I continued to protest, he told me all things must end. If it weren't those men, there would be others. Penalties for dealing in stolen antiquities had become severe in an attempt to stem the flow of Thailand's heritage out of the country, and jealous business rivals would be glad of an opportunity to turn him in."

"But he only pretended to sell stolen antiquities," Kerry said.

"It didn't matter. He became too successful, and he made enemies."

Kerry shivered. "Maybe his enemies are your enemies."

"I suppose it's possible," Bob said slowly, "but the men I saw in my room were Caucasian, and definitely American. You've got me thinking. I wonder if someone got wind of Hsiang-li's gold Buddha and figured I know where to find it."

Kerry's eyes grew enormous. "Gold Buddha? It sounds to me as if your life wasn't so quiet and uneventful after all."

"This isn't my story," Bob reminded her. "It's Hsiang-li's."

"Well, do you know where to find the Buddha?"

"No, and neither does Hsiang-li, but he sold his restaurant and went in search of it."

"All by himself? If you were so close, I would have thought you'd go with him."

"He wanted to go alone. A personal quest. Also, I have the feeling that one way or another he doesn't plan on returning to civilization."

"Jeez. Where did he go to look for the gold Buddha?"

"In the jungles of Northern Thailand and Burma." Bob closed his eyes. "I dream of the jungle sometimes. Hsiang-li is lost, and I have to find him. As I push my way through the foliage, vines strangle me, snakes entwine themselves around me, clouds of insects envelop me. Then I'm hurt, I don't remember how, and

I have to pull myself along on my belly, but the jungle goes on forever."

He rose and paced the room. A minute, two minutes ticked by.

Finally, Kerry patted the couch next to her. "Why don't you come back here. Maybe if you finish telling the story, you can get it out of your system and out of your dreams. I know he's your friend and you're worried about him, but he made his choice."

Bob's steps slowed. A minute later he settled beside her. She took one of his hands in both of hers, and he felt her warmth seep into him.

"Two months ago we were in the secret room. We had sold off Hsiang-li's inventory and all that remained were the tan and sepia figurines I mentioned. 'I found these figurines a long time ago during a period of great sorrow,' he said, and explained that he had not been prepared for such sadness. He'd lived in Ch'engtu, the largest city in Szechuan Province, which is the most densely populated province in China, but his own world was tiny, centered around his family's restaurant. He went on to tell me about his robust baby boy, about his beautiful wife who had a laugh like the tinkling of bells, and about how happy and complete they made his life.

"Then a high-placed friend warned him about his name on Mao's purge list, and his wife decided they should escape. They hired a guide to take them through the mountains and across the border into Burma, then on into Thailand. Although Thailand curtailed Chinese immigration, Hsiang-li figured they could blend into the Chinese community there with no one being the wiser. Before they left, his wife set her pet finch free. She could no longer stand the idea of any creature living in captivity."

Feeling Kerry moving restlessly next to him,

Bob said, "Maybe I should tell you the story some other time, let you get some sleep."

She shook her head; strands of her hair brushed against his cheek. "This is daytime to me. Normally, I'd be in the middle of the bar rush, being run off my feet. Besides, no one's told me a story since I was a little girl sitting on my grandfather's lap." Kerry moved closer to Bob and curled up against him. "You don't smell the same, though. He smelled of pipe tobacco and horses and old leather. You smell like Rimrock's meatloaf. You don't feel the same, either. He felt safe and secure. Settled. You feel . . ."

"Feel what?" Bob asked when she didn't finish.

"Dangerous." She spoke in a voice so low it barely qualified as a whisper.

He wanted to put his arms around her, assure her everything would be all right, but he couldn't lie to her. No matter how much care a person took, things still happened.

"All went well for Hsiang-li at first," he said. "They actually made it into Burma, maybe even Thailand. One evening Hsiang-li went off to collect firewood while the others remained behind to prepare camp. He returned to find his wife, his son, the guides all dead, knifed by bandits for the pittance they had managed to bring with them."

Kerry sucked in a breath. "Oh, that poor man."

Bob nodded, remembering the pain in Hsiang-li's eyes while he spoke of his grief, and the way his voice rasped, as if the words scraped the sides of his throat.

"The next morning he started to dig their graves. He had no tools, only rocks, sticks, and his hands. He dug for many days, wanting to be certain the bodies would be safe from the ravages of animals."

"His poor hands must have been raw and bleeding," Kerry said. Then, in an even softer tone, "I wonder what it would be like to love someone that much."

"I don't know," Bob said, but he was getting an inkling. "Hsiang-li had dug a very deep hole when suddenly the earth gave way, and he fell into a cave, or so he thought. As his head cleared and his eyes adapted to the dim light, he realized he had fallen into a man-made chamber."

"A treasure house?" Kerry asked breathlessly.

"No. An ancient kiln. Fragments of broken pottery littered the floor of the room. He also found many intact jars on long stone benches and a cache of—"

"Figurines," Kerry cut in. "The little ceramic creatures. No wonder he got so sad every time he looked at them."

Bob nodded his agreement. "Hsiang-li lowered the bodies into the kiln and laid them on the stone benches. He stuffed a backpack with the figurines, crisscrossed branches over the opening to the kiln, and refilled the hole he'd dug. Then, staggering under the weight of the pack, he left. He didn't get far when he came face to face with an immense sitting Buddha, perhaps twenty feet tall."

"The gold Buddha," Kerry exclaimed.

Bob smiled at her eagerness. "It makes me wonder who actually told the stories when you were a child. You or your grandfather."

She laughed. "I never like waiting for the ending. I want everything in a single gulp. Beginning, middle, and end all at once."

"Maybe I should stop here. Make you beg to hear the end."

"You can't stop! Not until you get to the part

about the gold Buddha." Snuggling closer, she took his arm and draped it around her shoulders. She smiled at him, her eyes dancing, as if daring him to move it away.

He fell silent for a moment, savoring the feel of her tee shirt- and jeans-clad body next to his. She smelled clean and fresh, like cucumber, or melon, or pear.

"Roots of a strangler fig enveloped the Buddha." Hearing a slight huskiness in his voice, he cleared his throat and continued. "The tree's foliage concealed it further. The dark green algae or fungus coating the Buddha added to its appearance of ageless wisdom and serenity. Hsiang-li thought it would watch over his family until he could return.

"Beyond the Buddha, barely visible through the dense foliage, he saw a building almost swallowed by the jungle. Hsiang-li found an open, vine-covered doorway and pushed his way inside. The beauty of the room he had entered awed him. Luminous golden brown tiles overlaid the floor. The walls and ceiling were also tiled, but in a pale green that shimmered in the shadowy light of the jungle. Except for patches of discoloration from a fungus, the room was remarkably well preserved.

"At the far end of the room sat a crude stucco Buddha about five feet tall that seemed at odds with the elegance of the place. Out of curiosity, he scraped off a piece of the lichen-encrusted stucco and discovered the glimmer of gold. With a pounding heart, he went outside for some mud to hide the scratch."

"Why was it covered in stucco?" Kerry asked.

"I don't know. He thought he had stumbled on a lost city, one, perhaps, that had been destroyed by Mongol hordes. In the days of Kublai Khan, gold Buddhas had often been stuccoed to hide then from the invaders."

Kerry sat upright and stared at him. "Are you telling me Hsiang-li discovered a lost city?"

"No. There were four buildings, one of which lay in ruins. He decided the place must be a monastery compound that had been long abandoned."

"But why would they leave the Buddha behind?"

"He didn't know and didn't care. He just knew it now belonged to him. He made his plans. He would find his way back to civilization, sell the figurines for the funds to mount an exhibition, then return."

Kerry settled back into Bob's embrace.

"Unfortunately," he said, continuing with the story, "things did not work out according to plan. First, he had no idea where he was or where he was going. Because of the vaulted canopy of the jungle, he could not even tell where the sun rose or set to give him a vague idea of direction.

"Second, there were no distinctive landmarks to tell him where he had been. All around him, everywhere he looked, he saw the same soaring tree trunks, giant ferns, tangled roots, dangling vines, and huge orchids."

An image of the jungle formed in Bob's mind. It seemed so real, he felt as if he were in that shadowy gloom with its suffocating aroma of moist, decaying vegetable matter, and the deafening din of insects, birds, tree frogs, and monkeys. He shuddered at the thought of a lone man lost in such an inhospitable place.

"Bob?"

Hearing his name, Bob gave a start and saw Kerry peering anxiously at him.

She touched his cheek. "You got so still, I

thought you were in the jungle of your nightmares."

Bob laid a had on top of hers. "I was."

"Then let's get you out of there. Finish the story."

"Hsiang-li didn't know how long he wandered, alone, starving, half-mad with grief, before he stumbled on a hunting party of Lahu. They fed him and showed him a trail to Mai Hong Son, a half-day's journey away. He sold a figurine, getting enough money to get to Bangkok where he sold a few more. By then he realized it could take years—and a small fortune—to find the abandoned monastery again, so he put the money into a restaurant instead."

"Then he met you," Kerry murmured, "and found contentment once again."

Bob swallowed. "Yes. After he finished telling me the story of the figurines, he said a consortium of Japanese executives had approached him. They wanted The Lotus Room for a conference center, and he decided to sell it to them. He said his dreams of looking for the gold Buddha had faded, but he wanted to find the remains of his wife and child, and give them a proper burial. 'I am getting old,' he said. 'If I don't do it now, I never will.'"

Bob grew silent, thinking about the last time he'd seen Hsiang-li. They were at Bangkok Hua-lompong Station; Hsiang-li had decided to travel north by train instead of airplane because he wanted one last look at rice paddies and open skies before disappearing into the jungle to begin his search. He bowed under the weight of the backpack containing the figurines, which he planned to restore to their rightful place.

Hsiang-li pulled an envelope out of his pocket and handed it to Bob. "This is for you, my son," he said quietly. Without waiting for a response, he swung into the train and was lost in the crowd.

Bob watched the train pull out of the station, then left to prepare for his own journey into the past.

Hearing a sigh, Bob turned his head to look at the woman in his arms. She slept, a peaceful expression on her face. He watched her for a minute, then closed his eyes. Soon he too fell asleep.

He did not dream.

8.

Bob's left arm, entwined around Kerry's shoulders, was asleep, but the rest of him was awake and rested, with only the tiniest twinge in the back of his skull to remind him of his problems.

Kerry stirred. Her eyelids fluttered and popped open. She lifted her head, looked around the living room, then up at Bob.

She smiled. "And you were saying?"

He disentangled himself from her. "I'm not telling any more stories. All I do is put us to sleep."

"You slept?" she asked. "No nightmares?"

"No nightmares."

She stretched. "I had such a delicious dream, hacking my way through jungles, finding lost cities and golden Buddhas." Two vertical lines appeared between her brows. "Was the story true? You weren't stringing me along?"

Shaking life back into his arm, he said, "I didn't make it up, if that's what you're asking. I told you the same story Hsiang-li told me."

"In that case, it has to be true. I doubt he'd have closed his restaurant and left his adopted son for anything less. Wow! A gold Buddha, five feet tall. No wonder someone is looking for you. I bet they think Hsiang-li gave you a treasure map and directions how to find the abandoned monastery, and those are the papers they're looking for."

"You're forgetting one thing—Hsiang-li and I were alone in his secret room when he told me the story."

She waved a hand in a dismissive gesture. "If those thugs in business suits are as powerful as you say, they could easily have bugged the place to make sure

Hsiang-li got out of the antiques business."

Bob stood and arched his back while he considered the possibility. If true, could they have also followed Hsiang-li to the train station and seen him handing over the envelope? But why wait a month before trying to nab it? Could it have taken them that long to understand the implications of what they'd seen and heard? It didn't make any sense, but neither did anything else that had been happening.

"How much do you think the gold Buddha is worth?" Kerry asked.

Bob shook his head, a faint smile playing on his lips. "I should never have told you about it. The next thing I know, you're going to be tramping through the jungles of Thailand and Burma looking for the Buddha yourself."

"I wish I could, but buying a ticket to Thailand, stocking up on supplies, hiring guides, and who knows what else would take more money than I could earn in a lifetime. Rats. I would have loved to be able to see it."

"If all you want to do is see a gold Buddha, that's a lot easier to arrange. There's one in a wat on the edge of Bangkok's Chinatown, near the railway station. Interestingly, stucco covered that one, too, but movers dropped it during a relocation, and some of the stucco came off showing the gold underneath. Five and a half tons of pure gold."

Excitement flared in her eyes, then died. "I don't even have the money for a ticket to Thailand. Now that I'm shucked of the cheat, maybe I can start saving."

Kerry was still in her bathroom when Bob finished showering and shaving. He pulled on the clean clothes he'd purchased the day before, and went out to the kitchen.

As he chopped onions, zucchini, and carrots for a stir-fry, Kerry entered the room. She stopped and stared wide-eyed at him.

He paused, knife in the air. "Do I frighten you?"

"No," she said quickly.

Noting the way she wadded her hands together, he laid down the large knife. "After you reminded me about the MSG in American-Chinese food, I went to the Asian market on Alameda and bought supplies, including a wok and a sharp knife. Whenever I cooked, my landlady hid behind the kitchen door, peering at me as if terrified, but I don't know why."

Kerry let her hands fall to her sides. "It's the way you use the knife, so fast and proficient. I've never seen a blade move so rapidly."

Bob picked up the knife and slowly finished chopping the vegetables. "I didn't realize. Wu Shih-kai always found my efforts to be hilariously clumsy."

Kerry watched him a moment. "Is there anything I can do?"

"Set the table. The food is ready." He gave a theatrical shudder. "Minute rice. Shih-kai would be horrified, but that's all I could find in the cupboard."

"This is fabulous," Kerry said after they filled their plates and took their first bites. "What's it called?"

"No name. It's just a stir-fry."

She took another bite and sighed in contentment. "You can cook for me whenever you want."

"Maybe next time I'll make whole pigeon or whole fish soup." He gave her a sly smile. "Those are delicacies you will never forget."

"Were they on the menu at The Lotus Room?"

"In the beginning, until I told Hsiang-li that

westerners were squeamish and didn't like to see eyeballs and feet in their food."

"Eyeballs and feet? Oh, ick."

After they ate and cleared away the dishes, Kerry drove Bob to City Park so he could peek at the boardinghouse. Each time he'd checked, he'd seen either a new blue Buick or a late model white Ford parked on the street where the occupants had a view of both the front door of the boarding house and the French doors at the side. Today it was the blue Buick.

They strolled around the park.

"Why don't you call the cops?" Kerry asked.

"They are more of a problem than a solution," Bob said.

"I take it you don't like cops."

"My father was a cop."

Bob hunched his shoulders, remembering how his father had swaggered about town in his uniform. The people Edward had dealt with on the job were "low lifes," as he called them, and this added to his belief in his superiority. Since he assumed no one obeyed the law, he treated everyone, from the most harmless witness to the most vicious criminal, with the same unmerciful arrogance. Bob had met many like Edward, people who became puffed with the weight of a uniform's authority.

"I can't go to the cops with a story about far away jungles and gold Buddhas," he said, "but you've given me an idea. First, I'll need to get some dark clothes."

"I have a warm-up suit I bought Pete's Porches for his birthday next week. It will probably be too big for you, but the pants have an elastic waistband, and you can roll up the cuffs. Will that do?"

"Perfect."

Her eyes sparkled. "What's the plan?"

At ten o'clock that night, Bob hid in the dark shadows of a honeysuckle bush, key in hand. He'd left Kerry at a phone booth on Colfax Avenue. If she followed the plan, she had called the local police station, claimed to be Ella Barnes frightened of the suspicious characters parked in front of her house, and immediately hung up.

As soon as Bob saw the police car stop behind the Buick and two cops get out and approach the vehicle, he stole across the yard. With one fluid motion, he put the key in the lock, turned it, opened the door, and slipped through. Crouching in front of the heavy drapes, he yanked out the thread he'd used to tack the hem, and removed his passport and traveler's checks. He glided from the room and strolled to the end of the alley where Kerry waited.

"How did it go?" she asked.

"Fine. I got what I needed."

"It's a shame you had to leave your paintings behind."

He shrugged. "Can't be helped."

"How did you know your things would still be where you hid them? And why did you hide them in the first place? Oh, right. Your nosy landlady."

"I didn't know my things would still be there," Bob said. "I had a hunch. They called me a nothing."

Kerry looked at him out of the corner of her eyes. "Do you know why I needled you that first day?"

"You didn't needle, you challenged, and yes, I do know why. You were upset with your boyfriend and wanted to get back at the whole male gender. You picked me because you thought I was a 'mousy little fellow' who wouldn't fight back."

She smiled sheepishly. "It's scary how well you read me." She drove back to the house in silence. As she stopped to let him out before continuing on to work, she said, "I don't imagine many people see you as you really are."

Bob woke at dawn, did his stretches, sit-ups, and push-ups, then went out for a run. Feeling fall in the air, he was glad he'd worn the warm-up suit Kerry had given him. He didn't even care that it bagged; he hadn't been so comfortable since he'd left Bangkok, where he'd dressed like the Thais in baggy, lightweight cotton clothes. Not only were those garments best adapted to the climate, while wearing them, especially with the ubiquitous lampshade-style straw hat, he'd melted into the crowds on the teeming streets.

When his work visa expired along with his job, he'd purchased western-style clothes, which he'd worn on the flight home, but he couldn't seem to get used to them. Maybe he needed a closet full of warm-up suits.

He covered the blocks in an easy lope and soon ran along Seventeenth Avenue at the edge of City Park. Passing the street where the boardinghouse stood, he noticed that a dark green Ford had replaced the blue Buick and the white Ford.

He could see two heads bobbing as if to music. Were the surveillance teams getting lax? Maybe he could sneak past them, jump into his car, and drive off.

Deciding it wasn't worth the risk, he continued his run, circling back to the church where the Vietnam vet support group met.

He found Scott Mulligan outside, cutting the grass.

Smiling warmly, Scott turned off the mower and

extended a hand. "Good to see you, Bob. Just last night Rose mentioned how much she enjoyed having you over for dinner."

"I enjoyed it, too," Bob said.

"How about if we do it again—say, tomorrow night?"

Bob hesitated. "I'm staying with a friend."

"Great. Bring her along. Or him."

"That would be nice. I'm sure she'd like meeting you."

Scott gave him a shrewd look. "What can I help you with?"

"Do you know anyone I could hire to tail a car, see where it goes? It seems my place is being staked out, and I'd like to know who's behind it."

"I have a friend at the police department. He'd run the plates for me."

"I'd prefer to keep the cops out of it."

Again that shrewd look. "Are you in trouble with the cops?"

"Not that I'm aware of."

Scott nodded thoughtfully. "I know a couple of Lurps, guys from the Long Range Reconnaissance Patrol, who are bored with civilian life. They might be willing to do the job, probably wouldn't charge a lot. How much are you willing to pay?"

"Whatever they ask. At the moment, I only have traveler's checks, and whoever's looking for me might be able to trace them and connect your friends to me, but I'll try to get some cash."

"If you can't, we'll work something out. Where's the car you want tailed?"

Bob gave him the address, described all three cars, and apologized for not knowing the license plate numbers.

"I never got close enough to get a good look," he said.

Scott wrote down the information. "Maybe I'll have something to report when you come to dinner tomorrow night."

Bob was preparing another stir-fry when Kerry came home from work.

Her eyes lit up at the sight of him. "I thought maybe you went back to the boardinghouse."

"I can't. The place is still being watched."

"So the cops didn't scare those guys away."

He shrugged. "I didn't expect them to. I just needed a diversion."

"Do you know what we should do?" She flicked the hair off her face. "Stake out the people who are staking you out and follow them when they leave, see where they go."

"I've already arranged for that." He told her about his conversation with Scott Mulligan, ending with the invitation to dinner.

"That sounds like fun," she said. "I probably ought to get someone to cover my shift in case we get back late."

She went into the other room to make the call. "I traded days off," she said on her return, "so I have to work tonight instead of tomorrow. What are we going to do after we eat?"

"Don't you need to get some sleep?"

"No." She yawned. "Well, maybe I could use a nap. Then what?"

"I need to go shopping, replace some of the things I had to abandon."

"Shopping! Why didn't you say so? I can always sleep afterward."

***

Kerry drove them to Bear Valley Mall in west Denver. They went to several stores, buying one or two items at a time. Bob paid for each small purchase with a large traveler's check. Since he wouldn't be returning to the mall, it didn't matter if they found out he'd been there, and he needed to get as much cash together as he could; he'd need plenty for motels after Kerry's roommate returned, and enough to pay Scott's friends.

Kerry shot him a curious glance when he added a child's watercolor paint set to his purchases, but she made no comment. She did remind him, however, that a bottle of wine would make a nice hostess gift for Rose Mulligan, and she even picked it out herself.

While Kerry slept, Bob painted a picture of his garden in Bangkok.

Soon after his arrival in that city, he happened to notice a narrow lane leading to a cul-de-sac containing several charmingly ramshackle teak houses with corrugated tin roofs, surrounded by shrubs, unpruned rosebushes, and oleander. In a window of one of the houses was a placard, written in English, advertising a room for rent.

A cadaverous Englishman answered Bob's knock and led him up a creaking staircase to a sparsely furnished room with stained walls and a scuffed wooden floor. A warped door opened onto a balcony where a rickety stairway descended into a garden with more shrubs and bushes, and a wild profusion of tropical flowers—jasmine, frangipani, orchids. Red-blossomed bougainvillea climbed the walls, purple wisteria dripped from the balcony, and a bushy ebony tree provided shade.

As Bob inhaled the glorious scent wafting

through the inhospitable room, he realized he could be content there.

Since the Englishman seldom stepped outside, the garden had been Bob's alone until three months previously when the man's recently divorced daughter had moved in with her many offspring.

Bob did not have to contend with their invasion of his garden for long; shortly afterward, Hsiang-li had announced he was closing his restaurant.

Bob stepped back and studied his painting. The bright, translucent tints of the watercolors had been the perfect choice. The garden looked so vibrant, the fragrance seemed to swirl out of the paper, and he thought it might be the best thing he'd ever done. Perhaps the thin paint, unlike the heavy opaque acrylics and fast-drying oils he generally used, allowed no place for menace to hide.

"It's lovely."

Bob turned around. A sleep-tousled Kerry gazed at the picture, a smile gracing her lips.

"Is it a real place?"

He nodded.

"The hand is interesting," she said. "It makes the garden seem like a living creature."

"What do you mean?" Bob glanced back at the picture, and for the first time noticed the clawed hand reaching out from the mass of blooms.

As if sensing his disquiet, Kerry put an arm around his waist and rested her head against his shoulder.

After a moment, she lifted her head and looked at him. "It just dawned on me. There are no people in your paintings. Don't you ever paint people?"

"No."

"Why not?"

He hesitated, then spoke in a low voice. "I'm afraid of what my fingers would see."

9.

Kerry stepped out of her bedroom, stopped, then turned around slowly. "What do you think?"

Bob swallowed. She looked stunning. She'd brushed her black hair off her face and loosely bound it at the nape of her neck, making her dark eyes appear enormous. The long-sleeved dress that he had last seen in the shop window at Buckingham Square skimmed her body, flared out at the hem, and bared enough of her breasts to tantalize. The deep rose color made her skin seem luminous and put a blush on her cheeks that no cosmetic could duplicate.

He nodded. "It's definitely your color."

She held out the skirt and frowned at it. "You're sure? I never much liked pink. Too little-girlish."

He smiled at her. "Believe me, you do not look like a little girl."

She put her hands on her hips and stared at him as if waiting for something more.

"You're beautiful," he said.

"Thank you. You look nice, too, but I wish I could have talked you into buying something dressier than those navy slacks and that pin-striped shirt."

"I don't wear suits, and I definitely don't wear ties. Shall we go?"

Kerry immediately took to the Mulligans and they to her. She chatted with them about her family back in Chalcedony: fiery-tempered mother, easy-going father, staid brothers—one older, one younger—both married with children. All lived on the family acreage, which included hayfields, apple orchards, and pastures for horses, cows, goats, and llamas.

During a lull in the conversation, Beth fixed her

with a challenging stare that reminded Bob of the way Kerry sometimes looked at him.

"Jimmy says girls can't like toads."

"Why not? I like toads. I think they're cute. Back home, we have a great big toad living in our garden. Whenever I'd go out and water the flowers, he'd turn his back on me like a little kid who thinks if he can't see you, you can't see him."

Beth threw a triumphant glance at Jimmy, who shrugged his shoulders good-naturedly.

"Sometimes after a heavy rainstorm in the spring," Kerry continued, smiling at both children, "there would be so many baby toads hopping around you could reach out and catch them."

"What did you do once you caught them?" Jimmy asked.

"Let them go, of course. I suppose it's silly of me since I'm from a ranching family, but I don't believe we have the right to deny any creature its freedom. Especially wild animals. I once had an orphaned baby cougar. I loved her, but when she didn't need me to feed her anymore, I let her go. She came back every day at first, but the periods between her visits grew longer and longer, until one day she didn't come back at all. I miss her, but I like to think of her out there somewhere, wild and free."

Beth scooted over on the couch until she sat next to Kerry. "What other pets did you have?"

"A baby llama, a raccoon, rabbits, lots of cats. I even had a prairie dog once. I called him Speck. When I came home from school, he'd run to the door and greet me with a happy little jump. My mother wasn't too thrilled with the way he kept digging holes in the sofa."

"Do you like video games?" Jimmy asked.

Kerry nodded.

"Do you want to come play?"

When Beth jumped up and took her by the hand, Kerry gave Bob, Rose, and Scott an apologetic glance, and let herself be towed out of the room.

"Your girl is delightful," Rose said.

The corners of Bob's mouth twitched. "Believe me, she's no one's girl but her own."

Rose excused herself and went to see about dinner.

Scott leaned forward. "I heard from my Lurp friends today."

Bob tried to keep his voice casual. "What did you find out?"

Scott handed him a small piece of paper containing an address. "They followed the green Ford to this place out in Broomfield—the corporate headquarters for ISI, Information Services Incorporated."

"I've come across the name," Bob said, barely able to hear himself over the beating of his heart, "but I don't know who they are."

"According to my friends, they're a closely held corporation, which means they do not fall under the jurisdiction of the SEC since they are not listed on the stock exchange. The stock is held by interlocking private trusts, so actual ownership of the corporation is shrouded in mystery and legal language. Ostensibly, they set up security systems for major corporations, and their research division awards grants to colleges, universities, private laboratories, and even individuals. They also seem to have a strong link to the intelligence community—they're supposedly involved in a lot of black ops stuff. In fact, many ex-CIA, ex-FBI, and ex-DEA agents work for them. That's all my Lurp friends found out."

Bob stared at him, his mind blank.

"They appreciated the challenge," Scott said. "When they saw they were dealing with a major corporation, not a couple of small timers, they got curious and did some digging." He gave Bob a level look. "If you tell me what trouble you're in, maybe I can help."

"I wish I knew." He thought about Herbert Townsend and the way the two of them seemed to connect. Like the veterans whose experiences in Vietnam had made them identifiable to one another, did both he and Herbert have ISI's name clearly stamped on their foreheads?

Then, recalling the concentration of U.S. government agents in northern Thailand because of the drug trade, he wondered if perhaps Kerry was right after all, and they had somehow gotten wind of Hsiang-li's gold Buddha.

Feeling Scott's eyes on him, he stirred. "How much do I owe your friends?" When Scott named an amount that seemed too small, Bob added a bonus. "For the extra work," he explained.

Scott pocketed the money. "They said to let them know if they could do anything else for you."

"I'll keep that in mind."

Rose appeared in the doorway. "Dinner's ready."

When the lasagna, garlic bread, and salad had been mostly consumed and Bob and Kerry's wine bottle emptied, Kerry glanced from Bob to Scott.

"How did you two meet?"

Bob and Scott busied themselves with the remains of their dinner, but out of the corner of Bob's eye he could see Rose and Kerry exchanging looks.

Rose shrugged. "I don't know what the big secret is. They met at a Vietnam veteran support group."

"My dad was a CO in the war," Beth said proudly.

Bob shot a questioning glance at Scott. "A commanding officer?"

Scott snorted. "Not hardly. I registered as a conscientious objector."

"He got sent into combat," Rose said. "Can you believe that?"

Bob drew back. "Combat? A lot of conscientious objectors, including Quakers have served in the military, but they were usually given duties like medic or clerk. I never heard of any being sent into combat."

Scott shrugged. "Well, they sent me. I don't know if it was a mistake or someone's idea of a sick joke."

"Dad wouldn't fire his weapon," Jimmy said. "He believes killing for any reason is wrong."

"He won't even kill bugs or spiders," Beth added.

Kerry laid aside her fork. "It must have been terrible."

Rose nodded. "They assigned him jobs of a particularly filthy or menial nature, like permanent latrine duty, trench digging, and retrieval of dead bodies."

"Someone had to do it," Scott said.

"I know, but they didn't have to harass you the way they did."

"They thought I was a coward, hiding behind my religious beliefs to get out of combat duty." He sighed. "Maybe I was."

"No you weren't," Rose said fiercely. "It took a lot of courage to maintain your dignity in the face of their hatred. And you always had to dodge bullets and skirt explosions on your way to rescue injured men."

She turned to Kerry. "During combat he had to get the wounded out of the line of fire and to help the medic care for them."

Kerry's eyes widened. "I can't even begin to comprehend the strength it must have taken to survive not only a combat zone, but the torment of one's own countrymen."

"I had my faith to sustain me," Scott said.

Beth shuddered. "They shot my dad."

"The bullet gouged a furrow on my thigh, a flesh wound." Scott smiled. "In the movies they always say, 'It's just a flesh wound,' as if it's nothing, but mine hurt like the dickens. They wouldn't give me many painkillers, either. One nurse pompously told me they didn't want us wounded soldiers getting addicted so they cut back, but another nurse whispered that the hospital workers had used the drugs themselves for fun. They must have received new supplies, because I didn't notice much after those first few days—they kept me doped—but I do remember being transferred to a hospital in the Philippines."

"Can you believe they sent him back to Vietnam after that?" Rose said. "It makes me furious thinking about it."

Scott reached across the table and grasped her hand. "When I got back, my sergeant said to me, 'Now that you know being a conscientious objector doesn't keep you from getting wounded or even killed, are you ready to do your duty as a combat soldier?' 'I have no control over the actions of other people,' I told him. 'If the VC choose to shoot me, there's not much I can do about it. The only choice I have is whether or not to shoot them, and I will not kill anyone.' He glared at me and ordered me to get out of his sight and to keep out of his sight, because I disgraced the U.S. Army."

Scott kept silent for a time while his family gazed sympathetically at him. Bob watched them, thinking the man had more than his faith to sustain him.

Scott drew in a breath. "Everyone still treated me the same until after the next engagement. We were under heavy fire, and many of our guys got wounded. I kept busy hauling injured men away from the front line. Afterwards, the sergeant came to me and said, 'Glad to see you finally got some balls.' The others guys stopped ostracizing me as if by getting shot I had passed some sort of test, like an initiation, but sometimes I could hear them snickering at me behind my back."

"Do you think maybe you changed?" Kerry asked.

"No. Well, in little ways, of course. I became more self-confident, knowing I had never wavered in my beliefs even though my faith had been severely tested, and occasionally I have nightmares that make me sick to my stomach, but for the most part I'm the same as always."

Kerry pushed aside her plate, folded her arms on the table, and gave him an intent look. "What kind of nightmares?"

Scott fidgeted for a few seconds as if getting ready to speak, but didn't answer.

"The reason I ask," she said, "is that Bob has nightmares, too, and I wondered if yours are anything like his."

Her gaze met Bob's across the table. He broke contact first.

"I've met lots of Vietnam veterans," she said,

"and so many seem to have an underlying sadness." She looked from Scott to Bob. "Do you have these sadnesses too?"

Bob blew out a breath. "No. I was a supply clerk. I never had to fire a weapon at another person, or have one fired at me. I never had to watch a buddy die."

"Yet you have nightmares. I hear you thrashing around at night, and sometimes you call out."

"I see things in my dreams," he said quietly. "Things I cannot explain."

"Besides the jungle, you mean?"

He glanced around the table. The Mulligans focused their attention on him, and he squirmed.

"What kind of things do you see?" Kerry asked.

Bob shook his head, but found himself responding to her question. "Surreal images of war. Sometimes the scenes are strobic, coming and going so quickly I don't get a good look at them. Other times they are kaleidoscopic, a continuous stream of fluctuating forms I can't clearly define." He nodded at Scott. "That's why I couldn't stay at the meeting the other day. Since I never saw combat, these dreams can't have anything to do with me. I must be receptive to other men's stories."

Kerry turned to Scott. "What about your nightmares?"

"I'm sorry," he mumbled. "I can't."

"Sure you can," Jimmy said. "You always say we can do anything."

Rose gazed at Scott with anxious eyes. "Maybe you should tell her, dear. You have always refused to talk about your nightmares, even to us, but perhaps it's time."

"Go ahead, Dad," Beth chimed in. "You can tell Kerry."

"But what if you find out my life is a lie?" Scott asked his wife. "What if you find out I'm an evil person?"

Rose looked at him in astonishment. "Evil? You?"

"In my dreams I am."

"But those are only dreams."

Scott held her gaze. After a moment he spoke in a voice so low Bob could barely make out his words. "In one of my dreams, the VC is firing on us. I see a man down. He's hurt badly and is trying to crawl away. I go to help him, but before I drag him to safety, I take his M-16 from him. I don't know why. I just do it. Then, as if it's the most natural thing in the world, I shoot the VC. I see blood spurting out of the men I shoot, and I hear their screams, but I keep shooting. When the rifle is empty, I return the weapon to the injured soldier, who is staring at me as if he can't believe what he saw. He laughs, and I awaken with the sound of his laughter still echoing in my ears.

"All the dreams I have are similar to that one, but they involve different firefights and different men, as if I killed many times.

"I don't know what these dreams mean. I don't know why I dream them. But the idea that I murdered people, even if only in my dreams, makes me so sick I have to vomit. Sometimes after I've thrown up I feel as if I've gotten rid of the evil, but other times I feel as if the evil is a permanent part of me, and I wonder if somehow I did do those things."

He looked at Bob with sad, sad eyes. "But it is only a dream, right?"

"Of course," Bob said.

"And you're not responsible for what you dream," Kerry added.

The Mulligans gathered around Scott, hugging each other and crying. Kerry caught Bob's attention and tilted her head toward the door. He nodded to show he understood.

Trying to make as little noise as possible, they arose and let themselves out of the house.

10.

"It looks more like a college campus than a place of business," Kerry said.

Nodding in agreement, Bob stared out the window at ISI's corporate headquarters. A dozen six-story red brick buildings and a couple of single-story ones ringed a grassy area so extensive it looked like a park. Paved pathways meandered among shade trees, bushes, and flowering gardens, providing a running track for the energetic; benches and picnic tables had been scattered about for the more lethargic.

An ordinary chain link fence surrounded the entire campus. A manned sentry booth stood at each entrance to the parking lot, but Bob saw no evidence of the high-tech security system he had expected at such a secretive corporation.

When they drove to the end of the campus and turned right, he saw a startlingly different aspect of the same company. Here was an entrance heavily guarded by armed men, a high fence topped by razor wire, and a proliferation of security cameras. Strangely, the parking lot on this side of the campus seemed absurdly large in relation to the small, squat building.

Bob had Kerry drive around the entire complex again so he could study the clothing. There seemed to be no dress code. Some men wore business suits, but most dressed casually in slacks and shirts. Several wore lightweight jackets in acknowledgment of the cooling temperatures; a few wore sweaters. Most of the women dressed in suits.

"Where are they going?" Kerry reached across Bob and pointed to a stream of people headed for a single-story building next to the tennis courts.

Noting that some of them wore workout clothes

or carried a gym bag, Bob said, "An athletic club, probably. Maybe I can find an empty locker to stow my gear during the day."

Kerry's eyes grew grave. "You're going through with it?"

"Yes. I need to get a feel for the place, see who these people are, then maybe I can find a way out of this mess and get on with my life."

"What will you do, go back to Thailand?"

"No. I'll find some place, but it won't be here. I'm beginning to think Denver is the seventh circle of hell."

Kerry chuckled. "Tell me about it."

Bob reached into his pocket for Herbert Townsend's ID. After borrowing the nametag, he'd gone to the photo booth at the downtown Woolworth's, cut one of the pictures to fit over Townsend's, and covered the whole thing with clear packing tape.

He held it up, squinting at the nearest group of people. About half of them had nametags clipped to their clothes.

"Does this look like the ones they're wearing? I don't know how long it's been since Townsend worked here. The design might have been changed."

"It looks the same to me." The sparkle returned to Kerry's eyes. "I don't know how you got him to lend it to you. I don't even know how you got him to talk. Must be more of your hidden shallows."

Bob tucked the nametag back in his pocket. "He didn't tell me much. He started working here after college graduation. They offered him a huge salary, great perks, interesting work, and he jumped at the chance without ever finding out what else the company did besides sell new security systems and analyze old ones. Then I lost him. He talked about the microchip they put in his head and how Issy's going to get me too if I don't watch out."

"So, watch out," Kerry said.

"I intend to."

After leaving the ISI campus, they drove around for a while scouting out motels and bus routes.

"I wish you could stay with me," Kerry said, "but my roommate is coming back tomorrow." She smiled at him. "At least we had the weekend."

The dinner at the Mulligans had been on Friday night, so today, Monday, had been the first chance they'd had to check out ISI. When their schedules had coincided the past two days, they'd popped corn, watched movies on television, and played silly games, making a point of not discussing Bob's plan to infiltrate ISI.

"What now?" Kerry asked.

"Shopping."

"How about Southglen Mall? That's about as far away from here as we can get."

"Sounds good."

Bob searched the mall until he put together the perfect costume: forest green pants from one store, pale gold shirts with a flap on the pocket from another. A third store yielded a green, gold, and brown sweater that would blend nicely with the foliage he'd seen at the ISI complex. He also bought a gym bag. As at Bear Valley, he purchased each item with a traveler's check, netting him more cash. Before they left, he dashed into a toy store for a two-and-a-half-inch-diameter pink rubber ball.

They were quiet during the drive back to Broomfield. At Bob's direction, Kerry parked a block away from the motel he'd chosen for the night, then they lapsed into silence again.

"This is ridiculous," Kerry said. "Just kiss me and go." She offered her cheek.

Bob leaned over, intending to give her a friendly peck, but at the last minute she turned her head. Their lips met.

All at once they were in each other's arms, mouths locked together. When they finally pulled apart, Bob felt dizzy, and his resolve had fled.

Maybe he should forget about ISI for now and stay with Kerry awhile longer.

He pushed the thought out of his head. He couldn't allow himself any distractions. He had work to do. Besides, her roommate would return soon.

He got out of the car, said goodbye, and headed for the motel. He did not look back.

Once he'd checked in, he sat on the bed, back propped against the pillows, squeezing his new pink rubber ball, first with one hand, then the other, squeezing and squeezing until time to retire for the night.

He rose at dawn for his run. He put one foot in front of the other, refusing to dwell on anything but the steady rhythms of movement and breath.

Before he left for work, he attached the ISI identification card to his shirt pocket and was pleased to see the pocket flap covering the last name as he hoped it would.

He and several others got off the bus at the stop outside the ISI campus. The guard barely glanced at him as he passed.

Acting as if he belonged, he headed for the building by the tennis courts. As he surmised, it was an athletic club, and he did find an empty locker for his gym bag. Reminding himself to buy a lock, he went back outside and walked among the ISI employees.

He wondered who among them had an interest in him. *Is it you?* he silently asked the bird-beaked man. *Is it you?* he asked the chipmunk-cheeked woman. *Or you? Or you?*

As Bob watched, he noticed as many people coming out of the office buildings as entering. He had expected the grounds to empty as people settled into their jobs, but many individuals and small groups milled around.

Listening, he learned that many of these people were on break, having been at work since six or seven. He overheard one young woman explaining to a trainee about ISI's open-door policy. Employees could arrive as early as six in the morning and stay as late as seven in the evening. As long as they worked a full forty hours each week, they could set their own schedules.

Bob moved toward the single-story building that seemed to have the most interest for the most people. The cafeteria, he discovered.

He stood in line for a hot chocolate, listening to the gossip swirling around him.

"My daughter Susie got braces yesterday. She refuses to smile, says she'll probably never smile again."

"Don't worry, she'll get over it."

"How do you know?"

"My son Jack acted the same way."

"Did you know that Jan in Accounting is having an affair with Richard in Human Resources?"

"No. Really?"

"Yeah. Becky saw them coming out of a motel together."

"What was Becky doing there?" Laughter.

"Mary's pregnant."

"Mary Carter?"

"Yes."

"But how? I mean, you know, she's a lesbian."

"Artificial insemination."

"Oh."

"Don't look now, but there's that hot receptionist."

"Where? I don't see her."

"You missed her. Next time I see her, I'm gonna ask her out."

"Yeah, right. Like you stand a chance."

Bob took his hot chocolate out to the campus lawn, grateful for the warmth of the drink. This early in the morning the air was a bit nippy, and even with his sweater he felt cold.

After he finished his drink, he still felt chilly. He jogged slowly for a few minutes, trying to get warm. Ahead of him on the pathway rambled a group of young people who seemed barely out of school. All talked at once.

"Can you believe the nerve of that woman? She planned her retirement for months, told Baxter she quit . . ."

". . . we gave her that retirement party . . ."

". . . when I think of all the nice things we said to her . . ."

". . . engraved a watch to the best boss ever. We'll miss you . . ."

". . . bitch actually believed we meant it . . ."

". . . feel sorry for Joyce . . ."

". . . so excited about her promotion . . ."

". . . came to work today all ready to start her new job as supervisor of the mailroom. When Joyce stormed into Baxter's office, he shrugged and said Enid decided not to retire after all."

"Enid told me she retired because she thought we all hated her, but when she found out how much we liked her, she decided to stay."

"But we don't like her."

"We're screwed. She'll never leave now."

Bob veered off the path into the shadow of a stand of young, bushy Siberian elms with green and gold foliage. Snippets of conversation wafted through the autumn air.

"I hear we're going to be downsized."

"Oh, no! I came here from a company that got downsized. I can't go through it again."

". . . best barbecue I ever had. Too bad I went with that asshole Jared."

"I thought you liked him."

"I did, but he . . ."

"I spent all day on my 679K report, now they tell me they inputted the wrong data."

". . . took the cocktease out to dinner and she wouldn't put out. You promised me a sure thing. That's the last time I ever listen to . . ."

And so it went.

Two days later, Bob was standing by a honeysuckle bush listening to the sound of hundreds of voices talking, whining, arguing, laughing, when suddenly a man on a skateboard crashed into him.

The man, about forty years old with a slight paunch and curly black hair, stared at him in astonishment. "Sorry, man. I didn't see you."

"No problem," Bob said.

"My wife tells me I'm too old for skateboarding. So does my doctor—he says my knees are shot. Looks like they're right. What a bummer.

Name's Don. Don Donati. Actually, it's Percival, but no one calls me that if they know what's good for them. I work in Advertising, administrative assistant to the department head. I'm also the liaison between the Advertising Department and Marketing. You're that new guy in Marketing, aren't you? Thought I recognized you, but, hey, man, what are you doing over here all by yourself? You'll never meet anyone that way. Why don't you come sit with me and my friends. We're right over there." He lifted a hand to wave at a group of people seated at one of the picnic tables; they all waved back.

"Sure, why not?" Bob followed Don to the table.

"Hey, everybody, this is—" Don glanced at Bob.

"Herb," Bob said.

Don sat down, shoving trays of dirty dishes out of his way, and motioned for Bob to do the same. Don finished the introductions, then said, "Herb's the new guy in Marketing."

A bony young woman named Julia snickered. "Marketing, huh? Good luck."

Bob turned to look at her. "What does that mean?"

"Don't listen to her," said John, a young man with the hopeful shadow of a goatee. "She thinks the Marketing Department is cursed."

"Well, it is," Julia insisted.

"Really?" Bob asked.

"Yes," Julia answered.

"No way," John said at the same time.

Bob looked at Don, who shrugged. "It's not cursed, of course, but some weird things have happened to the people in Marketing."

"Like what?"

"Like that guy who disappeared," chubby, blond Heather said.

"Who disappeared?" John demanded. "I never heard about anyone disappearing."

Julia bobbed her head. "Yes, you did. Remember Will Turnow?"

"Oh, him." John waved a hand dismissively.

"How did he disappear?" Bob asked.

"No one knows," redheaded Andy responded. "He went to Boston for a seminar, attended a few meetings, and no one ever saw him again."

"He acted like a jerk, anyway," John said.

Julia looked at him with a puzzled expression in her chocolate brown eyes. "What does that have to do with anything?"

John stared back at her. "It has everything to do with it. I mean, like, who cares?"

Julia held up a finger. "There was also that guy who got killed."

"Are you talking about Doug Roybal? He died in a rock climbing accident."

"But he still worked in Marketing. And there were those two guys who claimed to have been beamed aboard a space ship, and what about that guy who had terrible temper tantrums. What's his name?"

"Jerold Hancock," Don answered.

"Who's he?" Heather asked.

Julia spread her hands. "You know, that tall, good-looking guy in Marketing? The one who says hello to everyone?"

"But he's so nice." Heather glanced around the table at the others. "I don't get it."

John rolled his eyes. "There's nothing to get. Jerold is a valuable employee who had a vicious temper, so human resources sent him to a clinic in Boston where he learned how to control it. I don't know why you guys have to make such a big deal out of everything."

"What clinic?" Bob asked.

John stared at him. "Why do you want to know?"

"Hey, chill out, man," Don said. "What's with you?"

Heather giggled. "Maybe John needs to go to that clinic."

John glared at her, then turned back to Bob. "Well?"

Bob shrugged. "Just curious."

"It's at the Rosewood Research Institute," Andy said. "I know a few people who were sent there for treatment of personality disorders and came back completely cured. Those doctors have developed a program that works fast—usually takes a couple of weeks. It's miraculous."

"They are also involved in some of the most promising cancer research," Heather put in. She flushed when the others stared at her in astonishment. "I read that somewhere, okay?"

Julia tapped a finger on her chin. "Now that I think about it, the company sent those guys who saw the UFO to Boston for examination. I guess Issy wanted to make sure they weren't crazy."

John snorted. "They should have been sent to a mental hospital. Anyone who sees UFOs is obviously nuts."

"That one poor guy did go nuts," Andy said softly.

"No surprise there." John sniffed. "He was always unbalanced."

Heather sighed. "I wish I'd seen a UFO."

"Are you crazy?" Julia shrieked.

"No." Heather sounded wistful. "I've always wanted to be on television, and Michael Mortimer is on TV all the time talking about his experiences."

"What if you turned out like Herb Townsend instead?" John asked.

Bob remained still, though Townsend's nametag seemed to burn through his shirt.

"I wouldn't turn out like him." Heather shook her curls. "You said Herb was unbalanced, and I'm not."

"That's what you think," John said.

Heather lifted her chin. "Well, if I did go crazy, I wouldn't wear that ugly aluminum thing on my head. It's so . . . so . . . you know, ugly."

Julia giggled. "Herb never did dress well. I mean, really—plaid jackets? And that hair!"

"It's surprising he managed to get so many women interested in him," Don said. "He acted sort of crude, but he still seemed to be always having affairs."

John snorted. "Goes to show how desperate women are."

"You want to know why women liked him?" Julia glared at John. "He was charming, which is something you will never be."

John laughed. "I love it when you unsheath your claws."

She lowered her head, cheeks flaming.

He put a forefinger under her chin, raised her head, and gently touched his lips to hers. Giggling, she jumped up from the table and ran off, glancing behind as if to make sure he followed.

Heather watched John and Julia duck behind some bushes. "I don't get it. I mean, they don't even like each other."

"I'm not sure liking has much to do with love or lust." Andy stood. "Time for me to get back to work." He gathered his lunch tray and the ones John and Julia had left behind. He nodded at Bob. "Nice meeting you, Herb."

He walked off, balancing the three trays.

"Hey! Wait for me." Heather grabbed her tray and hurried after him.

Don took a squashed sandwich out of one pocket and an apple out of another. He smiled at Bob. "My six-year-old daughter makes my lunch for me. It's always something weird like peanut butter and banana with chocolate chips. I could never hurt her feelings by not eating it, but I get tired of the sarcastic remarks John makes when he sees it, so I wait until he's gone before I eat. I do leave the Barbie doll lunch box in the car. If I toted that into the office, I'd never hear the end of it."

He unwrapped the sandwich and offered Bob half.

"No, thanks."

"Do you have children, Herb?"

"No."

"I'm sorry."

Bob inclined his head, but remained silent.

While Don ate, he talked with glowing pride about his family: his brilliant wife, feisty daughter, and mischievous son.

When he finished, he said, "Feel free to come eat lunch with us anytime. We're always glad of a new audience." Laughing, he hopped on his skateboard and shoved off.

Bob looked around and noticed a small, dark-haired, tense young woman sitting at the next picnic table. She shot surreptitious glances at him. Yesterday he'd also caught her staring. Who was she? One of his hunters? He was debating whether to confront her when she looked at her watch, jumped up, and sped into one of the buildings.

11.

Like a well-oiled machine, Bob did one smoothly flowing push-up after another until his arms quivered with exhaustion. Giving himself no time to rest, he rolled onto his back and began to do sit-ups, completely relaxed except for the abdominal muscles pulling him up then setting him back down. When his muscles rebelled, he arose and went outside for a run, covering mile after endless mile in an easy lope.

A shower, a shave, and a leisurely breakfast, then he returned to ISI.

He had learned that admittance to some of the buildings required a card key and retina scan, but most had minimal security. He slipped into one of these buildings in the midst of a stream of people and looked around. Bright colors and a profusion of plants could not offset the depressing sight of so many humans encaged in tiny cubicles, staring vacantly at flickering computer screens while their fingers flitted spasmodically over the keyboards. He hurried back outside to the fresh air and the infinite blue sky.

As he moved about the campus, the conversations he heard filtered through his mind like plankton through the mouth of a whale.

Sue Ellen delivered her baby, finally. Neil Jr. starred in the school play. They fired Kathy. Brewster got his promotion. Joe quit. The computers are down again. Sara is on the verge of a nervous collapse. Alice, that bitch, is sleeping her way to the top. Well, at least she's not sleeping her way to the bottom, ha, ha. Robert Stark is starting to piss me off.

Bob froze, then stealthily stepped around a bush. Sitting at a picnic table twenty feet away, were the very men who hunted him.

He stood absolutely still, watching, listening.

"Starting to piss you off?" hooted the man with the deep voice. "Ever since he gave us the slip at the airport, you've been acting like a grizzly who found a hornet's nest when he went poking about for a honeycomb."

"The fuck you talking about, Sam?"

Sam laughed. "I forgot how much you hate being compared to a bear . . . Teddy."

Baritone glared at him.

Sam laughed again. "Lighten up, Ted."

"Asshole."

Except for an inch or two difference in their height, Sam and Ted seemed remarkably similar. They were both about thirty-five, well over six feet tall, broad across the shoulders, lean-hipped, flat-bellied, hard-eyed. Brown hair tumbled down their foreheads, giving them an utterly deceptive appearance of vulnerability.

"I don't get it," Ted grumbled. "Evans says Stark's been under surveillance on and off for sixteen years. He says Stark's retarded—never understood even the simplest joke. He also says Stark is a limp dick. All he does in a whorehouse is sit and drink tea. The guy was a waiter, for cripes sake. So how does this pathetic nothing, this wimp, manage to elude us—us!—for six weeks?"

"I don't know who Evans got his information from," Sam said, "but it doesn't add up. Stark acts like a professional. Not many people would walk away from everything they own on a moment's notice."

"He didn't own much and what he did own looked like junk." Ted shivered. "Those paintings sure gave me the creeps."

"Doesn't matter if it's junk. The less people have, the more they need to hold on to it."

Two men approached and sat across from Sam and Ted. One was black and the other white, but they too were a matched set. Both had the beefy, over-developed look of men who spend too much time in the gym, and both had the arrogant bearing of people who thought they were special. They would have been handsome, each in his own way, but for the identical smirks marring their faces.

The white man chortled. "I hear you two are in trouble."

"Yeah," the other said. "Not looking in the hem of the drapes for the papers. What amateurs."

"Evans's wonder boys aren't so wonderful after all."

The two newcomers high-fived and laughed uproariously.

"Assholes," Ted muttered.

Sam raised his eyebrows. "Weren't you the two staking out the boardinghouse when our little fugitive snuck back in?"

The laughter stopped abruptly.

The dark-skinned man pointed to his partner. "Grimes here—"

Grimes interrupted. "Don't blame it on me, Clayton, you know it was the cops—"

Sam overrode them both. "I don't care who did what or why. The point is that Stark is making us all look bad."

The other three nodded in agreement.

"I hate that fucker," Ted said. "When I get my hands on him, he's going to be one sorry son of a bitch."

Grimes stared at Ted in surprise, then turned to Sam. "What's with him?"

Sam shrugged. "PMS." When no one laughed,

he continued, "We've been looking for this guy for six weeks, and he's always a half step ahead of us. Ted has never had to deal with failure before."

"I'm gonna kill him first chance I get." Ted slammed his fist on the table. "No one, and I mean no one, gets the better of me."

"The thing is," Sam said, "it's like he's taunting us. He doesn't bother to hide—a lot of people have seen him, but we still don't know what he looks like."

Clayton smirked. "We do."

Sam raised his eyebrows. "Oh?"

"We went around to all the stores in Bear Valley where he used his traveler's checks. We got a good description from one girl."

"What does he look like?" Ted demanded.

"He's really, really short, and he's got like this gray hair and he's like really, really old." Clayton spoke in a singsong voice as if mimicking someone.

Sam roared with laughter. "You're kidding, right?"

"Nope, direct quote," Clayton said.

"Who was she? A six-foot-tall teenager wearing high heels?"

Clayton looked surprised. "How did you know?"

"Because the one thing we know for certain is that he's average," Sam said. "Average height, average weight. And he's in his late thirties."

Grimes poked his partner in the ribs. "Told you."

Clayton glared at him.

"We have a lot of pictures taken in Southeast Asia," Sam said, "but the guy in the photos looks like a Thai peasant or a Chinese waiter. I'm not even sure it's Stark. But I am certain no one who looks like that got off the plane at Stapleton when we were there." Sam rubbed his forehead. "Supposedly our Stark resembles the one you're now tailing, but it's hard to tell from the pictures."

"I thought you guys got a more recent picture," Grimes said.

Ted snorted. "So did we. That bitch."

"The old woman who owns the boardinghouse where Stark lives agreed to work with a sketch artist," Sam said. "She even swore the finished picture looked exactly like Stark."

"What's the problem?" Grimes asked. "How come we don't have a copy of the picture?"

Sam laughed humorlessly. "I take it you haven't seen it."

"No," Grimes and Clayton said simultaneously.

Sam turned to Ted. "Do you still have a copy?"

"Yeah." Ted dug a piece of paper out of his pocket and handed it to Clayton.

Clayton unfolded it with great ceremony. He stared down at the picture, then up at Sam. "Is this some kind of joke?"

"'Fraid not."

"Let me see." Grimes tried to snatch the piece of paper out of Clayton's hand.

Clayton held it out of reach. "Gimme a second."

He studied the picture, shaking his head, then handed it to his partner.

"What the hell is this?" Grimes asked, scowling. "Why're you showing us a picture of Charles Manson?"

"That's how the old woman described Stark," Sam said. "Wild, crazy eyes, masses of filthy hair, and all." He took the picture from Grimes and looked at it. "Makes you wonder what he did to her. We asked, but she wouldn't get specific. Just went on and on about knives."

"Knives?" Grimes questioned.

Sam nodded.

"Who is this guy?" Clayton demanded.

"Dead meat," Ted said.

Sam refolded the picture and returned it to Ted. "No one knows except Evans, and he's not telling."

"What I don't get is if Evans wants this Manson-type Stark," Clayton said, "why are we staking out a completely different Robert Stark?"

Sam shrugged. "Evans thinks our Stark will try to contact your Stark. Don't ask me why, because I don't know."

"Are they cousins?" Grimes asked. "A lot of times cousins have the same name, you know."

"I said I don't know," Sam repeated harshly.

After the hunters had dispersed, Bob returned to himself, though he remained in the protective embrace of the bushes for several minutes longer.

The words "sixteen years" kept going around and around in his head, like the refrain of a song too terrible to forget.

He tried to concentrate on who could have been watching him the entire time he had lived in Bangkok, and why. He even tried to focus on Ted's overt and Sam's covert hatred. But all he could think about was that someone had been watching him on and off for sixteen years.

Sixteen years.

12.

"I know you." Kerry held the door open. "Won't you come in?"

The light danced in her eyes, but Bob detected a slight distance in her manner. Or perhaps the distance lay in him. Like an automaton, he'd retrieved his gym bag from the locker at ISI and climbed aboard a bus. He hadn't even known he was coming to see her until he disembarked at the stop closest to her friend's house.

He gave a vague look around the living room as if it had been weeks since he'd seen it instead of a few days.

"Is your friend here?"

"She's at her office, but she'll be home soon."

"Oh." He felt himself swaying from exhaustion.

She herded him toward a chair and pointed at it. "Sit."

He sat.

"Would you like something to drink? Hot chocolate? I think there's also some of your green tea left."

"Green tea, please." He preferred that beverage, but he ordered hot chocolate when eating out because Denver restaurants usually served insipid herbal blends and pekoes.

He sipped the tea, feeling its warmth overcome the chill he'd felt ever since hearing the words "sixteen years."

Not wanting to think about that, he said, "Are you still working the same schedule?"

She waved a hand. "Don't bother me with trivial questions. What did you find out?"

"Lisa Donati beat up a bully at school, and her brother Josh sneaked into the girl's restroom. Amanda

Donati, their mother, is a partner at a downtown law firm."

Her brows drew together. "I don't know what you mean."

Bob put his empty teacup on the coffee table and stood. "That's mostly the kind of thing I found out."

She chewed her lower lip as she gave him a considering look. "You said mostly. That means you did learn something."

"Could be."

He moved toward the door.

"You can't leave now!" She jumped to her feet. "It's not fair."

"Your roommate will be back soon," he reminded her.

"Oh, right. It's safer for you if no one knows where you are."

"Safer for you, too."

"Me?" The questioning look in her eyes turned to one of astonishment. "You think I'm in danger?"

"It's possible. Until I know what's happening, it's best if I stay away. I shouldn't have come here tonight."

"Where are you going?"

"A motel."

She grabbed her keys and purse off the coffee table. "I'll drive you."

At his request, she took him to a motel on east I-70, far from ISI. She waited until he registered, then got out of her Toyota and gave him an impish smile.

"I better check out the room for you. See if it's okay."

"Can I stop you?"

"No."

She followed him up the stairs and along the corridor to the room at the back. "Typical," she said, stepping inside. "Like any motel room anywhere in the world." She sniffed. "It smells like someone tried to burn the place. Didn't you ask for a non-smoking room?"

He took off his sweater. "Of course."

She plopped on the bed. "Now what?"

"I need to take a shower, wash off ISI and all its filth." Looking pointedly at the exit, he unbuttoned his shirt, but she didn't take the hint.

Shrugging, he went into the bathroom, got undressed, and climbed into the shower. He stood motionless under the spray, letting the hot water cascade over his body and upturned face.

Kerry poked her head into the shower. "Looks like you can use some help." The next thing he knew, her naked torso nestled against his back and her arms encircled his waist, melting the last of the ice in his bones.

After a minute, maybe two, her hands inched downward. He turned around and looked at her through hooded eyes.

"Is this what you want?"

"Yes." She spoke in a hoarse whisper.

"Then first things first."

Reaching out from behind the curtain, he snagged both washcloths from the towel rack and handed one to her. By the time they'd washed each other slowly from head to foot, then stepped out of the shower and toweled each other dry, she was gasping, and her knees wobbled.

He scooped her up in his arms.

Her eyes widened and her lips parted. "I didn't realize you were so . . ."

"Didn't realize what?" he murmured as he laid her on the bed and brushed a string of kisses along the sweet curve of her throat.

A soft moan swallowed her response.

She sprawled half on top of him, one leg between his, her head resting on his chest. He could feel her breath on his skin and the beating of her heart. A sense of finally coming home washed over him.

"Wow," she said drowsily. "I think I still have orgasms backed up, waiting to land."

He kissed the top of her head and inhaled the scent of her hair: clean and salty like an ocean breeze. He could feel the growing tug and tingle of urgency.

She must have felt it, too, because she said, "Don't tell me you're ready again."

"If you want to."

"I want but I don't know if I can. I feel like a cat stretched out in front of a lit fireplace, all warm and boneless."

"Then you lie still, and I'll do everything."

He rolled her over, knelt with a knee on either side of her body and, cupping her breasts, caressed her nipples with his thumbs.

She let out a rumble of contentment that sounded like a purr.

In the early morning hours, they finally fell asleep.

When Bob awoke in the bright of day, Kerry lay on her side, head propped on one elbow, gazing at him.

A small smile played on her lips. "Where did you learn to make a woman feel like that?"

"From a woman."

"An old girlfriend?"

"No. Except for Lorena, I never had a girlfriend."

She blinked. "That doesn't seem possible."

"It's the truth. Jackson was two years ahead of me in high school. He was a good-looking football hero, student council president, and in the top ten percent of his class. Girls couldn't resist him.

"I dated some of the popular girls in my class and a lot of the not-so-popular girls. They went out with me to try to get closer to my brother, but I was young enough to hope that once they got to know me, they would like me for myself. It never happened. After a while, I felt like a court jester trying to entertain girls who never even bothered to feign interest. When I realized how much time and money I wasted on those dates, I stopped going out until I met Lorena in a college history class. We enjoyed each other's company, but she didn't like sex."

Kerry chuckled. "So how did she end up with all those children?"

"Technically she could have done it a mere six times."

"I guess. Then how did you . . . oh, I see. Patpong Road."

"Close. It was an exclusive establishment over by the American embassy."

"Did it have a name?"

He felt a rumble of laughter somewhere deep inside him. "That's all you want to know—the name?"

Her eyes twinkled. "Of course not, but it's a start."

"It had no official name, but everyone called it Madame Butterfly's after the woman who owned it."

"Her name can't really be Madame Butterfly, can it? Who is she?"

"No one knows much about her, not even her real name or nationality, but according to one rumor, she was working as a prostitute in Shin Yoshiwara, Tokyo's red light district, when a rich American enticed her to run off with him. He later abandoned her in Bangkok.

"Determined never to be that foolish again, the story goes, she learned everything about men and women and what went on between them. They said she was so good that simply by looking at a man she could tell exactly what he needed. Because of this, she could charge exorbitant rates. When she accumulated enough money, she opened her own brothel, catering to men who wanted the best and could pay the price.

"To add to her mystique, she dressed like a geisha, complete with elaborate makeup, so very few people know what she looks like."

Kerry's eyes grew bright with curiosity. "And did she?"

Bob sat up, arranged the pillow at his back, and leaned against the headboard. "Did she what?"

"Know what you needed."

"Apparently she thought I needed more from sex than mere physical gropings beneath the sheets and she decided to educate me in the art of seduction. This is hindsight, of course. At the time I didn't realize she had a plan."

"So she was your . . . your mistress?"

"No."

Kerry sat cross-legged on the bed, elbows on knees, chin cupped in her hands. "Then who was?"

"Several women. The first ones taught me about controlling myself, the next few taught me how and where to touch a woman, and the last one taught me the subtleties and ceremony of seduction."

Kerry batted her eyelashes. "Like this?"

Giving her a sidelong glance, Bob let the back of a hand graze her knee. "More like that. We'd sit in the reception room, drinking tea from fragile cups, talking of inconsequential matters, and touching as if by accident. Each tiny touch serves to arouse until the tension becomes unbearable, but you learn to bear it, and continue."

Kerry giggled. "It sounds like the Chinese water torture. Or high school."

Bob caressed her cheek with the knuckle of an index finger. "But infinitely more enjoyable."

Unbidden, a memory insinuated itself into his mind: Ted, at ISI, saying that all Stark does in a whorehouse is sit and drink tea. Bob shivered; while he'd been playing his innocent games, someone had been keeping watch.

"Bob?"

He turned toward the sound of her voice.

She peered at him. "Are you all right?"

"I'm fine." He tried to give her a reassuring smile, but it felt more like a grimace.

She sprang to her feet. "I'm going out to get us some food. You're probably starving. I know I am."

He watched her get dressed, noticing how unselfconsciously she pulled on her white cotton panties, lacy bra, jeans, socks, and the shirt that, as usual, she wore untucked.

When she finished tying her sneakers, she scooped up her purse. "Anything in particular you want?"

He shook his head no.

She opened the door and looked back. "I won't be long."

"I'll be waiting."

***

The aroma of breakfast—waffles and syrup, scrambled eggs, bacon, sausage, orange juice, hot chocolate and coffee—helped to dispel the stench of stale smoke that seemed to have grown stronger in Kerry's absence.

They sat side-by-side, leaning against the headboard, surrounded by Styrofoam take-out containers. As they ate, Kerry made a point of letting her hand occasionally graze against his. The glee in her eyes added to his enticement.

Bob smiled at her. "Now all you need is a cheongsam like the girls at Madame Butterfly's wear. There's something very seductive about that prim, Mandarin collar and the side slit showing off a shapely leg, and yours are especially alluring."

Kerry's eyes widened. "I used to have a dress like that. An aunt brought it back from a tour of Hong Kong." A grin appeared on her face. "Mother made me sew up the side. She said it was unseemly. I laughed and she got mad. She never did appreciate puns."

When Kerry continued to tease him with her touches, Bob gently put her hand in her lap. "If you don't stop, you won't be going to work tonight, either."

She flashed a radiant smile. "I don't have to go. I've been trading time so I could have the weekend off."

He slanted a glance at her. "You knew I would come back to you?"

"I didn't know. I hoped." Her smile faded. "You still haven't told me what you learned."

The bit of bacon he'd put into his mouth suddenly tasted of bile. He finished the laborious act of chewing and swallowing, then said, "I saw the two guys who searched my room. Their names are Sam and

Ted."

Kerry's eyes were enormous. "What did you do?"

"Watched. Listened. Discovered that two other guys, Grimes and Clayton, staked out the boarding-house the night I retrieved my passport and traveler's checks. Some time after that night my room must have been searched again because they know Sam and Ted hadn't looked in the hem of the drapes for the papers."

"Those mysterious papers again. Could they be identification papers, like your passport?"

Bob shook his head. "I don't think so, but I can't rule anything out."

"Did you find out why they're after you?"

"No." He stared at the framed mountain scene hanging crookedly on the opposite wall. "I think they want to kill me. Or worse."

Kerry's breath caught in her throat. "What's worse?"

"It seems there's a clinic in Boston affiliated with ISI that does behavior modifications."

"Behavior modifications? You mean like . . . mind control?"

"Yes." He forced air into his lungs. "I think they did something to Herbert Townsend, the foil man, among others."

Kerry's voice rose an octave. "And these are the people that are after you?"

He nodded.

She took his right hand in both of hers. "What are we going to do?"

"Not we. I."

"But—"

"People are being altered," he said harshly. "They are dying. I don't want the same thing happening to you that happened to Dr. Albion."

"You mean the doctor at the VA hospital? What happened to him?

"He had an allergy to alcohol, yet supposedly died in a car accident while drunk. Ever since Scott Mulligan told me many ex-CIA agents work for ISI, I've been wondering if Sam and Ted or their counterparts killed the doctor. Fatal car accidents are a specialty of that agency. I know it sounds nuts, but I can't help thinking someone wanted to prevent his inquiry into my military records."

She looked befuddled. "What would your military records have to do with the gold Buddha?"

"Nothing. In fact the Buddha is not part of this at all."

She swung around to face him. "How do you know?"

He looked away, unable to meet her bright gaze. When he glanced at her again, he saw that she still had her attention focused on him.

He felt the skin tightening over his face as he spoke the words. "They've been watching me on and off for sixteen years."

A sharp intake of breath. "Sixteen years!"

"That's what they said."

She studied him through narrowed eyes. "Does this have anything to do with you being a spy?"

He drew back. "A spy?"

"Don't you remember? At Buckingham Square when we watched your other self, I asked if you'd ever done that sort of thing before, and you said yes."

"Oh, right. The syndicate of sergeants." His mouth dropped open, and he stared at her, unable to believe what he'd said. He pushed the Styrofoam containers aside and scrambled off the bed. He had put on his pants and shirt when she went for food; now he grabbed his socks and shoes and headed for the door.

"Where are you going?" Kerry pressed her fingertips to her mouth. "Did I say something wrong?"

Bob turned around. Seeing the hurt in her eyes, he took two long steps toward her before he could stop himself.

"I'm sorry, but I can't afford the luxury of being with you. This person I am when I'm around you . . . I don't know who he is. He's not the real me. He's too relaxed and he talks too much. The real me is the man you first saw in the Rimrock Coffee Shop. You once referred to him as a mousy little fellow, and you were right. He is. And that's the person I need to be right now."

To his surprise, her eyes danced. "Another self. That makes three of you."

He frowned at her. "I'm being serious." ·

"So am I. Did it ever occur to you that the person you are around me could be the real you? In your whole life, no one tried to draw you out. You and Hsiang-li shared some sort of compact of silence. He didn't even tell you the most important episode in his life until the very end. Whatever friends you had, I bet they did all the talking while you sat there, never interrupting. And your parents. They were probably so enamored with their perfect Jackson they never paid any attention to you."

Bob sank onto the chair by the door and put on his shoes and socks. That she knew him so well did not alter the situation. He still had to leave to keep ISI from finding out about his relationship with this young woman who'd managed to penetrate his very soul.

He glanced up from tying his shoes. Her eyes appeared unfocused, staring at something only she could see.

She shifted her gaze to him. "I still don't understand what set you off. The last thing you mentioned was the syndicate of sergeants. That's the Khaki Mafia, isn't it?"

He shot bolt upright. "You know about the Khaki Mafia?"

She gave him a curious look. "Sure. Everyone knows."

"How?"

"William Henry Harrison wrote a book about it. I reread it not too long ago."

"William Henry Harrison wrote a book about the Khaki Mafia," he repeated flatly.

"Yes. He's that best-selling author—"

Bob nodded. "I know him. Tell me about the book."

"It's a novel called *Dark Side of Heroes* and starts out with this guy Bob Noone—spelled with an *e* like no one—sitting on the veranda of a hotel in a Vietnamese resort town called Nha Trang. Until I read the book, I didn't even know Vietnam *had* resort areas." She sighed. "One more place I never got to see, but it must have been beautiful with miles of white sandy beaches next to the turquoise waters of the South China Sea."

"Did Harrison happen to mention why Noone went there?"

"Sure. He was recuperating from an injury and waiting for his orders. A guy approached him and introduced himself as Michael Tate. Tate told Noone he was from the State Department and that the army had lent Noone to him for a temporary duty assignment. See, this organization of sergeant majors ran the NCO clubs, and they'd been misappropriating—that's the word Harrison used, I call it stealing—liquor, food, cigarettes, and anything else they could get their hands on and selling them on the black market, possibly to the VC. That organization extended all the way to the Pentagon. Tate wanted Noone to hang out at the NCO clubs, get a feel for the place, see who ran things, who drove the trucks. All the minor observations that could add up after a while.

"Noone protested that he was a private and didn't know anything about undercover work, but Tate gave him uniforms with stripes, the proper ID, and even a jeep so he could move from base to base. Tate wanted him because he seemed so plain and ordinary and non-threatening that nobody would pay attention to him long enough to notice he spent all his time at the NCO clubs."

Her eyes sparkled. "But Tate was wrong. Some people did notice."

She paused to gulp the last of the orange juice and sip her coffee. Bob moved from the chair to the unused bed and sat on the side, facing her.

She searched the take-out containers. "There's a couple pieces of bacon left, you interested?"

He shook his head. Even if he wanted to speak, he didn't think he could. There was something surreal about hearing this particular story from her lips, and it stripped him of all capacities and desires except to hear more.

Kerry ate the bacon, then settled back against her pillow. "One of the people who noticed Noone was a war correspondent named John Tyler. Tyler was a big, hearty man who usually wore a gauzy white suit. Since Tyler also moved from NCO club to NCO club, doing research for articles, he often hitched a ride with Noone, and the two became friends.

"Noone learned to recognize many of the people involved in the Khaki Mafia and reported his findings when he and Tate met."

"Did Harrison say what happened to the sergeant majors?"

A frown flashed across her face. "Nothing happened to them."

"What to you mean nothing? They were thieves on a grand scale. They were traitors. They sold out their country, pocketing tens and tens of millions of dollars, and left the American taxpayers to foot the bill."

"According to the book, very few criminal charges were ever filed and those charges were against the guys on the low end of the organization. Most of the others retained their jobs, some retired with full pensions. They even got to keep their ill-gotten gains."

Bob slumped forward, burying his face in his hands.

"There was more to the book than the Khaki Mafia," Kerry said. "After Tate terminated the surveillance of the NCO clubs, he sent Noone to Bangkok to spy on the CIA and NSA."

Bob's head jerked up. "Harrison knew? Did he say why Tate sent Noone to Thailand?"

"Something about the government needing to find out what the Chinese did to help the North Vietnamese. The NSA erected communication towers in Thailand to intercept military transmissions from China, and got college students and recent graduates who scored high on language aptitude tests to work there. A lot of those kids went to whorehouses and some talked about their work. The CIA owned the whorehouses, and a couple of their contract workers sold the information they heard to the communists. Tate wanted Noone to hang out at the whorehouses and try to find out who did the talking and who did the selling."

Bob shook his head.

Kerry put her hands on her hips. "That's what Harrison wrote."

"I believe you. I just don't understand how he knew about that. I never told him, and I doubt the man from the State Department did either."

13.

Kerry blinked. "What do you mean—you never told him?" Her eyes grew round. "Are you saying you're Bob Noone?"

"Apparently."

"William Henry Harrison, the author who's been on the bestsellers list every week for fifteen years, wrote a novel about you?" She threw a pillow at Bob. "How could you not tell me something like that?"

"I didn't know. I haven't read all of his books, and he seldom talked about them."

Kerry gaped at him. "I don't believe this. It's like I stepped into a different universe."

Bob nodded stiffly, trying to smile. "Welcome to my world. Tate, as Harrison called him, swore me to secrecy. I've spent the past sixteen years guarding my tongue, and now I find I've been protecting a secret the whole world knows."

"So, before when you said you knew Harrison, you meant you knew him personally?"

"Yes. We've been friends since Vietnam, like it says in the book. He's John Tyler."

"Weirder and weirder."

"Not really. He worked as a war correspondent when we met. He didn't become internationally famous until later. Back then, only us grunts knew him. Many American soldiers in Vietnam weren't too sure who General William C. Westmoreland was—"

"Who?" Kerry said.

"Exactly. But we all knew of William Henry Harrison, the one journalist who wrote stories that made us feel like heroes, as if perhaps we really were fighting for truth and justice, as if perhaps our presence meant something after all. The funny thing—" He stopped and shook his head. "See? Around you I always seem to be letting things slip."

"But you didn't," Kerry pointed out. "Besides, you can't stop there. What were you going to say?"

He regarded her for a moment, then shrugged. "He revealed me to the world. I guess I can reveal him to you. Some of the stories he wrote in Vietnam weren't true."

Laughter sparkled in her eyes. "You're kidding."

"No. He told me once the press hung out together and came to a consensus on what happened so all their stories had the same bias. Like the Tet offensive. The rest of the press corps wrote articles calling it a great psychological victory for the NVA, but Harrison saw it as a rallying point for the South Vietnamese. Before Tet, the war hadn't greatly affected the lives of the city dwellers, and they didn't care who won, but once their cities became war zones, on the most sacred day of the year, no less, they grew outraged. Harrison wrote that if the allied forces pushed their advantage, they would soon win. Instead of printing this story, his editor sent him a message telling him if he didn't stop writing his anticommunist bullshit and stick to the facts, he would be fired."

"But Harrison was right, wasn't he?"

Bob nodded. "His editor refused to print the article. He also rejected Harrison's story about the VC forcing whores to stuff glass up their privates before copulating with American GIs. And he rejected the one about toddlers being sent into bars with live grenades strapped to their bodies and getting blown up along with everyone else. The editor called these articles anticommunist propaganda."

"So those things did happen?" Kerry said in a

small voice. "I'd read about them, but didn't know what to think."

Bob shifted position. "It was not a pretty war."

She crossed her arms at her waist. "I'm glad you got to play secret agent instead of having to fight."

"I didn't play secret agent." He smiled at her. "I know this because secret agents have ingenious gadgets, fast cars, and gorgeous girls. I had a jeep and Harrison."

She chuckled. "Well, now you have the girl. What happened with Harrison?"

"He decided to prove his editor could not discern the difference between fact and fiction, so he sat at his typewriter and banged out an imaginary story. To make it as obvious as possible that he fabricated his story, he wrote that the hero's name was John Kane but his buddies called him Big Jake. He described Big Jake as a hellfighter with true grit."

"I remember that story," Kerry said. "We had to read it in school. The VC captured one of Big Jake's friends after an ambush. The sergeant refused to authorize a rescue mission, so Big Jake went off on his own and tracked the VC to a small compound where several Americans were being held. Big Jake picked the VC off one by one and rescued all the prisoners. When he led them back to base camp, his sergeant congratulated him and told him he was a real horse soldier who rode tall in the saddle."

"The story catapulted Harrison to fame. He decided if that's what people wanted, he'd give it to them. He told me, 'We're living in a strange new world where what people think is true means more than what really is, where fallacy is more powerful than fact. The illusion of John Wayne as the quintessential American war hero is much more real than the fact that he never went to war, never even enlisted in the military.' Years later, when Harrison got a contract for the definitive novel of the Vietnam era, he found he couldn't write fiction, even though he'd been doing it all along, so he wrote the truth."

Kerry laughed. "You're telling me his non-fiction was fiction, and his fiction was non-fiction?"

"Yes. He researched and wrote his novels as if they were nonfiction, then he added dialogue."

She gave him a sheepish look. "I guess I made a mistake before when I said your friends did all the talking. If he knew enough about you to put you in a book, he must have listened while you talked."

"You weren't wrong. I never told him anything about myself—that's what's so strange. Of course, he saw me in Vietnam, but the rest had to have been guesswork. He once mentioned that after I left Vietnam he heard talk of a secret government agency infiltrating the CIA-owned brothels in Thailand, but he never indicated he knew my part in the investigation."

Bob slowly shook his head. "I still can't believe he wrote a book about me, or that anyone bothered to read it. It was all so boring. Endless hours of listening to inane conversations and watching people drink, gamble, or play pool. I don't know how I'd have survived without Harrison's stories. He believed the ability to tell stories is the one thing separating humans from animals, and he always had a story."

"What kind of stories? No, wait a second." Kerry gathered the empty Styrofoam containers, threw them in the trash, then retrieved her pillow. She took Bob by the hand and led him over to the bed where they'd slept. When they had curled up together, she said, "Now you can tell me one of his stories."

Bob touched her shoulder-length hair, letting it

slide through his fingers. The sunlight shafting through the window made it glow like smoldering charcoal.

"You can begin anytime," she said.

"You'll fall asleep like you did when I told you Hsiang-li's story."

"So? I can use the rest. You kept me awake most of the night."

"Sure. Blame it on me."

"Well, it is your fault. Pete's Porches always finished in ten minutes and fell asleep a minute later."

Bob trailed a hand down her arm, then back up again. "You didn't mention how you two met."

"At a party. Boring. End of story. Now your turn. Tell me about you and Harrison."

"I was lounging in one of the NCO clubs when he came to me and said, 'If I could have been assured of a duty like yours, moving from base to base, drinking beer, I would happily have joined the army.'"

"I know," Kerry murmured. "I read it in the book."

"Shush. Who's telling the story, me or you?"

She snuggled closer, her breath warm on his neck. "You are."

"'I've been watching you,' Harrison told me. 'You're good at making yourself invisible, but some guys are so great at it, they seem supernatural. I heard about a guy they call The Sweeper.'"

Kerry let out a gentle snore, then lifted her head and grinned at him. "Just kidding."

Bob couldn't help returning her smile. All of a sudden he felt good, too good to be telling an unsettling story like The Sweeper's. "How about if I tell you about the Prince of Darkness instead? He made sure that during the day not the tiniest bit of light hit his eyes. Over a period of time, his visual purple built up, giving him an advantage when he went out on patrol with his unit."

"I'd rather hear the other story," Kerry said. "Tyler told Noone about the Prince of Darkness, but he never told him about The Sweeper."

"Harrison probably left it out since he planned to write a separate book about him. It was one of the many legends that came out of the war, but it seemed to capture his imagination more than the others. I heard it so many times over the years, I know it by memory."

"Don't you mean 'by heart'?"

"No. I know you by heart. I know the story by memory."

Kerry got very still, then let out a small sigh that spoke of contentment.

Bob drew her closer and kissed her. Her lips parted under his. His whole body seemed to hum with electricity as if he were a robot and she his power source. After a minute, she pulled away and looked at him with dancing eyes.

"You're not getting off that easy."

He smiled at her. "It was worth a try."

She raised her brows expectantly.

"All right," he said. "I've always found this to be a disquieting story, but if you want to hear it . . ." He paused to gather his scattered thoughts. "Up country where the Laos and Cambodia borders meet and abut South Vietnam, a large base camp had been set up in a bowl surrounded by jungled mountains. The troops might have appreciated the beauty if not for the Viet Cong snipers swarming over those dark green hills. Some of the snipers shot so poorly they were a joke. Others were deadly accurate.

"While most of the U.S. soldiers at the camp went about their duty of patrolling the borders, trying to control the VC and NVA infiltration into South Vietnam, The Sweeper went up into the hills to eliminate the accurate snipers. He was told to leave the rest alone since they were more of a nuisance than anything else, and if they got killed, they might be replaced by snipers who could hit what they aimed at.

"By all accounts, The Sweeper wasn't anything special, a typical grunt who got by the best he could, but he had one talent—an ability to blend. Because he melted into the jungle and became the jungle, he could go anywhere without detection."

"Like a chameleon," Kerry said.

"To a certain extent, all soldiers are chameleons. That's the whole purpose of camouflage. Harrison said this particular soldier seemed more like a shadow or a ghost mist. Supposedly The Sweeper could fade into the background so completely that sometimes those standing right next to him were unable to see him . . ."

"Bob? Bob?"

Bob gave his head a shake and looked into Kerry's concerned eyes. "What?"

"You drifted away."

"Oh . . . I was thinking about The Sweeper slipping into the jungle, hunting and eliminating his quarry. Harrison always wondered what it would have been like for the sniper. One minute he's going about his business picking off U.S. soldiers, and the next minute the jungle itself reaches out and kills him. But I was wondering what it would have been like for The Sweeper. A shadow, lost in the darker shadows of the jungle, he must have felt terribly alone."

Kerry reached out and touched his cheek. He tilted his head toward her hand, welcoming the warmth.

"No one knows how The Sweeper did his job," he said. "Rifle? Bayonet? K-bar? Garrote? They weren't even sure how many he took out since he refused to bring back trophies—ears, fingers, whatever—as proof of his kills. They did know he eliminated the snipers because they'd stop taking fire from a quadrant for a while. It would start again when a replacement arrived.

"One day an extraordinarily good sniper came to take the place of one who had been eradicated. This new guy was not VC but NVA, which were well-trained, well-equipped professionals. Normally, of course, a man of his caliber would have been reserved for much more important targets than those American GIs. Apparently, the North Vietnamese officers didn't like their snipers getting killed instead of the U.S. soldiers and had dispatched one of their master snipers to rectify the situation.

"The Sweeper set out to get rid of the NVA sniper, but the sniper continued to do his work. At first, no one realized something had happened to The Sweeper. He often stayed in the jungle for days at a time. All good snipers shoot once or twice then move on, and The Sweeper had to track them, following a subtle but noticeable trail deeper and deeper into the jungle."

Bob fell silent, the fecund stench of the jungle in his nostrils.

"What happened to him?" Kerry asked.

Bob inhaled her clean scent. "Supposedly he triggered a booby trap—possibly some kind of grenade, or perhaps shrapnel embedded in plastique—that had been set by the NVA sniper. Despite grievous wounds and a tremendous loss of blood, he did not die. He had a little water but no food, and since no one would ever find him so deep in the jungle, he had to save himself.

"Unable to walk, he began the long, desperate

crawl back to base camp. It must have taken days. Can you imagine? Every insect in the place would have converged on him. They'd get in his eyes, his nose, his ears. Even his privates. They'd sting and nibble and drink his blood, and they'd never shut up. Leeches would cover his body. And then there'd be the jungle rats, bit as cats."

Kerry sucked in a breath. "Jeez, Bob."

He gave her a sad smile. "I told you I found this to be a disquieting story."

"I can see why."

"Do you want me to stop?

"No. You'd better finish it, or I'll have nightmares for a week."

"There's no real ending. The Sweeper was found by a graves detail dispatched to collect the bodies of a patrol that had been ambushed the previous night by the Viet Cong. They assumed he was dead, but when they heard him groan, they sent for the doc.

"The Sweeper lay on his belly. Except for scratches, abrasions, leeches, insect and rat bites, there appeared to be no major damage, but when they turned him over onto his back, the doc, an experienced medic who thought he had seen everything, almost lost his breakfast—The Sweeper looked like one pulsating mass of bloated maggots.

"He was medevaced to Qui Nhon, where he died, some say. Others say he survived and is living in a stateside mental hospital. An orderly at the hospital in Qui Nhon told Harrison he thought he heard that The Sweeper had been flown to Okinawa or some other place with a major army hospital where they managed to save him.

"If so, the maggots saved him by eating his putrefying flesh and keeping his wound from becoming gangrenous."

Kerry wrinkled her nose. "I hope you're not expecting sex any time soon. This story didn't exactly put me in a romantic mood."

He gave her a lazy smile. "Let me see what I can do about that."

Bob sat propped against the headboard, squeezing the pink rubber ball, first with one hand and then the other. In the dim light filtering through the closed drapes, he could see Kerry asleep next to him, her black hair fanned out on the pillowcase. At least ten inches separated them, but he felt their bodies touching. He listened to the slow rhythm of her breathing and wondered how she could have become so dear to him. He'd never felt this way about anyone; in truth, he hadn't known he could.

Fear iced through his heart. How could he keep her safe? He'd known all along he ought to stay away from her, but that seemed to be the one thing he could not do. Then what? Run? But he doubted they'd be able to find a place beyond ISI's grasp. He would have to find out why they wanted him and somehow neutralize the threat.

He squeezed the pink ball until his hands ached. If anyone could help him discover the truth, it would be Harrison with all his connections, but Harrison was halfway into a six-month world tour promoting his latest best-seller.

"You're thinking so hard I can hear the gears grinding," Kerry said, opening her eyes.

He set the ball on the bedside table.

She sat up and yawned. "What are you thinking?"

"Trying to figure out how to contact Harrison."

Her eyes gleamed. "A séance?"

He drew his head back and studied her. What game was she playing now?

"His agent should know where he is," he said.

"You mean like where he's buried?"

"What are you talking about?"

Her eyes widened. "You don't know."

He frowned. "Know what?"

She put a hand to her mouth. "Harrison's dead."

"No."

"Yes. I saw it in the paper about six weeks ago. He died of cancer."

"That's not possible." He felt his throat tighten, and the words came out sounding strangled. "He looked okay when I saw him three and a half months ago."

"All I know is what the papers said."

He closed his eyes against the sympathy he saw in her face. "Papers don't always tell the truth."

"But what would they gain by lying?"

He jumped out of bed and yanked on his clothes. "I have to go make a call."

"There's a phone here."

"I'd feel safer at a payphone."

She nodded. "If you can wait a few minutes, I'll drive you."

While she dressed, he packed his gym bag.

"We're not coming back?" she asked.

"We've been here too long. I'll get another place tonight."

Kerry drove Bob to a phone outside a convenience store.

Armed with a handful of change gleaned from the bottom of her purse, he made the call to O'Riley's, a bar Harrison frequented whenever he stayed in

Bangkok.

The owner, Hamburger Dan, answered on the third ring. "O'Riley's."

"This is Bob Stark. I—"

"Bob? Is that you? Where the hell have you been? Everyone's looking for you."

Bob nodded to himself. So it was a mistake after all. Harrison must still be alive.

"The Lotus Room is closed," Hamburger Dan said, "and you haven't been around for a while. No one knows where you are."

"Denver."

"Denver? What are you doing in Denver?"

"Visiting. Who's been looking for me?"

"Two Americans who look like spooks. They say they're friends of yours, but I've never seen you with them."

"They're not friends."

"That's what I thought. Harrison's lawyer is also looking for you. He needs you to get in touch with him. He has papers for you to sign. Something about Harrison's will."

"His will? So he really is . . ." Bob could not continue.

"Harrison is dead," Hamburger Dan said quietly. "He died from cancer."

"He never told me he had cancer."

"He didn't know. He got sick shortly after returning to New York to get ready for his tour." A brief pause. "I thought I told you."

"This is the first I heard of it. I don't understand. If he just got cancer, how can he be dead already?"

A young man with spiked hair and a pair of miniature handcuffs dangling from one ear crowded Bob. "I need to use the phone."

Bob turned his back and strained to hear Hamburger Dan's words.

"The cancer was so extensive, he had to have had it awhile. Even if he had been feeling no pain, he must have known something was wrong. In the early stages of brain cancer, people often get paranoid and see elaborate conspiracies where none exist."

"Brain cancer?"

"Yes. But the lung cancer killed him."

Bob swallowed. "He had both lung and brain cancer?"

"Hey, dude," the young man said loudly. "You deaf or something? I told you I need to use the phone."

Hamburger Dan sighed. "It was a terrible thing. Before I forget, let me give you the lawyer's phone numbers. His main office is here, but he also has one in New York."

Bob wrote the information on the back of his motel receipt.

"You done yet, dude?" The young man thrust his face close to Bob's. "I got me some business to attend to."

"Did I mention that Robert Dunbar's been calling for you?" Hamburger Dan said. "He wants you to get in touch with him. Says it's about a game of golf you promised him. I have to go, but come see me when you get back, okay? We'll talk."

Bob hung up.

"It's about time," the young man sneered.

Bob trudged across the parking lot to where Kerry waited. He got in the car and scrubbed his hands over his face. He could feel the rumble of the engine as Kerry drove away.

"Did you see that?" she asked.

Bob lifted his head. "See what?"

She pointed to the white van that had pulled up close to the phone he had been using. Two men jumped out of the vehicle. They grabbed the surly young man and bundled him into the van.

"What do you think they want?" she said. Then she let out a gasp. "You! They thought he was you."

With an odd feeling of detachment, Bob said, "I think you're right."

"Then we better get out of here."

"Act casually. We don't want to attract their attention."

She nodded, her knuckles white as she gripped the steering wheel.

Bob could sense her alarm and knew that somewhere deep in his mind he felt alarmed too, but his struggle to comprehend Harrison's death overrode everything else.

He stared out the window at the passing scene and saw not Denver but Saigon, where they had met.

14.

As Bob headed out of the NCO club in Saigon, he could hear Harrison saying, "Two South Vietnamese generals got in a fight. This was not a matter of fisticuffs, you understand, but a mini war with heavy gunfire and bombing raids . . ."

The door closed behind Bob. For a second his ears felt empty. When they adjusted to the silence, the usual muted night sounds intruded: the rumble of traffic, the reverberation of distant helicopters, the chirping of insects.

He was trying to decide whether he should leave or comb his hair differently, put on a pair of non-prescription eyeglasses, and go back inside, when he heard voices wafting toward him. He could not make out the words, but he could hear the urgency behind them.

Glancing casually about, he caught sight of two men: Sergeant Major Jim Cole and Staff Sergeant Andrew Bishop, both of whom were involved with the Khaki Mafia. Cole disappeared into the rear door of the club; Bishop hopped into a jeep and drove away.

Bob hurried to his own jeep and took off after him.

Bishop drove sedately through the base, but once outside the perimeter, he sped along the streets, careened around corners, and several times barely missed running into pedestrians.

They soon arrived in a section of Saigon Bob had never seen before. The muddy, unpaved streets—alleys, really—weren't flat, but sloped toward the center, forming shallow ditches for the run-off of raw sewage. The shacks lining the alleys looked like the sort of houses small children build out of toothpicks and

Popsicle sticks. People and animals spilled out of the shacks into the alleys, impeding Bob's progress.

He parked his jeep. Even before he climbed out of his vehicle, children swarmed all over it.

Gagging on the smell of human waste, decaying vegetable matter, and rotten fish, Bob followed Bishop who drove by fits and starts toward a huge group of unkempt men milling around outside a bar/whorehouse. Most of the men carried weapons.

Bishop stopped and got out of his jeep. One of the men marched forward to meet him.

Unable to hear what they said, Bob inched closer. Seeing Bishop look around, he froze.

Bishop wrinkled his nose. "This place is a sewer."

"It's better than the fucking army," the other said in a New York accent.

Bob inhaled sharply, almost choking on the effluvia. Now he knew where he was. He had heard of this area where U.S. deserters, South Vietnamese criminals, and even VC congregated. Whenever the M.P.s tried to round up the deserters, pitched battles ensued.

He watched a rough-looking Vietnamese man approach the New Yorker. The two conferred for a moment, then the New Yorker said, "We have plenty of M-16s. We need ammunition."

"We don't want to get involved with that," Bishop responded.

An argument broke out. So many men talked at once Bob heard only a jangle of voices.

Finally, Bishop held up a hand. "Okay, but it's going to cost you." He leaned forward and spoke softly.

"No way," the New Yorker shouted.

He pushed Bishop. Bishop pushed back. The

other men held their weapons at the ready.

Bob felt a ripple of movement. He looked behind him. The bystanders melted away, leaving the streets empty. Then he noticed a long line of military vehicles approaching. M.P.s.

He inched his way back to his jeep, waited until the cavalcade of military vehicles had passed, then made a tight U-turn.

Behind him, the first shots rang out.

Bob was sitting at a table with a man who kept calling him Jimmy Ray, when Harrison breezed into the NCO club. Bob watched in amusement as the seasoned soldiers gravitated toward the journalist. In no time at all, Harrison was the center of a large group.

All at once, Bob felt the skin on the back of his neck crawl. He looked around.

Andrew Bishop was staring at him.

Wondering if Bishop had noticed him last night, Bob drew in his shoulders. The staff sergeant was only 5'9" or 5'10", but he had a powerful build with thick wrists, a massive chest, and hands that looked able to crush a larynx without any effort at all. His hair was cropped close to his skull, and a perpetual scowl compressed his face.

Still feeling Bishop's stare, Bob rose and strolled over to where Harrison held court. He pulled up a chair and sat, glancing back as he did so.

He did not see Bishop.

The next day, deciding it would be a good idea to get as far away from Saigon as possible to give Bishop time to forget his face, Bob drove to Da Nang.

As usual, Harrison hitched a ride.

On Bob's last night in Da Nang, he noticed

Harrison moving around the club, clapping some men on the back, giving others complicated handshakes, laughing with some, listening gravely to others, all the while gulping copious amounts of beer.

Harrison slipped into a seat next to a young man blubbering over a drink. The young man, with his freckled face and his shock of unruly blond hair, seemed no older than a junior high school kid.

"What's wrong?" Bob heard Harrison ask.

"Jamie, my fiancée, broke up with me," the kid said between hiccups. "She says she saw on the news that we're killing babies. She says she can't marry a baby killer."

Bob heard the soft murmur of Harrison's voice. Then in a normal tone the journalist said, "Do you want me to write Jamie a letter? Tell her you never killed a baby in your life?"

The kid looked at him with hope shining in his eyes. "You mean it? I know she'd believe you."

Harrison dug a notebook and pen out of his pocket. He wrote for a few minutes, ripped out the pages, and handed it to the kid, who accepted it with a broad smile.

Then Harrison moved on to someone else.

Bob stood and made his way to the can. As he finished urinating, the door opened.

A second later, a heavy weight crashed into his back, a vice gripped his head, and he was slammed against the wall above the urinal.

Pain exploded behind his eyes. As the first shock dissipated, he realized someone had one powerful hand at his back and the other on his head, keeping him glued to the wall.

Then he became aware that a second person held the tip of a knife to the soft spot beneath his ear.

He heard a toilet flush, footsteps moving rapidly across the floor, the door opening and closing.

"Who are you?" a voice growled in his ear. "I've seen you before. Are you following me, maggot?"

Bob recognized the voice. Staff Sergeant Bishop.

"Not following you," he said, trying to move his jaw as little as possible. "Following orders."

The weight disappeared from his back, while the pressure on his head increased.

He could feel Bishop groping through his pockets.

"What orders?" Bishop asked.

"I'm doing a survey of typewriters—"

"What kind of candyass job is that for a man?" the person with the knife asked.

The knife dug deeper into Bob's neck, and he could feel a trickle of blood.

"I'm supposed to find out how the typewriters are holding up under tropical conditions—"

"I can read, dumbass," Bishop said. "It's all here."

Bob could hear the soft whisper of paper fluttering to the floor, followed a moment later by a muffled thud—probably his wallet.

"How come I keep seeing your face all the time?" Bishop demanded.

"I do my job," Bob said. "After that I stop for a drink or two. What else am I going to do?"

Bob felt a slight draft as the door opened.

"Come back later," Bishop snarled.

"I need to take a leak," Harrison said in an overloud voice. There was a faint flick as if he were brushing lint off a shoulder. "I can see you're in the middle of something, but do you mind waiting until I'm through? I'd prefer not to get blood on my suit. I just got it cleaned."

Bob heard the sound of a zipper, then a steady stream of water hitting the urinal.

The pressure of the hand on Bob's head increased, but otherwise neither of his assailants moved a muscle.

He could hear the sound of a zipper again, the splash of water in the sink, then footsteps moving toward the door.

The door opened.

"By the way, I'd appreciate it if you didn't hurt him too badly. He's my ride."

The door closed.

"I don't like you," Bishop said, breathing hotly in Bob's ear. "If you see me again, you better run, you puke, because next time I won't be so nice."

He pulled Bob's head back, slammed it into the wall, and released it.

Bob had to put out his hands to keep from falling. He waited until Bishop and his sidekick left, then he pushed himself upright.

Noticing that his penis was still hanging out of his pants, he tucked it in and zipped up. He touched a hand to his neck and gazed at the blood smeared on his fingers.

After a moment he went to the sink, where he washed his hands and neck. He gripped the basin and bowed his head, waiting for the pain behind his eyes to subside.

The door opened. He turned to see Harrison step into the room and close the door behind him.

"You okay, pal?"

"I'm fine."

Harrison nodded. Bob retrieved his wallet and

his papers. Together they left the room.

Bob closed his eyes against the harshness of the Denver sun. First Hsiang-li had disappeared from his life and now so had the man who'd been more than a brother to him. He thought about the last time he'd seen Harrison and wondered how he could have missed seeing the symptoms of his illness.

"I don't believe in conspiracies," Harrison had said, banging his fist on the table in The Lotus Room.

"I know," Bob replied. "You've told me before."

"And why don't I believe in conspiracies?"

"You say whenever more than two or three people know a secret, always someone will let something slip."

"Abso-fucking-lutely right!"

Bob peered at him. In all the years he had known Harrison, he had never heard him talk like this.

"Are you all right?" he asked.

"No, I'm not all right," Harrison shouted. He lowered his voice and repeated softly, "No, I'm not all right."

"Are you sick?"

Harrison remained silent for so long Bob thought he might not answer, but finally Harrison said, "No." After another long silence he added, "Not physically, anyway."

"Being mysterious is not like you," Bob said. "The Bill Harrison I've always known never hesitated to blurt out whatever is on his mind."

"That Harrison never stumbled onto such a big story."

Bob grew still. "Tell me about it."

Harrison shook his head. "Just knowing about it

might put you in danger."

"I've been in danger before."

Harrison studied him for a moment, then he smiled. "So you have. I'd forgotten you were once the imperturbable James Bond." His smile faded. He looked to the right and to the left, then leaned forward. "I discovered something that happened during Vietnam."

"A lot of things happened back then."

Harrison settled back and toyed with his beer. "Do you know Donald McCray?"

"The big redheaded guy who owns a small air freight business?"

"That's the man. Shortly before my last trip to New York, I was sitting in a booth at O'Riley's when Donald approached me and said he'd heard of my interest in stories about Vietnam. He said he was tired of carrying the burden of his secret all by himself and thought he'd be safer if someone else knew."

"Knew what?" Bob asked when Harrison fell silent again.

Harrison pinched the bridge of his nose between a thumb and forefinger. "He claimed a private trauma hospital outside of Manila had experimented on soldiers during Vietnam. I couldn't verify it at first. Everyone I talked to, including a couple of generals, claimed to know nothing about the hospital. They also denied any knowledge of experiments. But someone had to have cut the orders."

"Even if you're right and there was some sort of conspiracy, it's nothing new. Soldiers have often been played with and manipulated in the name of science."

Harrison drained his beer. "I know. In the forties and fifties, they sent soldiers to the Nevada desert where they did the bomb tests. The scientists wanted to see first hand what effect radioactive fallout would have on humans. It's not that big a leap from purposely putting soldiers in harm's way to physically doing experiments on them."

Bob's brows drew together. "You are, or were, an investigative journalist. You discovered a drug connection with the CIA that affected a heck of a lot more people than these hypothetical experiments could have. Why is this so painful for you?"

"Maybe because I'm getting old. Or perhaps because it's personal."

"Personal how?"

Harrison responded with a shake of his head.

"If, in fact, someone experimented on soldiers in the Philippines," Bob said, "it happened a long time ago. Finding out now what had been done to them could only bring them more grief."

Harrison stared at Bob for several seconds. "Do you believe that?" he said at last.

"Yes. I do."

Harrison yawned and rubbed his eyes. "We'll have to continue this discussion another time. I'm beat. I have a long flight tomorrow, and then the book tour, so this might be my last chance for a good night's sleep." He sighed heavily and lumbered to his feet. "I'll stop by to see you tomorrow before I leave."

Bob was in the courtyard, cutting flowers for a banquet to be held later that evening, when he heard Harrison's voice inside the restaurant.

"Is Bob around?"

"He's out by the lotus pool," he heard Hsiang-li answer.

Bob watched Harrison walk out the door, look around, shrug, sit, remove his boonie hat, drop it on the table, then look around some more. He noticed that the writer looked old and tired, as if he'd aged ten years overnight.

When Bob finally stepped forward, Harrison glanced at him, then fixed his widened eyes on the knife Bob had been using to cut the flowers.

"Is something wrong?" Bob asked.

Harrison's gaze returned to Bob's face, and Bob could see the recognition dawning in his eyes.

Harrison's shoulders slumped. "I didn't recognize you, Bob. I thought . . ." He shook his head, looking bewildered. "I didn't see you come through the door."

"I've been out here the whole time."

"You have?" Harrison took a deep breath, and peered at Bob. "There's something different about you."

"I didn't sleep very well last night."

"Maybe that's it." He sighed. "I couldn't sleep either."

"Did you eat? We're not open yet, but I can fix you something."

Harrison massaged his neck, then dropped his hands between his knees, and stared at them. After a moment he raised his head. "I don't have time to eat right now. I have to go catch a plane. I came by to tell you . . ." He glanced at Bob, then averted his eyes. "I came to say goodbye."

He pushed himself off the chair. Bob accompanied him outside where they made their final farewells.

Harrison walked away. He stopped abruptly and looked back at Bob. They stared at each other for the space of several heartbeats, then Harrison turned and shambled off.

When Bob went back to get his basket of flowers, he found Harrison's boonie hat lying forgotten on the table. He grabbed it and dashed back outside, but Harrison had already disappeared.

Bob blinked, trying to bring the present into focus.

"I thought you were asleep," Kerry said.

"No."

"Where did you go?"

"The past. Harrison. He played a big part in my life. One time in Da Nang, I got in a spot of trouble and he rescued me in his own oblique way."

She nodded. "A couple of guys beat you up in the men's room. I remember."

"How . . . oh, right. Harrison's book. It's so strange that you know almost everything about me and I know almost nothing about you."

She shifted her gaze from the road to him, then back again. "There's nothing to tell. For as long as I can remember, I lived for some mythical future where fantastic adventures awaited me. I never had a present, only that longing."

"Still, something must have happened to you in your thirty years."

"I'm not thirty." She craned her neck to look at herself in the rearview mirror. "You think I look thirty?"

"You don't look a day over twenty, but that's beside the point."

"Not to me it isn't."

"Were you a cheerleader? I picture you as the girl on top of the pyramid who jumps fearlessly off into some brawny guy's arms. Or maybe you were a homecoming queen."

She giggled. "Not even close. I was too much of a daydreamer to get involved in school activities, and no one ever thought of me as one of the beautiful girls."

He studied her for a minute, taking in her glossy black hair, radiant skin, and eyes that sparkled like a clear midnight sky. "The kids in your class must have been blind." He gave her a sly smile. "I've seen better looking women than you. The girls in Chiang Mai are considered to be the most beautiful girls in the world, but you'll do in a pinch."

She reached over and pinched his cheek. "So will you."

Suddenly they were both laughing, though Bob did not know why. The exchange hadn't been that funny.

She stopped laughing. "I had a lot of boyfriends, but none of them were worth anything. One of my very first memories is of cuddling a sweet little baby chick against my face. It was so soft, the softest thing I had ever felt. Then it pecked me. It taught me that the world may be soft and cuddly, but it could still peck. And that's all I've met in my life, a bunch of peckers."

He didn't know whether she wanted him to laugh or commiserate, so he nodded, but she stared at the road and didn't look his way. He glanced out the window and realized they were far from the city. Long stretches of open field alternated with new housing developments. The air smelled of diesel fuel and onions.

"Where are we?"

"On the Valley Highway heading for Wyoming. I thought we could cash a few of your traveler's checks in Cheyenne. Lay a false trail."

Bob nodded reflectively. "Good thinking. Then what?"

"Circle back, I guess, unless you have a better idea."

"No. Besides, I have to return to ISI."

A breath caught in her throat. "Why?"

"I met a girl—a young woman—who seemed inordinately interested in me. I need to find out why."

"I wish I could come with you."

"I'll be better on my own. You're too much of a distraction."

"It's supposed to rain."

"Then I know what we'll buy in Cheyenne. Khaki pants, a plain white shirt, a blue jacket, and maybe a clip-on tie and non-prescription eyeglasses."

"I see. You want to be able to keep changing your appearance like you did in Vietnam so people won't notice you hanging around the cafeteria all day."

"You know me much too well." He tried to sound severe, but he could hear the smile in his voice.

15.

It rained all day Monday.

Although Bob spent the day in a corporate cafeteria in the United States instead of an NCO club in Vietnam, he had a strong sense of continuity, as if the intervening years had simply vanished. He kept glancing at the door, expecting Bill Harrison to come breezing in to enliven the room with his ready laugh and his steady stream of stories.

No Harrison, of course, and no sign of the intense young woman, either.

After a tasteless meal from a fast-food restaurant, Bob checked into a motel.

He sat on the bed, propped against the headboard, squeezing the pink rubber ball, first with one hand and then another. Squeezing. Squeezing. Squeezing.

In the early morning hours, still not tired but knowing he needed to rest, he put away the ball and turned off the light. He laid his head on the pillow, pulled the covers to his chin, and fell instantly asleep. It was as if, in some remote past, he had trained himself for such a contingency.

Tuesday dawned bright and clear.

Bob thought he detected a hint of pine in the air, blown down from the mountains on a rain-washed breeze. His fingers ached to lay on canvas the images the scent evoked, but he closed his mind against the desire and went on the prowl at ISI.

Around noon, he sat at a picnic table, letting himself be seen. Shortly afterward, the young woman laid her tray on a nearby table.

She glanced at him. He gave her a nod.

She dropped her gaze to her plate and ate her food as if it were the last meal she'd ever consume.

When she finished, she walked by Bob's table and tripped over her high-heeled shoes. She landed at Bob's feet, the contents of her tray strewn around her.

"Help me up," she said out of the corner of her mouth, "but act like you don't know me."

"I don't know you," Bob said.

"That's real good. Keep pretending."

As Bob leaned over to give her a hand, she said, "You're not the new guy in marketing, are you?"

"No."

She stood and brushed herself off. "That's what I thought. You're here to investigate Doug Roybal's murder, aren't you?"

"Yes," Bob said, agreeing as he usually did. He stooped to retrieve her dishes and utensils.

"Meet me at Pignoli's at five o'clock," she said. "It's on One Hundred and Twentieth Avenue, just past the highway."

She picked up her refilled tray and strode off, good-naturedly parrying jeers and catcalls from the witnesses to her tumble.

At four o'clock, Bob entered Pignoli's, ordered a draft beer, and took it to a table at the rear where he had an unimpeded view of the entire bar and its patrons.

Pignoli's, decorated with dead animal heads, seemed a strange choice for an office worker, especially a woman. The bar seemed to cater to construction workers, day laborers, and old men with grime permanently imbedded in the wrinkles of their leathery skin. No one who crossed the threshold had the pampered arrogance of Evans's men or the soft hands of a corporate drone. No one exhibited any interest in

Bob.

The young woman entered at five o'clock exactly. Bob remained seated and watched her. She perched on the edge of a barstool, facing the door. After a minute or two, she shrugged, turned around, and ordered a beer. She drained it in long gulps.

An old man slapped a bill on the table. "Another for the lady."

"No thanks," she said. "I can get my own."

"Aw shucks, honey. Humor an old man for once."

She smiled. "All right, Mr. Tonetti, you win, as always."

"I keep telling you to call me Tony," he said.

When her second beer arrived, she took a long pull. "Do me a favor, will you, Tony? I'm meeting a guy I don't know very well. Will you watch to make sure nothing happens?"

Tony puffed out his meager chest. "Sure, honey, you can count on me."

She slid off the barstool, mug in hand. "I'll be in a booth at the back if anyone comes looking for me."

"Okay, I'll keep an eye out."

Bob continued to watch awhile longer. No one but Tony showed any interest in the young woman. When the old man's attention wandered, Bob crossed the room and slipped into the seat across from her.

Her eyes widened. "I didn't see you come in."

Bob gestured with his head. "I was sitting over there."

"I didn't see you." She nodded in approval. "You're good at what you do."

"You're not so bad yourself."

She narrowed her eyes. "What's that supposed to mean?"

"The tumble you took at lunch today looked artistic."

"Oh, that." She laughed. "Ten years of gymnastics and all I have to show for it is the ability to trip over my own two feet."

"What do you want with me?" Bob asked.

"I want to help you with your investigation into Doug's murder. No matter what anyone says, he didn't die in a rock climbing accident. He was afraid of heights. I know Issy killed him."

Bob studied her, noting the determined tilt of her chin, the fierceness of her expression. "What's your name?"

"Tracy." She made a sweeping gesture. "This was our place, Doug's and mine. Nobody from Issy would ever be caught dead in a place as unsophisticated as this, so we felt safe here."

"Safe from what?"

"Issy and their stupid corporate policy. If two employees are dating, they have to sign a letter of intent. Supposedly, it protects the company if the romance goes sour and one of the employees decides to sue the other for sexual harassment. Doug and I wanted to keep our love away from Issy's prying eyes, so we had to sneak around. If Issy found out about us, we'd both be fired."

Her eyes filled with tears. "We were going to get married this Sunday." A single tear brimmed over and slid down her face. "I can't believe he's gone." She rubbed her eyes with her fists like a little girl.

Mr. Tonetti hurried over to them and glared at Bob. "He bothering you, Tracy?"

Her lower lip quivered. "I'm okay, Tony. Really."

He didn't leave, but continued to glare at Bob.

"Thanks, Tony," she said. "I can handle it. I'll let you know if I need you."

Mr. Tonetti walked away slowly, turning around several times to stare at Bob.

"Why do you think ISI killed Doug?" Bob asked.

"A friend of his, Will Turnow, hacked into Sven Berquist's home computer. A couple days later, Issy sent Will to Boston for a seminar, and nobody ever heard from him again. Doug thought someone at Issy murdered Will, and he tried to find out what Will learned that got him killed." An unreadable emotion flared in her eyes. "I guess he found out."

"Who's Sven Berquist?"

"Director of Research and Development at Issy. I remember Will laughing when he told Doug that this powerful man didn't even bother to put any security features on his computer. A simple password, but nothing else, like he couldn't imagine anyone breaking into his computer. Mostly he used it to write his memoirs, Will said, so maybe Berquist didn't care."

"Do you know what Will learned from the memoirs?"

"Some. Usually I tuned out when Will and Doug got on the subject of computers, but I wanted to hear about Berquist. Until Will hacked into his computer, I didn't know anything except he's nearing retirement age, he's still tall and imposing, and his eyes are a bright, piercing blue."

Bob leaned back and waited for her to tell the story in her own time.

"Will said Berquist is a Swedish Jew who attached himself to the OSS during World War Two. An interpreter, I think. At twenty years old, Berquist knew he was meant for great things, and he saw the

OSS as a means of getting there.

"Then he met the guys from Issy. Issy had sent some people to Sweden to see if they could meet German scientists who'd be willing to share the secrets of their research into biological warfare. Berquist arranged the meetings. After the war, Issy offered him a job, but he kept his ties with the OSS people. He built the Research and Development Department into a vast private intelligence agency modeled after the CIA."

She covered her face with her hands. Bob thought she was crying, but when she took her hands away, her eyes looked dry and feverish.

"I didn't know," she said. "None of us did."

"Didn't know what?"

"The kinds of things Issy is involved with. They've got scientists all over the world working for them, and they own controlling interest in all kinds of businesses, especially research laboratories and think tanks. They're like a huge octopus sitting on the world, tentacles reaching everywhere."

"What kinds of things are they involved with?"

"I just know about old projects. Berquist didn't get further than the Korean War in his memoirs. Doug found out about some of the more current projects, like what's going on at the Rosewood Research Institute, but he wouldn't tell me. He said it was too dangerous." She flexed her biceps. "As if I couldn't take care of myself."

"Yet Doug is dead," he reminded her.

"Don't you think I know that?" she said, a throb of anger in her voice. After a long pause, she continued in a more subdued tone. "I haven't been able to do much work since they found his body, so I stare out of my office window a lot. A few days ago I noticed you. You'd be there, and then you'd seem to vanish, kind of like those blinking eyes that used to come in Cracker Jack boxes. That's when I realized you must be working undercover, investigating Doug's death."

"What are the old projects ISI worked on?" Bob asked.

Tracy frowned. "Why do you want to know about that?"

"No reason. Just curious." Then, remembering something the man from the State Department had told him long ago, he added, "In an investigation, it's important to look for the unusual, even if the unusual has nothing to do with the matter at hand."

She nodded slowly. "I can see that." She ran a finger around the rim of her beer mug. "The subject of one project was a man who'd been hypnotized, then sent to wait tables at a very secret, very important dinner for some of the key people during the Korean War. In his hypnotic state, the waiter could remember everything everyone said and did. After he parroted it back, they erased his memory and brought him out of the trance. He resumed his normal life without ever knowing what he'd done. I remember Doug and Will joking about a secret agent so secret he himself didn't know he was an agent, but I thought it sad. And creepy."

Bob tried to ignore the acrid taste in his mouth. "Do any other projects come to mind?"

"They tried to desensitize soldiers to the act of killing. During World War Two, less than fifteen percent actually shot at the enemy." Her hands clenched into fists. "They must have learned how to get soldiers to kill, because I read that in Vietnam over eighty-five percent shot to kill. They had all sorts of projects. They developed an aerosol spray for use in biological warfare and something called a micro-bio-innoculator that's so tiny the victim feels nothing when it penetrates. And since the body absorbs the innoculator, no one can find a trace of the dart. They also developed lasers so tiny they can zap a single molecule. And Cerberus."

"Cerberus? Like the three-headed hound guarding the gates of hell?"

She nodded. "Berquist had a special interest in that project. During World War Two, he had met several amputees. They all told him the loss of the limb devastated them, the pain debilitated them, and dealing with the stump humiliated them. But the absolute worst was the phantom pain, the cramping, twitching, itching, in the missing limb. You can't scratch an itch or massage a muscle in a body part that is no longer there.

"Berquist reasoned that since the brain apparently retained a memory of the limb, he could erase the phantom pain by erasing the memory of the limb."

"Did he succeed?" Bob asked.

She shrugged. "I don't know. Will said they experimented on some of the soldiers who lost limbs in South Korea, but that's as far as Berquist got with his memoirs."

She finished the last of her beer, snatched her purse, and started to slide out of the booth.

"Do you have time for a few more questions?" Bob asked.

She sighed heavily. "A few, then I have to go."

"Who is Evans?"

"The only Evans I know is Alex Evans. He's the Assistant Director of Research and Development, but the guys who work for him don't look like scientists." She winced. "They give me the chills. They seem way too mean and menacing, and they all have those hard, cold eyes. They don't belong with the rest of us, so people are always spreading wild rumors about them."

"What kind of rumors?"

"Oh, you know, like they're Evans's secret police, or like they're killers." Her eyes widened. "They must be the ones who killed Doug."

"Tell me about Evans."

"I don't know anything. I've heard people say he's a megalomaniac who wants power at any cost and doesn't care who pays as long as it's not him. And he's going to take over when Berquist retires, which may be soon. Berquist has prostate cancer."

"What does Evans look like?

"He's about fifty and still good-looking, but not as good-looking as Berquist, and he has dark hair with streaks of silver in it."

"Can you be more specific—height, eye color, distinguishing marks?"

She shook her head apologetically. "I only saw him once or twice."

"What about the kind of car he drives?"

"I don't know. The suits have their own private entrance on the other side of the campus."

"Where the razor wire is?"

"That's the computer center. Supposedly, beneath the building is an installation containing acres of computers, but I've never been over there. The private entrance for the suits is around the corner from the computer center. It's a garage door leading to an underground parking lot that has about as much security as the computer center. Everyone uses the commons, even the suits. The commons is what we call the park-like area, in case you didn't know. I often see Mr. Evans's men on the commons, so maybe Mr. Evans comes sometimes, too. If you want, I can ask around about him."

"That's not a good idea. You don't want to bring yourself to his attention."

Tracy stared at the ceiling, as though trying to make up her mind about something. Finally, she looked at Bob.

"I work in accounting, and I discovered that during the past couple of years, huge amounts of money have been pumped into the Research and Development Department. They've obtained unsecured, interest-free, multi-million dollar loans from dozens of savings and loan companies all over the country, like Silverado here in Denver and Lincoln Savings and Loan in Irvine, California."

She clutched her purse to her chest like a shield. "What's strange is there's no repayment schedule. It's like the savings and loans gave away free money. Most of the money was transferred to a couple of different accounts in a bank in the Cayman Islands, but when I went back to double check my figures, all trace of the loans had disappeared.

"I think I stumbled on something I wasn't supposed to see. Except for Doug, I never told anybody else about my discovery." She shivered. "Is it cold in here?"

Bob nodded, but he knew the chill they both felt had nothing to do with the ambient temperature.

16.

Bob found Scott in the basement of his church, mopping up after the Vietnam veteran's support group.

Scott gave him a warm smile. "I'm sorry you missed the meeting."

Bob tried to return the smile but without much success. "I came to see you."

"Always glad of an excuse to put off work." Scott set the mop in the bucket. "Would you like some coffee?"

"No thanks."

"What can I do for you?"

"You seem to be well acquainted with the veteran community. Do you know anyone who could tell me about mind control experiments done on soldiers during the Korean War?"

Hearing the words hanging in the air between them, Bob wished he had phrased his question in a more roundabout manner. Spoken bluntly, it sounded outlandish.

"I do know someone." Scott got out his wallet, extracted a small piece of paper, and handed it to Bob.

Bob glanced at it. It was an address and phone number for Dr. James Willet in Omaha. He shifted his gaze to Scott, unable to keep his incredulity from showing.

"How did you know what I wanted?"

Scott tugged at an ear. "I didn't. I got it for me. Dr. Willet's a psychologist specializing in the problems of veterans. He has a particular interest in memory dysfunctions and debilitating nightmares, especially those arising from possible abuse or interference. I heard about him at a meeting once, and after talking about my nightmares the other day, I asked around until

I found someone who knew how to get in touch with him."

Bob tried to return the paper to him, but Scott waved it away.

"I decided against going." He looked at Bob with serene eyes. "I know I did those things I saw in my dreams."

"You weren't responsible. The people who programmed you are the ones to blame."

Scott shook his head. "I fired the weapons. I have to accept that. And I do. But I decided I don't want to live in the past. It's more important to be in the present with my family and my work. They deserve all of me now, so I have to handle it, get over it, and forget it."

"An admirable goal."

"A necessary goal. I have you and Kerry to thank for making me finally face what I did." He gave Bob a shrewd look. "You don't seem surprised by my revelation."

"No. It seems as if mind alteration is much more prevalent than I ever realized. I'm just sorry it happened to you."

"I've come to see that we're controlled every minute of every day. We're bombarded with ads, commercials, newspaper articles, television shows, all of which program us to think and act in certain ways, to accept modes of behavior that were anathema a couple of generations ago." Scott's mouth twisted in a wry smile. "I'll get off my soapbox now."

"I don't mind."

Scott grabbed hold of the mop. "I'd better finish here. Rose will be expecting me. You're welcome to come to dinner. We can talk afterward."

"I wouldn't be good company tonight. Maybe

another time."

"I'll hold you to that. And bring Kerry. We all love her."

Bob smiled.

The sodium vapor lights gave Colfax Avenue an unearthly glow, like an alien world with a dying sun.

The hookers teetered on their platform shoes and tugged at their miniscule skirts. Here and there a tattered old man smelling of urine, vomit and cheap whiskey slept fitfully in a doorway, while the homeless women pushed their shopping carts, doggedly steering clear of grifters, drug dealers, and crazies.

Bob walked among them. He'd detoured by the boardinghouse to see if it was still being staked out—it was—and now he had nothing to do but wait for Kerry to show up for her shift at the coffee shop.

Feeling twitchy, as if someone were following him, he cut diagonally across the street and glanced over his shoulder.

Herbert Townsend weaved through the crowd. He didn't rant but peered anxiously into the faces of the people he passed. He turned his head toward Bob, and their gazes met. Townsend loped toward Bob, hand outstretched.

The man wanted his ID back, Bob realized. He paused under a streetlight, pulled his picture off the nametag, and returned it to Townsend. He planned to return to ISI, but as long as he didn't try to enter any building except the cafeteria or health club, he could do without it.

Townsend carefully stowed it in a pocket of his jeans and curved his lips into something resembling a smile.

"Are you hungry?" Bob asked.

A brief pause as if the words filtered into his head through the aluminum foil helmet, then Townsend nodded.

Bob headed for Rimrock Coffee Shop, Townsend close on his heels.

"Let's go in here," Bob said, pausing outside the brightly lit restaurant.

Townsend shook his head no.

"It will be okay."

Bob entered the coffee shop. The taller Townsend followed, trying to hide behind Bob's back

The dark-skinned, frizzy-haired waitress dropped her towel on the table she'd been busing and hurried toward them.

"You can't come in here."

"Who? Me?" Bob said.

The waitress pointed at Townsend. "No. Him. If he doesn't leave, I'm calling the cops."

Narrowing his eyes, Bob stared at her. "He's with me."

She took a step back. "He better not bother anyone."

"He won't." Bob led Townsend to an unoccupied booth.

The waitress put her hands on her hips. "Ya want coffee?" she asked, making the innocuous words sound like a threat.

"Yeah," Townsend answered, head bowed.

"Hot chocolate," Bob said. "And menus."

Despite the inauspicious beginning, the waitress treated them with an efficiency that could almost be called courtesy, and in short order placed steaming plates of food in front of them.

Hunching over his plate, Townsend shoveled huge bites of roast beef and whipped potatoes into his mouth, and washed them down with noisy gulps of coffee.

When the waitress came to clean away the dishes, Bob slipped a ten-dollar bill into her hand.

"Keep the coffee coming."

"Sure. Whatever." She left with the dishes, returned immediately to refill Townsend's cup, then took off again.

"What happened to you?" Bob asked softly.

Townsend shrugged.

"Did you and Michael Mortimer see something?"

A barely perceptible nod.

"A space ship?"

"No!" The word exploded out of Townsend.

"Lights?"

"Yeah."

"Where were you when you saw the lights?"

Bob had to strain to hear Townsend's whispered reply. "San Luis Valley. Michael's grandmother lives there. We went to visit her."

"You and Michael are friends?"

"Then. Not now."

"Why not now?"

"He believed them when they made us think we'd seen aliens, but we didn't."

"Who made you think you'd seen aliens?" When Townsend didn't respond, Bob said, "Was it the doctors at the Rosewood Research Institute?"

"Maybe. Yeah."

"Can you tell me what happened?"

"We saw strange lights in the sky. Blue lights. Michael said they were UFOs, but they weren't. They were round and trans . . . translucent, like ball lightning, or earth lights."

"Is the San Luis Valley on a fault line?"

Townsend nodded.

"So you could have seen earth lights," Bob said, remembering reading once that when tectonic plates on a fault line rub together, they generate great energy, which is sometimes manifested by balls of light called earth lights. "What happened next?"

"Nothing, for a while. Michael kept talking about the UFOs. Then after a couple of weeks, our boss came to us and said his boss said our work suffered because of our UFO experience, and they wanted us to see a UFO specialist in Boston."

"What's that?"

"I think they made it up." Townsend's voice had been getting louder and shriller the longer he talked; his last comment caused heads to swivel in their direction.

"Drink your coffee," Bob said.

Townsend obediently raised the cup to his lips. When Townsend set aside the empty cup, Bob signaled for a refill. Within a few minutes, Townsend had calmed enough to continue.

"Michael agreed to go to the specialist. He was sure we'd been beamed aboard a spaceship, and he wanted to remember. I refused to go, but they said they'd fire me if I didn't. So I went." He was silent for a long time, then he added, almost inaudibly, "I can't believe I was such a fool."

"What happened in Boston?" Bob asked.

"I don't remember." Townsend looked as if he were about to cry. "I can't remember things that happened, but I can remember things that didn't happen."

"What do you mean?"

"When we got back to Denver, we both remembered being on the space ship. You know. Bright lights. Rectal probes. Long tweezers poking something far up our nasal passages. Tall, beautiful, blond aliens. Short gray ones with huge slanty eyes."

Townsend gulped his coffee. Putting down his cup, he gave Bob a surprisingly perceptive glance. "The aliens even warned us about nuclear bombs, like we're dumb enough to believe anyone living on a planet light years from here would be affected if we blew up our planet. If we did blow it up, it wouldn't generate even a fraction of the nuclear energy our sun does, so who would care? Besides us, I mean."

The waitress came and refilled Townsend's cup once more.

Bob waited until he drank it, then asked, "How did you know the memories weren't real?"

"I didn't. You trust your memories. All you are is what you remember. I figured I was wrong about the earth lights."

"So how did you learn the truth?"

"I found the computer chip they planted. One of them. The other is still in my head." Townsend showed Bob a red, puckered scar on the top of his wrist. "I took a knife and dug it out. Then I knew for sure."

"That the memories weren't real?"

"Yeah. I recognized the chip. Issy markets them. They sell them to ranchers to keep track of cattle, but they're trying to get prisons to use them to keep track of convicts, and then . . . They already keep track of everyone through satellite pictures and computers. What will happen if everyone is implanted with one of these chips? No one believes me," he added softly, as if to himself. "I try to warn them, but no one listens."

"I listened," Bob said as quietly.

Townsend looked at him for a long time, then he nodded once.

***

Townsend slipped away while Bob paid the bill.

Pocketing his change, Bob opened the door. When he stepped outside, two young men flanked him. They stood so close Bob could smell the acrid odor emanating from their large, well-muscled bodies. One had a smooth, baby face and tiny, feral eyes. The other had a pimply forehead and the merest wisp of a mustache. They didn't seem to fit with the other denizens of Colfax, probably because of their expensive jeans and brand-new running shoes.

"We need some shit, man," Baby Face said.

Bob pushed by them without responding.

They stayed right with him.

Pimples bounced on the balls of his feet. "We got money."

Bob kept walking.

Baby Face planted himself in Bob's path. "We said we got money, now give us the shit."

Bob stopped and glanced from one to the other. "You're making a mistake. I'm not who you think I am."

He started to walk around them, but Pimples grabbed him by the arm. "You playing games with us, asshole?"

"No." Bob jerked his arm out of the young man's grasp. "I'm telling you the truth."

Before he could take more than a few steps, they shoved him into a passageway between two buildings. He heard the distinctive sound of a switchblade being flicked open.

"Give us the drugs or I'll stick you," Baby Face growled, waving the knife.

Bob spread his hands. "You're mistaking me for someone else."

179

"Stick him," Pimples said in a high, excited voice.

Looking at the gleaming blade, at the young men towering over him, Bob was surprised to find he had no fear. His muscles felt loose and fluid, his mind alert.

He bent his knees slightly and stared into Baby Face's eyes.

"This is the last time we tell you," Pimples shouted. "Give us the drugs."

Baby Face lunged, aiming for Bob's abdomen. Bob grabbed the young man's wrist with his left hand, pulled him forward, and smashed the heel of his right hand into his nose. As Baby Face started to fall, Bob twisted his wrist.

The knife clattered to the ground.

Baby Face continued to fall; Bob maintained his iron grip.

The bone snapped. Baby Face screamed. He rolled around on the ground, blood on his face, cradling his wrist.

Pimples froze, then all at once he dived for the knife. His fingers closed over the handle. He sprang at Bob. Bob kicked him in the face. Pimples's head snapped back. He collapsed on the ground.

Bob seized the switchblade. Without looking at the two young men, who twitched and moaned and muttered curses, he walked away.

Back on the street, he tossed the knife into the second trash receptacle he passed.

17.

Bob entered the skin flick theater, intending to remain out of sight until eleven o'clock when Kerry's shift started, but he fell asleep and didn't wake until after her shift had ended.

He stepped out of the dark theater into the bright of day. He felt disoriented, as if the world had continued without him, and now he had to scramble to catch up.

The thought of seeing Kerry helped steady him.

"I hoped it was you," Kerry exclaimed, opening the door of the house. She pulled him inside, locked the door, and threw herself into his arms.

Bob hugged her closely, inhaling her clean, fresh scent and letting her warmth seep into his soul. An invisible hand seemed to close around his heart at the thought of having to leave her yet again.

He leaned back and gently brushed her hair away from her face. "I came to say goodbye."

"No," she said swiftly, without equivocation. "You can't."

"It's for a few days. I need to see a doctor in Omaha."

She sucked in a short breath. "Are you okay? I mean, outside of the obvious."

"I'm fine. He's a psychologist who might have some information for me."

"How are you getting there?"

"Bus or train, whichever works out."

A brilliant smile lit her face. "Then it's not goodbye. I'll drive you." She held up a hand to keep him from answering. "If I don't come, who's going to check out the motel room for you?"

He stroked his chin, but it was a parody of deliberation; he could refuse her nothing, especially when she smiled at him like that.

She pointed to his empty hands. "Where's your gym bag?"

"I left it at ISI. I had a meeting with the young woman I told you about, and since I didn't know whether she was friend or foe, I wanted to be unencumbered."

"Was she friend or foe?"

"Yes."

He could feel her gaze, a kind of heat on his skin.

"You're teasing me," she said, smiling.

"A little."

Her eyebrows shot up. "Well?"

"Friend."

"Why did she want to see you? Was she pretty?"

He laughed. "I don't know if I'll ever get used to the way your mind works. Yes, she was pretty, in an intense sort of way. And it's a long story. I'll explain on the way to Omaha."

She gave a business-like nod. "When do you want to leave?"

"As soon as possible. I called the doctor before I came here and made an appointment for tomorrow evening at five. There's plenty of time, but the way my life's going, I don't want to take any chances."

"We'll have to stop somewhere to get you some clothes. You left a few things here, but I don't know if there's anything presentable to wear to your appointment."

He sighed. "I feel fractured, always having to leave bits and pieces behind."

"Did you have anything important in the gym bag?"

"No."

"Then, why are we standing around talking? We should either go or . . ." She pressed against him, her mouth sweet and firm on his.

Desire swept through him in a warm rush.

Well, perhaps he didn't have to leave right this minute.

Kerry trailed her hand through Bob's chest hairs, tracing his scars. Her touch felt like drops of summer rain.

She lifted her head to look at him. "Where did you get the scars?"

"A hunting accident in my youth." He spoke the words by rote, as if they had no connection to him.

She didn't seem to notice. Giving a delighted laugh, she said, "Do the deer come armed with knives now?"

"No. Jackson shot me."

The amusement died out of her eyes. "Your brother shot you? By accident, I hope."

He shook his head. "When I was ten, my father took us to the prairie east of Denver to hunt quail. I didn't want to go, but he insisted, saying I needed to learn how to be a man. I hated the idea of killing and refused to fire the shotgun, but Jackson fired at anything he could.

"In the late afternoon, not content with merely killing defenseless animals, he deliberately took aim at me. I was looking at a flock of geese flying overhead and happened to glance at him as he pulled the trigger, which is how I knew it was no accident. Luckily, I stood far enough away the shot didn't kill me, but the pellets blasted the front of my chest.

"My father blamed me for getting in Jackson's way." A memory popped into Bob's head; something he'd forgotten until that very moment. "My father always called Jackson 'son,' but he called me 'kid.'"

"When we were at the cemetery, I noticed that your father passed away a long time ago."

"I was fifteen. He died in a bar fight. The last words he ever spoke to me were, 'Why can't you be more like Jackson? You're such a cold son of a bitch.' But I wasn't cold. Just empty."

"What was your mother like?"

"Aloof. She'd been a beauty queen and never forgave me for my terrible sin of being average."

Kerry frowned. "Why would someone so pretty marry a cop?"

"He played professional football when they met, but two years in he destroyed a knee. Why the interest in my family?"

"Not them. You. I was curious why you took so long to return to Denver. Now I know."

She jumped out of bed. "Weren't you anxious to get to Omaha? Well, what are we waiting for?"

"I wish we could go someplace far away and forget all your problems," Kerry said. They'd left Denver behind and were driving through open country. "I can get us fake IDs, even passports if we needed them."

Bob smiled at her. "You're an amazing woman, Kerry Casillas."

Her eyes laughed at him. "You're just now noticing?" She swung out from behind a semi. "The guy I know used to work at the restaurant, and now that he's off parole, he's back in business. Nobody can tell his paper is fake because he gets it input into the proper computers, like it's for real."

"If he's so good, how did he get caught?"

"He didn't. He went to jail for possession of drugs." She passed the truck and moved back into the right lane. "He charges a lot. Too bad you're not rich."

"How much does a person need before you consider them to be rich?"

"I don't know. Maybe a half million. I don't suppose other people think that's much, but it sure would make me feel rich. I'd be able to travel and then settle down in a nice little house somewhere."

"Then I'm rich."

She swerved into the left lane. When she had the car under control again, she glanced at him. Her eyes appeared to be all pupil.

"You have a half million dollars?"

"More, actually."

"Where . . . how . . ."

"From Hsiang-li. He was always giving me money. He paid me a handsome salary, and at the end of each year he gave me a bonus—a percentage of his considerable profits. And, of course, the money for my paintings. Since my expenses were minimal—Madame Butterfly's was my one extravagance—I saved most of it. Also, when Hsiang-li left, he gave me an envelope containing a check that doubled what I had."

"But the boardinghouse, the cheap clothes, the junky car . . ."

"Things don't mean much to me. I've always been more interested in being at peace."

She made an exasperated sound. "You want peace? I'll give you peace. A piece of my mind."

He smiled. "At least it won't be anything weighty."

185

There was a moment of stunned silence, then she burst out laughing. Wiping her eyes with one hand, she said, "It always takes me awhile to recognize when you're being facetious. You were being facetious, weren't you?"

"Of course. I think you're exceptionally smart."

"Yeah, well, if I'm so smart, how come I'm out of a job?"

Bob jerked his head toward her. "What!"

"My boss wouldn't let me take tonight off, so I quit." She gave him a sidelong glance. "You can hire me to be your agent."

"If that's what you want."

"What I want is . . ." She drove in silence for a mile or two. "You don't have any more surprises for me, do you? I mean, every time I get to figuring I know who you are, you throw another surprise in the works."

"No more surprises. You know everything about me I know."

"Okay. Now tell me about your meeting with the girl. What was she wearing?"

18.

"How can I help?" Dr. James Willet rested his chin on his steepled fingers. The backs of his hands were crepey and mottled with age spots, but he seemed only about ten years older than Bob.

"I'm doing research for a book," Bob said. "A friend told me you specialize in the problems of soldiers who had been abused or interfered with."

Dr. Willet nodded. "That is correct."

For a moment Bob thought he caught a glimpse of buried sadness, then the look of patent interest reappeared in the bluish-gray eyes.

"This friend has been plagued with recurring nightmares," Bob said. "He was a conscientious objector during Vietnam, and he dreams that several times he grabbed a weapon and fired on the enemy, though it goes against everything he believes. He now thinks he really did do it."

"Does your friend have a name?"

"I'd prefer not to say."

"What does your . . . friend think happened to him?"

Noting the slight hesitation, Bob realized the doctor assumed he was the friend. He thought of correcting the assumption, then decided it didn't matter.

"He has a vague idea someone programmed him, possibly during a visit to a hospital after receiving a flesh wound."

Dr. Willet tapped the tips of his fingers together. "I see."

"It's as if someone tried to turn a less than ideal soldier into a perfect cog in the military machine, and I became curious about what went on back then. I think there might be a book in it."

Dr. Willet's lips twisted in a sardonic smile. "So do I. I've been working on it for twenty years, but since I don't have anything more than circumstantial evidence and hearsay, editors aren't interested. Also, patriotism is big right now, so an exposé of military malfeasance isn't in hot demand."

"Malfeasance? Is that what you call it?"

He gave a bitter laugh. "No. That's what my agent calls it. I call it criminal behavior. I call it murder."

His hands fluttered in an agitated manner. He set them flat on the desk, took a deep breath, and exhaled slowly.

"Sometimes it seems to me as if the prevailing American attitude is 'I want mine and I don't care what happens to anyone else as long as I get it.' And always, throughout history, the combat soldier got screwed first. In the 1800s, the Chicago meatpackers sold their tainted meat to the army. Many soldiers died on the frontlines not from bullets but from beef. In this century, soldiers have been forced to use leech repellents that didn't repel leeches, shark repellents that actually attracted sharks. They've been supplied with weapons that sometimes failed to fire and weapons that blew up in their hands. And they've been experimented on, like lab rats or guinea pigs."

"It makes a certain sense," Bob said. "The military, particularly the infantry, is a captive population that can be easily controlled and, unlike prison populations, they have little recourse to lawyers since basically they have no rights."

Dr. Willet nodded. "Exactly. And if they ever mentioned that something had been done to them, chalk it up to battle fatigue. If they got injured or killed, that's easily explained too, even if the country isn't at war. If any serious questions are ever asked, all that's necessary is to call it a snafu, and everyone understands because people have come to accept incompetence from the military."

"I heard about a scientific test," Bob said, "where they sent some soldiers to the tropics equipped with winter gear, and posted other to sub-arctic areas with tropical clothes. The soldiers sent to the tropical areas had it easy. They took off their clothes. But those sent to the cold regions could not put on winter gear they didn't have. Most got frostbite. The military laughed it off as another snafu."

Dr. Willet leaned back in his chair; the brown leather groaned. The look of professional interest in his eyes became more personal.

"You've been doing your homework, I see."

Bob nodded, taking the credit, though Harrison had once mentioned it to him. Thinking about Harrison, Bob realized that despite Harrison's expansive ways and the doctor's air of self-containment, the two men were alike in their concern for the plight of the common soldier.

"They deserved better from their government," Dr. Willet said, as if he had heard Bob's thoughts. "Besides the experimentation, some of the most reprehensible measures concerned POWs. After Korea, the government changed the status of the remaining POWs to KIA. They assured the country they left no American POWs in North Korea, but those were just words. The POWs had been moved to China and the Soviet Union."

"Why did they get listed as killed in action if they were still alive?" Bob asked.

Dr. Willet rubbed a thumb over his fingers in the universal sign for money.

Bob's eyebrows drew together. "Who makes money off POWs?"

"The American military. By removing someone from MIA status and placing them on the KIA list, there is a one-time insurance payment. This saves the government a fortune in monthly service pay—which includes promotions and pay raises—over the life of the POW. And it saves a great deal of embarrassment for military officers and politicians who do nothing to secure the release of their men.

"They did the same thing to the POWs after Vietnam, but in that case they had a reason to keep the POWs from coming home. Many had been sent to northern Laos and were held among the poppy fields, where they couldn't help but learn of the American involvement in the drug trade. The U.S. government certainly did not want those soldiers to return home and talk about what they had learned. In fact, one man did manage to escape and make his way back to America. When he tried to tell what he saw, they court-martialed him for being a deserter."

Not knowing what to say, Bob remained silent. He glanced around the office with its homey touches designed to put patients at ease: the restful blues and greens of the landscapes on the walls, the comfortable couches and chairs, the simple wooden desk. The only incongruous note in the room was the table shoved in a corner and piled with stacks of paper. Underneath the table lay cardboard boxes overflowing with more paper.

"My research," Dr. Willet said. "None of those interviews or snippets of information mean much by themselves, but the preponderance of material has proven to me, if no one else, that American soldiers have, in fact, been experimented on."

Bob related what Tracy had told him about the

secret agent from the Korean War who was so secret even he didn't know he was an agent.

Dr. Willet nodded. "They began using such agents during World War Two and continued right on through Vietnam, but more than simple hypnotism was usually involved. I don't know what procedures they're using now. Light, sound, and color, perhaps. I do know there are several drugs that help overcome the mental and moral blocks we all have, and make us more susceptible to suggestion.

"In nineteen fifty-three, the director of the CIA said they had to find effective and practical techniques to render an individual subservient to an imposed will or control. The CIA created pain, produced headaches, used drugs, did anything they could to make the subject open to manipulation. They strove to induce amnesia, a way of gaining control over people's memories by wiping out certain areas of experience and leaving intact only what the agency wanted them to remember."

Bob felt a chill on the back of his neck. "Have you ever heard of a project called Cerberus?"

"I don't believe I have."

"According to my informant, it originated to help amputees overcome the discomfort in their phantom limbs by removing the memory of it."

Dr. Willet froze. There was a crack in the calm façade at that moment, a lowering of the guard, and Bob saw the extent of his pain.

The doctor's voice shook when he spoke. "What do you know about the memory removal?"

"Only that ISI—Information Services, Incorporated—funded it and that they experimented on amputees during the Korean War."

"Cerberus," the doctor said, as if to himself. "An apt name. Similar to cerebrum. And, like the three-headed hound, the brain has three parts—hindbrain, midbrain, forebrain. It too sometimes guards the gates of hell, an internal hell composed of terrible and unbearable memories."

"I'd appreciate anything you can tell me about ISI," Bob said.

Dr. Willet sounded abstracted. "I don't know much."

"Will it help if I promise not to use anything you tell me?"

"No. I *don't* know much. I've come across the name a couple of times in the course of my research, but that's all. And if I did know, I wouldn't care if you used it. I'm more interested in getting the information exposed than in getting credit."

"How did you get involved in this research in the first place?"

Dr. Willet studied him a moment, but didn't respond.

Bob returned his look.

"My brother," Dr. Willet said at last. "Daryl was eight years older than me, and my idol. We grew up in a farming community here in Nebraska, and life seemed perfect.

"Then Daryl got drafted. He left home a happy-go-lucky kid and returned a morose, remote stranger with one leg. I endured rebuff after rebuff trying to get close to him. One morning before school, I went looking for him, hoping that maybe, this time, I could help him. I found him in the barn, crying. I hugged him, and for once he didn't push me away.

"When he got control of himself, he said, 'I can't remember.'

"'Can't remember what?' I asked.

"'What it was like before,' he answered. 'I

vaguely remember you and the rest of the family, this farm, a dog we used to have named Butch, but nothing else.'

"'You don't remember Jake?' I asked.

"He gave me a blank look. 'Who's Jake?'

"'Your dog,' I told him. 'The one you had before you left. A car ran him over a few months ago, and we've all been wondering why you haven't asked about him.'

"'I can't remember,' Daryl cried. 'I can't remember. Can't remember.' He banged his head against the wall.

"I was scared. I wanted to run get my parents, but I couldn't leave him. I stayed with Daryl until he calmed, then, reluctantly, I went to school."

He drew in a ragged breath. "If I could change one moment of my life, it would be that one. Years of therapy, and I still can't help thinking if I'd stayed with him, he'd be alive."

"What happened?" Bob asked softly.

"He killed himself. I found him hanging from the rafters when I returned home from school that day. Everyone assumed he couldn't deal with the loss of his leg, and I didn't tell them any different."

His smile had more teeth than humor. "You should have my job. You're certainly good at getting people to talk. I've only told my therapist and my wife about that morning in the barn." He paused for a moment, then continued in a harder tone. "That moment defined my life. It was thirty-six years ago and I now have a family of my own, but my brother's suicide still haunts me, still drives me to understand. That's why I became a therapist for veterans."

He gestured toward the stacks of paper on the corner table. "As I pieced together what little my

193

patients knew, a story gradually emerged about a hospital in the Philippines where many had been subjects of mind control experiments."

Bob stiffened, remembering that Harrison had told him the same thing. So the conspiracy had been real after all and not a fabrication of the journalist's diseased mind. A frightening notion popped into his head.

"Is it possible to give someone cancer?" he asked.

With a visible effort, the doctor pulled his attention back to Bob. "Lab rats are given cancer all the time."

"But people?"

"Yes." He rubbed the back of his neck. "A colleague discovered a cluster of cancer victims at Leavenworth several years ago and is convinced they had been purposely infected. The cancer took hold and spread so rapidly, they were dead within a month. From the extensive growth of the tumors, the prison doctor assumed they'd been sick for months, perhaps years, without anyone knowing, but my colleague doesn't agree."

Dr. Willet rolled his chair over to the table, shuffled through a stack of papers, pulled one out, then rolled back to his desk.

He handed the paper to Bob. It was a photocopy of an interview published in a journal called *Scientific Revolutions.*

"It won't be long before we can completely cure cancer," bragged Dr. Martin Reed of the Rosewood Research Institute. "We're making tremendous progress due to a new, super-fast-acting cancer I have developed."

"How does a new cancer help cure the old

ones?" the interviewer asked.

"It doesn't," Dr. Reed responded. "What it does is allow us to speed up the whole process. Protocols that used to take months can now be completed in a matter of days."

Bob stared at the picture accompanying the article. Did this man create the cancer that killed Harrison? With his thin, pale face, aquiline features, and mop of unruly brown hair, he looked like a scientist, not a murderer. But looks don't tell the truth.

After Bob seared the man's face in his memory, he returned the paper to Dr. Willet.

"What do you know about the Rosewood Research Institute?"

"Not as much as I'd like to," Dr. Willet responded. "I do know they're endowed by ISI and are involved in all sorts of innovative and highly successful treatments of behavior disorders, but there's something not quite right about the procedures. I've tried to use the techniques they describe in the journals, but I've never been able to achieve their spectacular results. I have yet to find a therapist who has."

"What do you think they're doing?"

Dr. Willet looked Bob straight in the eyes as if he wanted to catch even the smallest reaction. "I think they're using laser surgery."

Bob didn't blink. "According to my source, ISI has developed a laser so fine it can zap a single molecule."

Dr Willet nodded. "And I've heard of a scientist who created a remote-controlled radioactive isotope that can find the location of any memory in the brain. To be precise, it is not the memory itself the isotope locates. A single memory is not stored whole in a specific location but is diffused throughout the brain.

What the isotope actually finds is the spot on the brain responsible for the retrieval of a particular memory. Her research was funded by ISI."

He lifted his chin. "I think someone has been using the isotope and the laser to remove memories and undesirable character traits."

"Who?" Bob asked.

"A psychiatrist named Jeremy Rutledge, for one. He now runs the Rosewood Research Institute. In the sixties, he had a patient, a little girl who suffered such severe abuse she became catatonic. He theorized if he could physically prevent her brain from being able to retrieve those memories, to erase them, in effect, she could grow up to have a normal life.

"It sounds farfetched, but the same thing occurs all by itself every day. If you forget something, the memory is still there, but the retrieval breaks down.

"They never planned to keep the procedure secret, but were going to submit a paper to the journals as soon as the girl had been restored to mental health. Before they could proceed, a lab technician leaked the information to the newspapers. The press called it 'The New Lobotomy,' and Rutledge was hauled into court.

"Rutledge, backed by ISI's money and a whole battery of attorneys, argued that the operation was not a lobotomy, not even open surgery, but a simple, humane procedure done with a laser. The time consuming part was finding the precise spot to hit.

"He testified that this procedure would greatly benefit mankind, but the courts didn't agree and enjoined him from ever performing the operation.

"The psychiatrist lost, but so did the little girl. She's grown now, but that poor woman is still imprisoned in her private hell."

Dr. Willet rummaged through his papers once

more and pulled out copies of the newspaper articles detailing the story.

Glancing through them, Bob noticed a picture of Dr. Rutledge. He seemed vaguely familiar with his round face and expression of cheery innocence, but Bob knew he'd never heard the name before.

"I have a theory," Dr. Willet said, "that even before Rutledge tried to cure the little girl, similar procedures had been tested on amputees during the Korean War. I believe they used my brother for one of their guinea pigs, and they destroyed more than the memory of his limb. I believe they continued with their research during Vietnam. I run a therapy group for Vietnam veterans with missing limbs, and some of them have never felt a single twinge of a phantom limb. Many of those men remember being sent to a hospital in the Philippines during the course of their treatment."

"But it's a good thing, isn't it?" Bob asked. "I mean, the doctors saved them a lot of agony."

Dr. Willet's mouth thinned. "It does sound nice and humanitarian, doesn't it? But not one of the amputees gave their consent. Also, I think somewhere along the line the doctors got giddy with power and started doing all sorts of experiments, venturing into eradication of anti-social behavior. I may never be able to prove it, but I'm going to spend the rest of my life trying. I owe it to my brother."

19.

Kerry's roommate left town for a few days, and once again Bob stayed at her house. Though he and Kerry had returned from Omaha late last night, he still rose early for a run.

Later, after a leisurely breakfast, Kerry went to the restaurant to pick up her final paycheck, and Bob went to the Denver Public Library on Broadway and Fourteenth—the only quiet and private place with a payphone that he knew about.

He roamed the library, familiarizing himself with the layout of the first floor. The library had two main entrances, but since they faced each other, giving someone entering one door a clear view of anyone leaving by the other, they would not serve as an escape route.

Toward the back of the library, beyond the history and biography departments, he found a more secluded exit.

He returned to the front of the library, walked down the stairs to the basement, and made his way along a darkened hallway to the telephones.

A child answered his call.

"May I speak to your father?" Bob asked.

"Da-a-addy," the child screeched. "It's for you."

A minute later a man with a pleasant but tired-sounding voice said, "Yes?"

"Robert Stark? I'm from the American Association of Prosthesis Manufacturers. We're trying to update our files."

"How did you get my name?" Robert asked. "I've never sent you people any information. I don't even know who you are."

"Maybe your doctor filled out the questionnaire.

Yes. It's signed by a Dr.—sorry, but I can't make out the name."

"She does have terrible writing, doesn't she?"

Remembering Dr. Albion and his question as to whether Bob's left foot had been blown off, Bob said, "Hmm. Let's see. It says here you're missing your left foot."

"Yes."

"Any problems with your prosthesis?"

"No. It's comfortable enough."

"What about phantom pain? Are you still experiencing any itching, twitching, anything like that?"

"No. To be honest, I never did have any phantom pains. I used to belong to a support group for amputees, but I quit. A lot of them had problems with those pains, some on and off for years, and they resented the fact that I didn't."

"You're lucky," Bob said.

Robert laughed humorlessly. "If I were lucky, I'd still have two feet."

"How did you lose your foot?"

"Vietnam."

"A mine?"

"Yes."

"On Highway One? Near Qui Nhon?"

"How did you know?"

"It's right here on the questionnaire."

"It was one of those things," Robert said. "I was a supply clerk, but one day I got orders to ride along on one of the supply trucks. It was the first time I had been outside of Saigon, and I was enjoying the trip, then all of a sudden we ran over that mine. It shouldn't have been there—the minesweepers supposedly had cleared the road. Heck, *I* shouldn't have been there, but that's life, I guess."

"Did you sustain any other injuries?"

"Just minor ones."

"Any scars?"

"Other than around my stump? No."

"What about old scars? Maybe scars on your chest?"

"What does that have to do with my prosthesis?"

"Nothing, as far as I know, but it's on the questionnaire, so I have to ask."

Robert sighed. "I have a tiny scar on my chest where my brother shot me when we were kids. I was standing a long way off, so only one shotgun pellet hit me, but it still left a mark. Do you have any more questions? I have to get ready for work."

"One more. What hospital did you go to after your injury in Vietnam?"

"The one at Qui Nhon at first, then they transferred me to a hospital in the Philippines."

"Thank you for your help," Bob said. He would have liked to talk to his other self longer, maybe find out how else their early experiences varied, maybe find out why Robert had married Lorena despite that cold letter, but he knew his time was running out.

He hung up the receiver and strode back to the stairs, took them two at a time until he neared the top, then slowed to a more casual pace. He turned to the left and made his way to the tall shelves of fiction where he felt secure enough to glance behind him.

It was as he expected. Sam and Ted were crashing through the front door, suit coats unbuttoned for easy access to their guns. They shoved their badges in the face of the old man standing at the door making sure everyone had checked out their books.

"Where are the phones?" Ted demanded.

The old man pointed a trembling finger to the steps leading downward.

Sam and Ted pushed past him, almost knocking him over in their haste, and hurried to the staircase.

As soon as they sprinted down the stairs, Bob moved away from the protection of the shelves and headed for his emergency exit.

Once outside, he crossed Fourteenth Avenue, seeking the relative safety of the Greek amphitheater in Civic Center Park. Standing as still and as silent and as cold as one of the statues adorning the amphitheater, he watched the action unfolding across the street.

A half dozen cars came screeching to a halt outside the library and double-parked. Ignoring the honking horns and the obscenities from irate drivers, the teams of ISI operatives jumped out of their vehicles and ran into the building.

More cars arrived, further snarling traffic. Within minutes, stern-faced, self-important men and women surrounded the library.

Some of the operatives guarded the entrance, refusing to let anyone go in or come out of the library. They demanded to see identification from all who approached and studied the faces of those who held back.

Others searched the grounds, the parked cars, and everywhere else a man might have hidden. They interrogated everyone in the vicinity.

Not a single city cop arrived at the scene.

Bob saw Ted come out of the library.

"I can't believe you fuckers let him get away again," Ted yelled at the milling agents. "We had him. He was right here."

One of the agents responded, speaking too

quietly for Bob to hear.

"He is not a phantom," Ted bellowed. "He is not a shape shifter. He is not a shadow. Anyone, and I mean anyone, who ever mentions any of that supernatural shit again will be fired on the spot. Got it?"

Bob heard no more of Ted's harangue. The crowds that had gathered to watch the spectacle began to disperse. He slipped among them and made his way to Colfax where he caught a bus.

As the bus lumbered up Capitol Hill, Bob saw Herbert Townsend trudging along the opposite side of the street.

Townsend seemed sad and listless, as if his inner fires had burned low. Even his aluminum foil headgear seemed lusterless. Occasionally Townsend would turn to accost someone, but when they maneuvered out of his way, he made no attempt to detain them. Mostly he plodded along, head bowed.

Will I end up like him, endlessly roaming the streets with a message no one wants to hear? Bob flexed his fingers and found his answer: no.

Townsend seemed a frail creature without inner reserves of strength to sustain him. Bob, on the other hand, was a finely turned instrument at the height of his mental and physical powers.

More importantly, he had Kerry on his side.

Bob was sitting on the porch swing when Kerry came home, a troubled expression on her face.

He jumped to his feet. "What's wrong?"

"Yesterday a man and a woman came into the restaurant asking about someone who matched your description, and they used your name."

He felt as if his heart had skipped a beat. It was one thing to realize how close they were to finding him.

It was another thing to realize how close they were to connecting him to Kerry.

"We have to leave," he said. "I'll never forgive myself if something happened to you on my account."

She gave a shaky laugh. "I'm pretty sure I'll be okay. If they find me, I'll tell them where you are, then I'll go back to Pete's Porches."

He laughed because she wanted him to, but he scrabbled around in his mind for a way to keep her safe. "You'll have to come with me."

"Anywhere." After a moment she said, "Where are we going?"

"Thailand."

A joyful light appeared in her eyes, then slowly faded. "I can't."

"Why not? Isn't this what you've been living for—a chance to travel? And besides, if you don't come, who's going to check out the hotel room for me?"

She set her jaw. "I don't have the money."

"But I do."

"I can't take your money. I made a promise to myself when I left Pete's Porches that I'd never give myself away again. Don't you see? If I won't give, I can't take."

"I understand," he said gently, "truly I do. But having ISI operatives appear at your place of business changes everything. We're in this together. I can no longer assume you'll be okay, and I can only protect you if you're with me."

He took a step closer. She stopped him with a hand on his chest.

"I don't need you to protect me."

He put a hand over hers. "Maybe I need you to protect me."

She gave him an uncertain look.

He lifted her hand and kissed it. It felt cold against his lips. "You must be sorry I came into your life."

A smile lit her face, and laughter was in her eyes. "You didn't come into my life. I dragged you in, remember?"

"Then it's settled. First we need to go shopping and cash the rest of my traveler's checks, then we need to buy IDs from your friend."

"I don't even know what kind of clothes to get," Kerry said as she drove them to a new mall southwest of Denver. "What's the weather going to be like?"

"This is still monsoon season. By noon, dark thunderclouds will appear on the horizon, and the air will become thick with humidity. Later, torrents of rain will fall. Lots of rain. Sometimes the streets of Bangkok get flooded, creating massive traffic jams, but the rain also washes away the smog, and each day dawns bright and cool. Of course, by noon thunderclouds appear again."

"So I guess we need raincoats. What else?"

"Mesh socks if we can find them, otherwise cotton will do, and canvas shoes or sandals. Also whatever cotton touristy clothes we can find."

"The stores will be stocked with late fall and winter things."

"We need the bare minimum, whatever fits into carry-on bags. We can buy everything else in Thailand. Since you like to shop so much, you should have fun. In addition to small shops and street markets, there are some very modern department stores and shopping centers."

Kerry bounced in her seat. "I can't believe I'm

actually going to Bangkok. Did I ever tell you I saw *The King and I* at least four times?"

Bob put a finger to his lips. "Don't mention that movie while we're in Thailand. It's so full of misconceptions it offends the Thais, and it's disrespectful to the king."

"You never said what you're going to do once we get there."

"Talk to a pilot named Donald McCray. I need to find out more about the hospital in the Philippines. And I'll probably stop in to see Hamburger Dan."

"Wouldn't it be easier to call?"

"I have to convince McCray to tell me what he told Harrison, and for that we have to be face-to-face. And obviously Hamburger Dan's phone is tapped, so I can't call him, either."

"Are you talking about *the* Hamburger Dan? The hero of Harrison's book *A Separate War*?"

"Yes."

"Wow!"

After a mile of silence, she said in a more subdued tone, "I've been so excited about the trip, I forgot to ask you about talking to your other self."

Bob recounted his conversation with Robert and, after a brief hesitation, told her about the ISI operatives who'd stormed the library.

She drew in a sharp breath that sounded like a sob. "They do want you, don't they?"

"Whatever their original objective, it's become personal for Sam and Ted. I'm afraid they're never going to give up."

She gave him a lopsided smile. "You were right about needing me to protect you." She accelerated, shot through a yellow light, then eased up on the gas. "Why do you think they're after you?"

"I still don't know."

"You've talked to a lot of people and done a lot of thinking. Haven't you begun to connect the dots?"

"Of course, but I could be connecting dots that don't exist."

"So what's your theory?"

He felt a sudden need to be moving, but only had room to shift in his seat. "I think Robert got snagged for the Cerberus experiments, and they gave him a new identity. Mine."

"Why would they do such a thing?"

"Maybe for no other reason than to see if they could."

She chewed on her bottom lip. "But why are they after you?"

"I think they wanted to keep me away from their ringer, but things got out of hand."

A slow nod. "It must have been a shock when they discovered you were coming home after all these years."

Seeing a look of sadness in her eyes and something akin to pity, he turned his head and stared out the window at the distant mountains.

Snow already dusted the peaks.

20.

"I thought this would be fun," Kerry said, turning away from the airplane window. "But there's nothing to see. Just night."

Bob opened his eyes. "Go to sleep. It helps pass the time."

"I can't. My brain won't shut off." She gave him a crafty look. "Maybe if you tell me a story . . ."

He laughed. "I've never known anyone with such an insatiable appetite for stories. Harrison's going to love you."

He felt a jolt as it dawned on him, once again, that Harrison was dead. Maybe murdered.

Kerry reached out and touched Bob's hand. Her voice was as soft as her caress. "What was he like? In *Dark Side of Heroes* he described the journalist John Tyler as a big man with big appetites."

"Sounds like him. He drank big, ate big, laughed big. He was extravagantly generous but so offhand nobody resented him for it. When Kalia and Dave Marconi were ready for college, he made sure they got into Columbia University, invited them to live in his New York brownstone, and helped them get acclimated to the United States."

Kerry leaned her head against his shoulder. "Did he ever fall in love? Marry?"

"Not that I know of. I heard a rumor that his housekeeper in Bangkok, a woman from Chiang Mai, did more than take care of his residence, but he never confirmed it."

"What about his early life? The biography at the end of his books doesn't say anything except that he divided his time between New York City and Bangkok."

"That's about all I know. He talked constantly while we were together, but he never mentioned his past. It seemed as if he sprang forth fully grown from the soil of Vietnam where we met."

"Another conspiracy of silence," Kerry said. "You men!"

Bob tilted his head to look at her. "What are you talking about?"

"I read somewhere there are two ways of saying nothing, to be silent or to hide your silence behind words. You and Hsiang-li shared one kind of silence, you and Harrison shared the second."

"You could be right."

"I know I am. Who are Kalia and Dave Marconi?"

Bob waited a beat until his less nimble mind caught up with hers. "They're Hamburger Dan's children. Since Hamburger Dan can never return to the United States, Harrison acted as surrogate father to Kalia and Dave."

"How come he couldn't return?"

"Did you read Harrison's novel *A Separate War*?"

"Yes."

"Then you know the answer as well as I do. I read the book, and it's all there."

"But I want to hear the real story about Hamburger Dan and O'Riley's Bar. I think it's romantic—a typical New York neighborhood bar set in the middle of Bangkok."

"Harrison loved the place. When he arrived back in Bangkok after a stay in New York, he stopped at O'Riley's first thing. He told me it helped him bridge the gap between east and west.

"Hamburger Dan's real name was David

Marconi. He's Italian, but he grew up in an Irish neighborhood in Brooklyn where a bar sat on every corner, or so he said. In the summer, when he opened his bedroom window to catch the breeze, David could hear snatches of song coming from O'Riley's, the nearest bar, and he could smell its strange and wonderful odor.

"Before he grew old enough to legally patronize the bar, he enlisted in the army. He took and passed every advanced training course possible, and eventually became one of the elite—a Green Beret. They sent him to Vietnam to organize a remote tribe of Montagnards into a combat unit. The Yards, as the Green Berets called them, were anxious to fight the North Vietnamese, but they always had more important things to do than attend training sessions.

"In desperation, David went to one of the tribal elders and explained his predicament. The old man told him the people didn't trust him because he wasn't one of them, but he promised to help."

Kerry lifted her head. "I like this part. The old man brought a shy young girl to Dan—David, I mean— and said, 'You marry.' David didn't want to get married, but the old man insisted it was the way to get everyone to trust him. So David got married and later fell in love with her. Was she as beautiful as Harrison wrote?"

Bob nodded. "Very beautiful. Creamy skin with a bloom of roses on her high cheekbones, sparkling dark eyes set at an exotic slant, long lustrous black hair, surprisingly full breasts for such a delicate body."

Kerry poked him in the side. "A simple yes would have been sufficient."

Bob grinned at her. "I can't help it. I like black-haired women with sparkling dark eyes."

"Oh." She laid her head back on his shoulder. "After the wedding ceremony, David had no more trouble organizing and training his combat troops."

"Do you want to tell the story?" Bob asked.

"No. You go ahead. You're doing fine."

Smiling, he said, "The respect the troops had for David was often tinged with ribald humor, but David accepted the teasing good-naturedly.

"The longer he lived among those indigenous mountain peoples of Vietnam, the more he identified with their plight. At one time the vast section of South Vietnam known as the Central Highlands belonged to the Montagnards, but they had been pushed further and further back into the hills by the Vietnamese, who considered them to be little more than animals. In fact, after a bombing raid in North Vietnam, the South Vietnamese often expended any unused ordnance on the mountain villages."

"The South Vietnamese did that to the villagers even though they were both on the same side? And the government allowed it?" Kerry asked.

"Ancient hatreds are stronger than modern political alliances." He paused, but she had no more questions. "When David's tour of duty ended, he refused to leave. His commanding officer flew in to order David's return.

"David Marconi was a towering, muscular man with curly black hair, a classic Roman nose, and flashing brown eyes. He stood his ground and glared defiantly at the officer. In the end, it was not David's intimidating stance that induced the officer to leave, but the menacing arc of Montagnard soldiers with their M-16's at the ready.

"David gave little thought to the consequences of his actions. He and his troops were too busy fighting their war. Even after the American military pulled out of Vietnam, even after Saigon fell, the mountain tribes continued to fight. The South Vietnamese may have surrendered, but they had not.

"One day word reached the little village that the NVA was capturing any Montagnards who had not turned in their weapons and were taking them away to be shot by firing squads. Hundreds were being slaughtered.

"No coward, David would have remained, but he worried about the safety of his wife and their two young children. He prepared for departure. Although he begged his beloved Yards to go with them, they refused. The village was their whole life, and they would live and die with it.

"David and his small family slipped away in the night. On foot, they crossed the border into Cambodia and then into Thailand, following trails known only to the mountain tribes, who used them to move freely from one country to another, disregarding national boundaries.

"Once David had safely settled his family in Bangkok, he fell into a state of deep despair. He felt he had betrayed his Yards who had been betrayed too many times before. And he had no job. Unless he wanted to become a mercenary, his military days were gone forever. Even worse, he could never return to the United States. Refusing to obey a direct order from a superior officer in time of war is a serious offense, and if the military caught him, the best he could hope for would be to spend the rest of his life doing hard time at Leavenworth.

"I was tending bar in The Lotus Room one evening when David came in and tried to find the answers to his problems in a bottle of whiskey.

211

"Harrison sat on the barstool next to him. Between gulps of whiskey and an occasional belch, David poured out the entire tale. Several times he got sidetracked and lamented he'd never be able to have a drink at O'Riley's in Brooklyn. During the rest of the evening and late into the night, Harrison kept dropping casual remarks about Bangkok needing a good Irish pub.

"David opened O'Riley's Bar and Grill a month later.

"When Harrison wrote his book *A Separate War*, he used the real name of the bar, but he called the owner Hamburger Dan, a reference to an old song no one but Harrison ever remembered hearing.

"The book became an international bestseller, and O'Riley's became the most famous bar in the world.

"Hamburger Dan, as everybody now called David Marconi, took it all in stride. He made no secret that his family was the most important thing in his life. He boasts that his children, born in the jungled hills of Vietnam to a Montagnard woman, are now attending college in the United States and have the whole world at their feet."

Bob chuckled. "I still remember that night in The Lotus Room. Harrison thought he was subtle, but Hamburger Dan saw the truth. He told me once he would never forget how much he owed Harrison, not just for the success of the bar and for financing it, but for steering him into it in the first place."

Bob listened for Kerry's answering chuckle, but all he heard was the soft whuffling of her breath as she slept.

Bob dreamt.

The heavy warmth of the jungle wrapped around him like a familiar blanket. He felt at peace, knowing he'd become part of this green world. He paused in his journey and looked up at the small patches of pale blue showing through the canopy of leaves. From a nearby branch came the clear song of a finch accompanied by a chorus of tree frogs.

He took a deep breath, filling his nostrils with the rich smell of earth and vegetation. As he exhaled, a chill stole over him. Noticing movement to the left, he turned and peered into the shadows. A darker shadow, a ghost mist, slipped between the tree trunks.

Suddenly the jungle closed in on him. The smell suffocated him, the taste of the air choked him. His chest ached with the effort to breathe.

He felt a touch on his hand . . .

Gasping, Bob sat bold upright. He stared wildly about him.

Where am I? Who am I?

He became aware of the young woman gazing anxiously at him and of her hand resting on his. Then he became aware of the room and the intricately designed bamboo furniture.

All at once he knew. He was in a hotel room in Bangkok, in bed with Kerry. They had registered as Timothy and Louanne Prather, the names on their new drivers' licenses and passports.

"Are you okay?" Kerry asked. "You panted like you were in pain."

He rubbed his chest. "I couldn't breathe. The jungle . . ."

She put her arms around him.

His body registered her touch with a strange sense of numbness. She pulled away from him, a

213

puzzled look in her eyes. He hugged her close and buried his face in her hair. The numbness disappeared. He could feel the strength of her arms.

21.

Bob opened his eyes, then squeezed them shut against the light. From the heaviness of the air and the brightness of the day, he presumed it was mid-morning. He opened his eyes again and this time managed to keep them open.

He turned his head toward Kerry. She lay on her back, hands behind her head, eyes focused on the ceiling. Following her gaze, he realized she was staring at one of the ubiquitous green lizards. Her body vibrated with excitement.

He smiled to himself. Leave it to Kerry to be thrilled with this small reminder they were no longer in Colorado.

"Isn't this great?" she said in a hushed voice. "We have our own private watch lizard."

Bob brushed away a fly buzzing around his head. "We could use a few more."

A knock sounded.

He tensed.

Kerry patted him on the arm. "It's room service. I ordered breakfast. Green tea, coffee, rolls, and fruit." She jumped out of bed, snatched her red paisley wrap, and slipped into it as she headed for the door.

The spring within him wound tighter.

She paused to tie the belt around her waist, then put her hand on the knob.

He was sitting up, cursing the sluggishness of his wits, when she pulled the door open.

A young Thai waiter entered and set a tray on the table. He accepted a tip from Kerry, gave her a small *wai* and a large smile, then left, closing the door behind him.

Bob let out the breath he'd been holding, and

some of the tenseness seeped from his body.

Inspecting the contents of the tray, Kerry pointed to a round object of such a deep reddish brown it almost looked black. "Is that food?"

"It's a mangosteen. You need a knife to cut through the tough skin, but the white pulp is delicious."

She laughed. "I wondered why they sent a sharp knife for soft rolls and bananas." She cut through the rind and took a big bite of the pulp. "You're right. This is delicious."

She cut off a piece and held it out to him.

He shook his head. "I need to take a shower first."

She stuffed another piece of the fruit in her mouth. "Good. More for me."

When Bob came out of the bathroom, he found Kerry dressed in her new cotton pants, a vividly colored shirt, and sandals.

"I can't wait another minute." Her smile was incandescent. "I'm going for a walk. My very first walk in a foreign country." She opened the door. "Do you want me to wait for you?"

"No. Go ahead. Be careful, okay?"

"I will." She ran back, gave him a hug, then dashed out the door.

The hotel was built around a courtyard accessible from all the rooms. Bob took his breakfast out to the courtyard, but couldn't enjoy the fountain, the bushes, the flowers. He kept stealing glances at the windows, wondering if anyone was watching him.

When dark clouds rolled across the sky, pushing a stifling humidity before them, he took refuge in his room. It did not have air-conditioning, but the slowly revolving ceiling fan offered a modicum of relief.

He paced the floor, feeling as if he were a stranger in this land. It didn't matter that he had lived here for sixteen years, he realized; any place would seem alien when he wasn't with Kerry. She was his home.

He tried not to worry about her all alone on the streets, but as time passed, the worry grew too strong to ignore.

Then the rains fell. There was no light spattering gradually increasing in intensity as in Colorado, but an abrupt opening of the skies as if someone had turned on a spigot.

Fifteen minutes later Kerry returned, dripping wet and laughing.

"I got lost. I kept pointing and asking people if this was the way back to the Fountain Hotel, and no matter which direction I pointed, they said yes."

Bob felt a pang of remorse. "I should have told you. It's considered polite to agree. You have to ask direct questions like, 'Where is the Fountain Hotel?'"

"I know. I finally figured that out. What's wrong?" She narrowed her focus on him. "Did something happen?" Then her eyes widened to normal. "You were worried about me. That's nice. When are we going to O'Riley's?"

"As soon as we get you dry."

Bob stepped into O'Riley's and paused until his eyes adapted to the dim light. When he could see clearly, he noticed Hamburger Dan, hair now more gray than black, serving a drink to Jim Keating, an ex-Marine reputed to be a drug dealer. Bob could not make out Keating's words, but he could hear the rumble of his deep voice underlying the ambient noise.

A gaunt, stringy-haired man sat at the piano,

played a soft rendition of "Yesterday."

Kerry glanced about, dark eyes gleaming with excitement. She leaned close to Bob and spoke in his ear. "This place is exactly the way Harrison described it. I feel like I'm in his book."

Bob smiled at her. With the smile still on his face, he let Kerry tow him to a vacant table where they'd have a good view of the whole bar.

He nodded to Hamburger Dan as he passed. Hamburger Dan frowned as if he could not place him.

"Hey, bartender," a portly man at the end of the bar called out. The man pointed to the skinny woman perched on the barstool next to his. "The missus needs another a those drinks with a umbrella."

Hamburger Dan gave Bob a second look then fixed the drink.

"This is great." Kerry took off her dripping raincoat and draped it across the back of her chair.

Bob took his off, too. In his short-sleeved shirt imprinted with red, green, and yellow parrots, he felt like a tourist. He even found himself gazing around as if he'd never visited the place before.

He saw a couple of the other regulars, a German and an American—both mercenaries—but most of the people were strangers to him, including the four men sitting at the next table. They seemed to be Americans of the right age to have fought in Vietnam. A man in a Yankees baseball cap waved his arms for emphasis.

"I did my job," Bob heard him say. "Then I got out and continued on with my life. Everything's great. My life is full. It happened so long ago. I don't understand what the big deal is."

The haunting strains of "Hey Jude" filtered through the room.

"What are you going to have?" Kerry asked.

"A Singha in honor of Harrison. It's a local beer he liked. Also a hamburger with fries."

When a giggling young waitress approached, Kerry ordered hamburgers, fries, and Singhas for both of them.

Hamburger Dan brought their drinks.

Setting them on the table, he gave Bob a penetrating glance. "It is you. I wasn't sure at first. How've you been—"

Before Hamburger Dan could speak his name, Bob said quickly, "Gandy. I'm Rick Gandy and this is Julie Walsh."

Hamburger Dan's eyebrows rose. "I see. Does this have anything to do with the two men sitting in the booth across the room?"

Bob lifted his drink to his lips and gazed over the top of the mug. The men in question leaned back in their seats with studied nonchalance, but their eyes were hard and way too alert—cop's eyes.

"My supposed friends?" Bob asked.

"Right. They've been in and out for the past six weeks or so, but after you called they started spending a lot of time here."

"Something you should know. Your phone is tapped."

Hamburger Dan stiffened. "What's going on? What are you involved with?"

"To be honest, I have no idea, but I'm looking into it."

"You?" Hamburger Dan had the grace not to smile, but Bob could sense his incredulity.

Seeing the light of battle in Kerry's eyes and her mouth opening to come to his defense, Bob laid a hand on her knee. She closed her mouth, but her jaw remained set.

The waitress brought their hamburgers. The delicious aroma of grilled meat made Bob's stomach growl with hunger.

"I'll leave you to your food," Hamburger Dan said. "I shouldn't stay here too long anyway, don't want to draw the attention of your friends."

Kerry's gaze followed him as he moved off, then it shifted to Bob.

"How come he talked to you like that? Doesn't he know you're the Bob Noone character in *Dark Side of Heroes*?"

"I doubt it. Now that Harrison's gone, you're probably the only one who knows. And if by chance Hamburger Dan does know, he still wouldn't be impressed. He'd think Noone was a wimp."

"Oh." She took a big bite of her hamburger and ate it slowly. "How did you come up with the names Rick Gandy and Julie Walsh?"

"They slipped out. I decided we shouldn't advertise the names we're traveling under."

"Good thinking." She chewed on a French fry. "I'm beginning to have as many identities as you. It's confusing."

Bob nodded. Munching on his own hamburger, he let his glance fall on the other bar patrons.

"Mike seemed like a brother to me," the man in the Yankee baseball cap said, tears brimming over. "I tried to save him, but there was nothing I could do."

The men with the cop's eyes stood, took a final look around, then sauntered out of the bar, still maintaining their casual air.

Bob felt his shoulders sag with relief.

As he continued to eat, he could hear the gaunt man playing "Let It Be."

"Who's the piano player?" Kerry asked. "He's

good."

"Alan Pierce. He's an Iowa farm boy raised in a strict Methodist family. He got hooked on heroin in Vietnam. He came to Bangkok after the war, and he's been drifting from job to job ever since. He's clean now, but he's still too ashamed to go home."

"So many stories," she said softly.

"That's what Harrison used to say."

After the waitress cleared away their plates, Hamburger Dan returned with two more beers. "On the house." He set the beer in front of them. "Have you two known each other long?"

"Yes," Kerry said while Bob was saying "No."

They looked at each other and grinned.

Hamburger Dan shook his head. "No wonder I didn't recognize you . . . Rick. You're so different.

"Different how?" Kerry asked, eyes bright.

"Younger. Happier. I don't think I've ever seen him smile before."

"Happier?" Bob gave a snort of unamused laughter. "With people after me for no reason I can fathom?" But something deep inside him said it might be true.

Hamburger Dan chatted a few minutes, bringing Bob current on the activities of his regulars.

"I don't see Donald McCray," Bob said. "Is he around?"

"Haven't seen him for a while. He took Harrison's death hard. Blames himself, but I don't know why. It's not like he had anything to do with Harrison getting cancer. Strange. I didn't think they were that close."

"Does he still use that old air strip west of town?"

"As far as I know. You planning on seeing

him?"

"I might."

"Well, go see Harrison's lawyer, too. And call Dunbar. Get them off my back." Hamburger Dan's quick grin took any sting out of the words. "Are you here to stay?"

"Not this trip."

"Be sure to stop by before you leave. Take care, you hear? You too, Julie."

Bob and Kerry finished their beers, then threaded their way around the tables to the door. A few notes of "Imagine" followed them outside.

It was still raining.

Despite umbrellas and raincoats, by the time they found a taxi, their pant legs and sandal-clad feet were soaked.

Kerry sneezed. "Are you going to see McCray now?"

"It's too late."

"Would it make you sad to take me by The Lotus Room?"

"No." Bob gave the cabdriver the address, then settled back into the damp seat, which smelled of mildew and sweat.

When they pulled up in front of the familiar building, Bob paid the driver to wait for them. He and Kerry climbed out and stood staring at the place where he'd spent most of his waking hours for sixteen years. Seen through sheets of rain, it seemed shuttered and remote, though its lines were still pleasing.

Kerry looked from the pagoda-like building to Bob and then back again.

She shook her head. "I can't picture you in there."

"Neither can I."

They climbed back into the cab.

"Where should we go?" she asked.

"To the hotel. I need to get some sleep. I'm still tired from the trip and not as alert as I need to be."

He shuddered, remembering how slow his reactions had been to the knock on the door earlier in the day. It had only been the room service waiter, but what if it had been the operatives from ISI?

Panting and shaking, Bob jerked himself awake.

He lay quietly, trying to remember the dream, but the images hovered out of reach, like chill emanations from a ghostly presence.

His breathing slowed. Calm settled over him.

He fell back asleep, back into the same nightmare. This time when he awoke, he remained edgy.

Realizing he wouldn't be able to sleep again, he got out of bed and did his exercises. When he finished, he went out for a run in the predawn dark. He ran long and far, but could not outdistance his edginess.

He paused in front of the Siam International Hotel to enjoy its unique roof of overlapping eaves representing an ancient Thai warrior helmet, and found a moment's respite, but as soon as he raced on, his disquiet settled over him again.

When he returned to the Fountain Hotel, the first fingers of light were stealing across the sky. He sat in the courtyard, watching the night-blooming flowers bow their heads, watching the sun lovers open to welcome the new day. He breathed deeply of the fragrant air and let his thoughts and feelings waft away.

When he finally went back inside, he found Kerry sitting cross-legged on the bed, talking on the phone.

She placed a hand over the mouthpiece. "I'm ordering the breakfast special for us. Something called a Thai Omelet. Is that okay?

"Fine, but be sure to order a glass of whole milk."

Hanging up, she said, "I didn't know you drank milk."

"I don't. It's for you."

She drew back. "Don't you know by now I never touch the stuff?"

He smiled. "You will."

The omelets came, sitting innocently in the middle of thick white china plates.

Kerry poked at hers. "Looks like a plain old western omelet to me." She put a forkful in her mouth. All at once her eyes widened, and tears streamed down her face. She dropped the fork and frantically fanned her mouth with both hands.

Bob passed her the glass of milk.

She grabbed it and gulped a mouthful. Eyes still watering, she said, "How can you sit there so calmly eating that stuff? I think I burned a hole in my esophagus."

"I'm used to it. You can order something else if you want."

"No, no. It's good. Just . . . not what I expected." After a few more bites of food and gulps of milk, she lifted her chin. "I'm not going with you to the airfield."

He raised an eyebrow. "We decided we needed to stay together."

"No. You decided." She held out her hands and juggled them like a scale. "Sitting in a boring old office waiting for you or going on a tour of Bangkok. That's a toughie."

He opened his mouth to protest, but she hurried on. "You want to talk to Donald McCray alone so we'd be separated anyway, and it's a guided tour. There's safety in numbers, right?"

He found himself momentarily at a loss for words.

A smile spread across her face. "Good. That's settled."

McCray seemed older and paler than Bob remembered, but his thatch of red hair burned as brightly as the tip of his cigarette.

He squinted at Bob through the smoke. "Haven't seen you around for a while. Thought you took off." His voice sounded rough from decades of smoking.

"I came back to talk to you."

McCray coughed. "Yeah? What about?"

"A private trauma hospital operating in the Philippines during Vietnam."

McCray's eyes shifted to the left as he took a deep drag. Blowing out the smoke, he said, "Don't know what the hell you're talking about."

"Before Harrison died, he told me you'd talked to him."

"So what if I did?"

"He said you told him about the hospital."

McCray set his half-smoked cigarette on a cracked ceramic ashtray, fumbled in his shirt pocket, and brought out a pack of cigarettes and a cheap disposable lighter. He shook out a cigarette, then dropped the pack on the dusty invoices littering his gray metal desk.

He narrowed his eyes at Bob. "You fixing to get yourself killed, too?"

"No."

McCray lit the cigarette, cupping his hands around the flame. "Wish I'd never told him. Those bastards killed him."

The smoke stung Bob's eyes and scratched his nostrils. "Do you know for sure, or are you guessing?"

McCray flicked a shred of tobacco from his tongue. "Don't know for sure, but it's more than a guess. Those people can do anything."

"I know how dangerous they are," Bob said. "I promise they'll never know you helped me."

"Why do you care what happened?"

"Harrison was my friend."

McCray puffed a couple of times. The smoke swirled toward the ceiling fan.

"Kept my mouth shut for nineteen years," he said. "Now look what I started." He set his cigarette on the ashtray next to the first one, which had burned down to a long ash.

"We flew transport planes out of Bien Hoa, me and my co-pilot Hap. Barry Hapworth. We loved flying, being above it all. We talked a lot about staying in Southeast Asia when our time was up and opening our own air cargo business. Everyone always complained about the shitty weather in Vietnam, but not me and Hap. I came from Chicago, and he came from Detroit, and we had no intention of going back home to face the frigid winters.

"When we had about six months left of our tour, they ordered me to fly with another pilot, and they sent Hap on a special assignment.

"Hap was a quiet guy who seldom talked, which is probably why the brass chose him for those missions, but nobody seemed to realize his curiosity made him stick his nose where it didn't belong.

"Hap knew from the beginning there was something very odd about his assignment. For one thing, he flew solo with a plane full of injured men, which seemed risky to him. For another, he took them to a privately owned trauma hospital on the outskirts of Quezon City, not to a military hospital. And to top it all off, too much secrecy surrounded what should have been a routine flight.

"He kept his eyes open and discovered that most of the patients were injured badly, but some seemed to be relatively healthy men in drug induced stupors. One day he returned from his special mission really upset. At first he refused to tell me the trouble, but finally the truth burst out of him."

McCray lit another cigarette and dragged hungrily on it. When it burned down half an inch, he stared at the ash as if he couldn't bear to get rid of it. Finally, he tapped it into the ashtray.

The smoke made Bob want to cough, but he held it back, afraid to disrupt the flow of the story.

"Hap told me they did human experiments at that hospital," McCray continued. "He said they did something to his passenger's brains. Then he clamped his mouth shut and refused to say another word.

"Two weeks later he had another solo flight to Quezon City. Right after he took off to return to base, his plane crashed. He ended up in that trauma hospital.

"When he got back, I asked him if he found out anything more about the human experiments, and he acted like I was crazy. I didn't see Hap much after that, but when it came time for us to be rotated out, I went searching for him and asked him if he still wanted to go into business with me. He gave me a blank stare and asked what business. I reminded him we were going to open an air cargo business here in Southeast Asia, and he said—I'll always remember this—'I hate flying. I hate the tropics. I can hardly wait to get back to Detroit.'"

McCray finished his cigarette. "If they can scramble a person's brain like that, they can do anything, anything they want."

"Do you know who they are?" Bob asked.

"Not really. By chance, several years ago I got a charter to take this guy to Singapore, and we got to talking. You know how it is. Well, maybe you don't know, seeing's how you're not much for shooting the bull. We found out we were in the service at the same time. He'd been some kind of orderly stationed at a hospital outside Quezon City. He mentioned that the military didn't run the place. Some corporation owned it. ISS, I think."

Bob gave him a sharp look. "ISI?"

McCray nodded. "Could be."

"Did he give you a name?"

"Fowler? Crowley? Something like that."

"Is there any way to find out? Maybe from an invoice?"

"No. It happened too long ago." McCray lit another cigarette. "I kept asking the guy about the hospital, but he didn't remember much." He inhaled, held the smoke for several seconds, then exhaled it with a cough.

"But he did remember something," Bob said.

"Nothing important. When you were in Nam did you ever hear that story about the freak they called The Sweeper? No, I guess you wouldn't have since you were just a REMF."

"I heard Harrison tell the story many times."

"Well, this guy said that when he was stationed at the hospital, he heard rumors the freak died there.

That's about all he remembered, except that after the war when the hospital closed, one of the doctors stayed behind and opened a clinic in the slums of Manila. Four, five years ago when I was in the Philippines I checked it out. What a shithole."

"Do you know the doctor's name?"

"Brewer. I remember because me and my charter joked about it being a better name for a bartender than a doctor."

Bob leaned forward. "What's the address of the clinic?"

"I don't know exactly, but I can draw you a map like I did for Harrison." He scribbled a few lines on a piece of paper then pushed it across the desk. "Don't blame me if you wind up dead."

22.

The skies were deep gunmetal gray, but it did not rain.

Bob perched on a stone bench in the courtyard, a tablet of 12x18 ready-to-paint canvases steadied in one hand, a brush tipped with forest green acrylic paint in the other. He dabbed paint on the canvas, then cocked his head, listening for Kerry's return.

Telling himself she was safe—she had to be— he dabbed another bit of green onto the canvas.

Knowing Kerry's tour would last most of the day, he'd bought the painting supplies as a way of passing the time, but he couldn't seem to get into it. His depiction of the courtyard seemed lifeless and disjointed.

With a forearm, he wiped away the sweat trickling into his eyes and continued to dab color onto the canvas. He had almost finished with his painting when he heard the door bang open, Kerry's voice call out his name, and the sound of her quick footsteps.

"There you are," she said, entering the courtyard. "I wish you could have come with me. It was so much fun. I got to see the gold Buddha! It's nine meters tall—I didn't realize it would be so big. We also saw the marble temple, Chinatown, and all sorts of fascinating places. We even had lunch at the terrace restaurant at the Oriental Hotel where Somerset Maugham used to stay." She wrinkled her nose. "You were right about the smog. I'm surprised you don't have emphysema or something after so many years of living here. All the times I dreamt of having adventures, I never considered that the places might smell terrible. What are you working on?"

She leaned on Bob's shoulder. "Oh." She spoke

the word in a flat tone. "What happened? It looks like one of those paint-by-number things my grandmother used to do."

"I tried to stay focused in the present."

She moved in front of him and put an index finger to her chin as she studied him. "You're afraid," she said softly. "You're afraid if you let go you might get lost in your own picture and not be able to find your way out."

A denial formed in his mind, but before he could voice it, he realized she was right.

"How do you know so much about people?" he asked.

She smiled, but he thought he detected a hint of sadness in her expression.

"Not people," she said. "Just you." Then her smile broadened, and the dancing light returned to her eyes. "Feed me. I'm starving."

"Do you want to go out?"

"I've been out."

"Room service it is. Let me put away my paints first."

She gestured to the picture with her chin. "What are you going to do with that?"

He glanced at it with a feeling of distaste. "Paint over it."

"Good choice. I'm sure Hsiang-li would agree."

They feasted on lemon chicken soup, spinach salad with peanuts and shredded carrots, grilled chicken and shrimp dipped into a sweet-and-sour sauce, stir-fried vegetables, and a coconut and squash custard for desert. To drink they had tead ice: tea that had been frozen then crushed and served in a glass.

Listening to Kerry rhapsodize about the sights

she had seen and watching her attack the exotic food with enthusiasm, Bob found himself wondering what his life would be like if he could spend it with her. He pushed the thought away, knowing all he had to offer was an uncertain future filled with unknown dangers, but it left him with a dull ache in the vicinity of his heart.

When they consumed the last of the food, she took his hand. "Tell me."

Obediently, he repeated everything Donald McCray had said. As he spoke, he saw her eyes grow dark, and the dull ache expanded until it choked him. She might not regret having become involved in his affairs, but he regretted it on her behalf, wishing he could have spared her this knowledge of human perfidy.

"I try and try to figure it out." She touched her temple. "I understand here that they're doing all these things you're telling me about, but I don't understand it here." She touched the left side of her chest.

He hunched his shoulders. "I don't know how to explain it to you."

Her chin jutted out. "Why? Because I'm just a waitress?"

"No. Because you're a good person. You care about others. You empathize."

"And the experimenters don't?"

"They care about their own interests. They do these things to learn, but more than that, they do them because they can. Human interaction is all about power, and those who have it use it. Power is like money. Everyone wants it. No one ever has enough. And the more one has, the more one needs."

"Not everyone. I don't want power. You don't either, do you?"

"I want the power to live my life without interference, and sometimes I think that's the hardest thing of all to achieve. If you're not out there trying to grab power, you're perceived as weak, and that makes you fair game."

"It doesn't make it right."

"No. It doesn't."

"What comes next? Where do we go from here?"

"Tomorrow I have to see Harrison's lawyer, also stop by O'Riley's to say goodbye to Hamburger Dan, then we fly to Manila."

She gave a shiver. "To talk to that doctor."

He nodded.

She cuddled next to him and said defiantly, "At least we have tonight."

Twining her arms around his neck, she brought his mouth to hers. The kiss was hard and short, but immediately her lips sought his again.

He gathered her closer. Their kiss deepened.

All at once she pulled away and hopped out of bed. "Omigosh!"

"What?"

"I forgot. I have a present for you." She flashed an impish smile and darted into the bathroom. She emerged a few minutes later wearing a dark rose cheongsam that accented the swell of her breasts and the taper of her waist. "I bought it in Chinatown. What do you think?"

He couldn't speak, couldn't breathe. She looked flushed, radiant, beautiful.

She jutted out a hip. The side slit parted, giving him a glimpse of shapely leg.

He felt a shock that started in his groin and radiated upward. From the glint in her eyes, he knew she was aware of the effect she had on him.

He slid off the bed and moved toward her, stepping slowly and carefully as if he were in danger of falling off a precipice. As he neared her, he smelled her new perfume—frangipani. From now on, he knew, whenever he caught a whiff of that scent, it would remind him of this moment, of her, of the teasing look in her eyes.

He knelt on one knee in front of her and skimmed his hand along her bare leg. It was as if he had touched fire. Heat surged through him.

He rose. Reverently, his hands moved over her, exploring her breasts, her back, the slope of her shoulders. He could feel the warmth of her through the cool silk.

He kissed the hollow of her throat. She let out a soft gasp, and her back arched. He kissed her breasts, first one, then the other. She trembled. He laid his hands on her hips and drew her closer. She stopped him with a palm on his chest and unbuttoned his shirt. The blood ran faster in his veins.

When he was naked, she wiggled out of the dress and leaned against him. He held her gently, wanting nothing more for the moment than to be close to her, smell her, feel her breath against his skin. She lifted her head, and her mouth took his.

In a single fluid motion, he scooped her up and laid her on the bed, their mouths still locked together. He was aware of hot little jolts sweeping through him, of the feel of her in his arms, then his body became fire, consuming all thought.

They lay in each other's arms, a sheen of perspiration on their bodies. Bob ran his fingers through Kerry's hair. It was as soft as the silk of her cheongsam.

"This is all so new to me," he said.

She looked at him with laughing eyes, as if they shared a private joke. "What? Sex?"

"No. Making love. Being in love."

She grew still.

He touched her cheek with the back of a hand. "I worry about you all the time."

"My grandmother always said that was the price you had to pay for love."

"Now you tell me."

"Anyway, you don't have to worry. I can take care of myself. I had two brothers, you know." She leaned close, her lips a whisper from his. "You love me?"

"Very much. I've never loved anyone before. I don't know how to deal with it."

Her lips brushed his. "I've never loved anyone either, not the way I love you."

His heart seemed to thrust in his throat, beating there with such force he had trouble swallowing. He wanted to remind her of the differences in their ages, of the problems that dogged him, but when he saw the joy reflected in her smile, he held his tongue.

"Here, put this on." Bob held out a brown two-inch-wide belt.

Kerry lifted her shirt and showed him the waistband of her dark cotton slacks. "It's elastic, see? I don't need a belt."

"It's a money-belt. I got two of them yesterday, one for me and one for you. There's ninety-five hundred dollars in each of them—"

"Ninety-five hundred dollars?" Her eyes grew round. "In cash?"

"Yes. I would have liked to get more, but that's

all we're allowed to bring into the United States without having to fill out forms, and in our situation, that can get sticky."

"What would happen if we brought in more than that and didn't declare it?"

"Maybe nothing unless we got caught, but since we're traveling with fake IDs, I'd prefer not to complicate matters. When the problem with ISI goes away, I can have some of my money wired to an account in Colorado or wherever."

"Just some? Not all?"

"It's safe where it is." When she gave him a narrow-eyed look, he laughed. "I don't seem to be able to keep anything from you. It's in a private bank in Chinatown. Hsiang-li sponsored me, otherwise I'd have to use the same banks as everyone else, and ISI would probably have found my account by now."

"Wouldn't ISI have already traced the bank through your traveler's checks?"

"My bank doesn't offer that service. I paid cash for them at another bank that does, and since they don't know me, that's a dead end for ISI."

Becoming aware he still held out the money-belt, he said, "Well, are you going to put it on?"

She took it from him, fastened it around her waist, and smoothed her shirt over it. Turning sideways to look in the mirror, she asked, "Does it make me look fat?"

"I don't even notice it."

She gave him a laughing glance. "Aren't you afraid I'm going to run off with your money?"

"No. In fact, you can have it."

She looked at him aghast. "I can't take your money." Reaching under her shirt, she started to remove the belt.

He put a hand on her arm. "Keep it for now. If we get separated, or if anything happens to me, you'll need it to get back home."

"Nothing's going to happen to you," she said fiercely.

He nodded as if he agreed and did not mention the sense of foreboding that made his shoulder blades itch.

23.

They found Bernard Goldman's office in a glass, steel, and concrete building. It was furnished with towering mahogany shelves full of law books from the United States, Thailand, China, and several others in languages Bob did not recognize. Behind the massive mahogany desk, a window overlooked the Chao Phraya River.

Bob and Kerry perched on uncomfortable seats, while Harrison's attorney lounged in his well-padded burgundy leather chair.

"You're a hard man to get hold of," Goldman said, huffing and puffing and sweating profusely in the air-conditioned room. Though he was heavy, his skin hung loosely as if he had recently lost a lot of weight.

He took a monogrammed handkerchief out of his jacket pocket and mopped his face. "Most people come running when they think there might be an inheritance." He stuffed the handkerchief back in his pocket. "Let's get to business, shall we?" He seized a thick sheaf of papers and began to read Harrison's will.

Bob cleared his throat to catch the lawyer's attention. "A brief summary will be fine."

"In short, you inherit William Henry Harrison's estate, but you won't see a penny for years. Harrison's will is very extensive—he mentioned more than a hundred people—and you inherit after all the other bequests have been made. As things stand now, by the time everything has been distributed, all that will be left for you are Harrison's New York brownstone and future royalties from his books, but—"

Goldman shuffled through the will. "Yes, here it is. Dave and Kalia Marconi have the use of the brownstone for as long as they are going to school. Since the estate is paying for their tuition, they will probably be going to graduate school, also. So you can see, it will be years before you can sell the place. With the state of the New York housing market, however, when you do sell it, you will be a very rich man."

Bob closed his eyes. A rich man? Harrison himself had enriched his life. No amount of money could ever make up for his loss. Besides, he was already rich.

He felt Kerry's fingers touch his hand. He opened his eyes and smiled at her. She gave him an inquiring glance; he nodded to let her know he felt okay.

Goldman looked from Bob to Kerry. "If we may continue?"

Kerry folded her hands primly in her lap, but her body seemed to vibrate with suppressed excitement.

"Mr. Harrison left you one other bequest, Mr. Stark," Goldman continued. "Because he gave it to me before he died, there's no need to wait for probate. Unfortunately, it's in a safety deposit box in New York. I'll be there in a few days. Perhaps I could send it to you. Do you have a business card?"

Bob shook his head.

Goldman waved a hand toward the door. "Leave your address with my secretary." He hunted through the accumulation on his desk, obviously signaling their dismissal.

Bob remained seated. "What did Harrison want me to have?"

Goldman looked up. The expression on his face clearly said, "Are you still here?"

He mopped his brow. "He left you a satchel. He called me from the hospital and told me they were after his papers. He said he made Dave bring them to him for safekeeping. He wanted me to come get them. I was in

New York at the time, so I agreed. When I got to the hospital, he gave me the satchel, said it contained notes for his work in progress, and told me to protect it until I could give it to you.

"I don't imagine it will come as any great surprise when I tell you I tried to talk him into donating the papers to a library or a university. I'm sure you know the papers of such a great man are valuable and not to be treated lightly, but he wanted you to have them. When I asked him why, he said, 'Because if I ever get well, he will immediately return them to me, and if I don't, he will know what to do with them.' Anything else, Mr. Stark?"

Bob shook his head, wondering what Harrison meant. He didn't expect him to finish writing the book, did he?

Bob left the office and headed for the elevator. Realizing Kerry wasn't with him, he retraced his steps. He found her talking to Goldman's secretary.

"What was that about?" he asked as they waited for the elevator.

"I gave her my address so the lawyer could send you the satchel. You do want it, don't you?"

"Yes, but not at any risk to you."

She held up her palms. "Don't worry. I didn't give her the address of the house where I'm staying. When I decided to leave Pete's Porches, I got a box at one of those mail outlets. I planned to have my mail forwarded there since I didn't know where I was going to be living and I didn't trust the cheat to save it for me. I never got around to sending the change of address card to the post office, so no one knows about the box." She finished the last few words in a rush as the elevator doors opened.

Three people stood in the elevator when they

entered. By the time it reached the main floor, four more had joined them. Bob waited until he and Kerry left the building before responding.

"I appreciate your letting me use your address."

"I wanted to make sure you got Harrison's papers." She stopped short and had to run a few steps to catch up to him. "Harrison's papers! That's what those guys were looking for at your boardinghouse."

"You could be right."

She elbowed him. "'Could be'? All I get is 'could be'? No 'That's a brilliant deduction, Kerry'? Or what about 'I don't know what I'd ever do without you, Kerry'?"

"I *don't* know what I'd ever do without you, Kerry," Bob said.

A blare of horns drowned out the quietly spoken words, but she must have understood because he saw her nod in satisfaction.

A taxi pulled out of traffic and discharged a young couple. Bob and Kerry dashed for the vehicle. Climbing inside, Bob gave the address for O'Riley's Bar.

Bob stood under the green domed canopy, a hand on the brass doorknob. He tried to peer in through the diamond-shaped stained glass window, but all he could see were vague shadows.

"What's wrong?" Kerry asked.

He felt the itchiness between his shoulder blades. It was as if an ant had crawled under his skin and was now trying to find its way out.

"I don't know." He released the knob. "Let's find a telephone."

They passed three phones. By the time they reached the fourth one, a few blocks away from the bar, the itchiness had abated somewhat.

A female with a young-sounding voice answered the call. Bob asked to speak to Hamburger Dan.

A minute later Hamburger Dan picked up the phone. "Yes?"

"This is—" Bob paused, trying to remember the name he'd given in the bar.

"I know who you are," Hamburger Dan said. "We missed you yesterday. Jim Keating has been speaking of you. But just you."

"I understand." Bob kept his voice even. "We're taking the train to the gulf, maybe stay at Bangphra for a few days. I wanted to let you know I talked to Harrison's lawyer. He told me Kalia and Dave have the use of the brownstone while they're going to school. Harrison left the place to me, but I have no interest in it. They can stay as long as they wish."

"That's good of you. I'll let them know." A significant pause. "Take care."

"I will. And thanks."

"Why are you thanking him?" Kerry asked when he hung up. "You're the one giving away a fortune in real estate."

"Lending, not giving. And I thanked him for the warning."

"Warning?" Her voice rose. "What warning?"

"A guy I know told those men with the cop's eyes that I'm here, but at least he didn't mention you."

"So we're not going to the gulf? You said that for the benefit of the people who tapped his phone?"

"Exactly." Bob looked around for a cab. "As soon as we get a taxi, we'll be heading for the airport to catch a plane to Manila, then back to Colorado before they figure out where we are."

At that moment, it started to rain.

***

The monsoon delayed their flight. It was still raining when they finally landed in Manila six hours later.

The taxi inched its way through the crowds of people spilling over into the narrow muddy street in a part of Manila tourists generally did not see. Bob stared out the window at the makeshift shacks. The stench burned the lining of his nose.

Hearing Kerry gag, he turned his head toward her. She had a hand to her mouth, and she breathed shallowly.

"How can people live like this?" she said.

"Maybe they have no choice."

"Isn't this the country where the first lady had five thousand pairs of shoes?"

"Yes."

"I guess all countries are alike. The public servants are better off than the public they serve."

Smothering another gag, she clamped her mouth shut and held it shut until the taxi pulled up in front of a long, low building that seemed well built. In the rain it looked as gray and as dreary as its surroundings.

After Bob paid the fare, he held out three fifty-dollar bills.

A look of longing crossed the cabdriver's face.

"They're yours if you wait for us," Bob said.

The man snatched at the bills, but Bob held them out of reach.

"One now, the other two when we're finished."

The cabdriver nodded eagerly, never taking his eyes off the money.

Bob handed him one bill, then folded the other two and put them in his shirt pocket. "These are for later."

"How long I wait?"

"Thirty minutes. No longer than an hour."

"Okay."

Bob climbed out of the cab, opened an umbrella, and offered Kerry a hand. He slammed the door shut. The cab driver pulled away.

"Hey," Kerry yelled.

The cabdriver waved an index finger. "I come back one hour."

Huddling under the umbrella, Kerry asked in a small voice, "Do you think he'll come back?"

"Yes," Bob responded, hoping he sounded more certain than he felt.

To his surprise, she laughed. "You don't lie very well, do you? At least not to me. I like that in a man." She linked arms with him. "Let's get this show on the road."

Dr. Brewer looked about fifty. He had a sallow, heavily lined face and wiry gray hair. Dark-framed eyeglasses kept sliding down his ski-slope nose. He didn't act friendly, but once he got to talking, he was open and effusive about his work.

In the clinic's business office, Bob and Kerry sat on a faded red couch. Springs and wisps of horsehair protruded from a fist-sized hole between them. Bob heard a rustle in the hole, and he expected to see a rodent head come popping out at any moment.

Kerry seemed unaware of the sound; she was still struggling to breathe. The overpowering stench of industrial-strength disinfectant made the air inside worse than the air outside.

Bob tried to look interested as Dr. Brewer droned on about the success of the clinic and his plans for expansion.

When the doctor paused, Bob said, "You're doing a wonderful thing here, but to be honest, we wish to speak about your work at the private trauma hospital operating outside of Quezon City during the Vietnam War."

Dr. Brewer stared at him for a long time as if taking his measure. Finally, he sighed.

"You're the second person to ask me about that in the past few months."

"Who else asked?" When Dr Brewer didn't respond, Bob asked, "Was it William Harrison, the writer?"

"Why, yes. How did you know?"

"He passed away, and I've been hired by the estate to finish his last book, which touches on the works of that hospital."

"I'm sorry to hear he's dead—he was a personable fellow—but I would just as soon his project died with him."

"Why?" Kerry demanded. "Don't people have the right to know about the human experimentation you did?"

"Human experimentation?" Dr. Brewer took off his glasses, polished them with a corner of his handkerchief, then put them back on. "Trauma care, especially during war time, does tend to be cutting edge—I suppose some may call it experimental—but I assure you, every single procedure was safe and precedented."

"How did you get a job at the hospital?" Bob asked. "You must have been very young."

"I was young. I had finished my residency at Boston Memorial when I received an invitation to apply for a position at a new hospital associated with the military but neither owned nor controlled by it. The successful applicants would have all the benefits of being a military doctor, meaning a lifetime of experience in a few short years, together with all the benefits of working in a well-equipped civilian hospital. Also, pay would be generous, and for every year of service, a large chunk of our student loans would be paid off.

"It sounded like a dream come true. Most of the doctors I had gone to school with started out idealistic, wanting to help humanity, but by the time they got to their internships, they were so sick of being poor, they wanted as much money as they could get their hands on."

Dr. Brewer laughed, gesturing to his shabby office. "As you can see, poverty doesn't bother me, but being in debt does. Also, I never lost my desire to help people. I was thrilled when Dr. Rutledge hired me to work at his hospital."

He looked from Bob to Kerry, his brown eyes serious. "No matter what else ISI might have done, they did one very good thing. They brought me here. This is where I was always meant to be—these people need me.

"By the time the Americans pulled out of Vietnam, making that private hospital redundant, my school loans had been paid off, and I had saved enough to get this clinic started. Dr. Rutledge arranged for a grant from ISI to keep it going. Also, before he shipped the hospital's equipment back to the States, he let me have my pick. So you can see why I don't believe those people did anything unethical."

"I understand," Bob said noncommittally. "What happened to the hospital?"

"ISI had leased a sugar plantation for the duration of the war. We used the house for the hospital. It reverted to its owners after the peace accords were signed."

"This Dr. Rutledge you keep talking about," Bob said. "Is his name Jeremy by any chance?"

"Yes. Do you know him?"

"I've heard of him."

"He's a great man. A visionary."

"What about Cerberus?" Kerry burst out.

Dr. Brewer pushed up his glasses with an index finger. "Cerberus?"

"That's the codename for the project concerned with eradicating phantom pains."

Dr. Brewer's brows arched above his glasses. "Is it? I didn't know that. Of course, by the time I got involved, it was an established procedure, well beyond the codename stage."

Kerry's mouth dropped open. "You don't deny there was such a project?"

"No. Why should I? Saving patients years of agony is a great advancement in medicine."

"A great advancement? How can you say that?"

"Look, Miss—what did you say your name was? Alice Baker?"

Kerry nodded.

"Look, Miss Baker. I don't have to justify a damn thing. Have you ever seen a man driven crazy because of an itch he couldn't scratch? Have you ever heard a man scream in agony because he has a cramp in a muscle that no longer exists? I have. The relief of such pain is justification enough."

"Did you perform the procedure?" Bob asked.

"No. I created the pain by removing rotting body parts and limbs mangled beyond repair. I'm glad someone could keep them from suffering another horror on top of that one."

"But they didn't give their consent," Kerry protested.

"Did they give their consent to get drafted? Did they give their consent to get blown up?"

Kerry raised her chin a notch, but her voice sounded subdued. "I guess not."

Dr. Brewer made a sweeping gesture over the file-laden desk. "As you can see, my day doesn't end when the clinic closes."

"I understand. Thank you for your time." Bob rose.

"One more thing," the doctor said.

Bob settled back on the couch. "Yes?"

"When you write Harrison's book, I'd appreciate it if you left off any mention of the man in the locked room."

24.

The man in the locked room?

"Why don't you want us to mention him?" Bob asked, hiding his lack of knowledge behind a bland tone.

Dr. Brewer took off his glasses and rubbed his eyes. "I was pleased when Harrison told me he planned to write about what we accomplished back then, but toward the end of the interview all his questions centered on that particular patient. I was afraid he would make that patient the focus of the book. I'm proud of the work we did and proud of the direction my life has taken. I'd hate to see all that overshadowed by a mystery figure when in truth there was no mystery, just a lot of rumors and myths and fanciful stories."

Bob sat straight and tried to act as if he knew what the doctor meant. "How fanciful were these stories?"

Dr. Brewer scowled at the eyeglasses in his hand, then repositioned them on his nose. "Oh, the foolishness of gossip. They called him the Freak, the Switcher . . . no, not the Switcher, The Sweeper? The Sweeper, that's right. They also called him The Human Chameleon, as if he were a comic book hero. It always happens. Whenever access to a patient or a room is restricted, the rumors fly."

Kerry's eyes were bright. "The Sweeper lived!"

"This may not be the same sweeper," Bob pointed out.

"Of course it is. How many people with chameleon-like abilities can there be?"

"At any rate," Dr. Brewer said, "he didn't live long. The doctors at the hospital in Vietnam patched him up, but he was in critical condition when I saw him."

"Do you know his name?" Kerry asked.

"I'm sorry, I don't remember." He sighed. "We treated so many . . ."

After a moment he gave himself a shake. "Not only had the poor man been severely wounded, but his ordeal had been so great he was completely spent. He was awake a lot of the time, he might even have been aware of his surroundings, but he was non-responsive.

"I'm sure you've heard people say, 'I was wearied to death,' when all they meant was they were tired, but that patient truly *was* wearied to death. It seemed that any exertion, no matter how trivial, would drive him right over the edge.

"Eventually his physical wounds healed, but not his mental ones. I recommended sending him to a stateside psychiatric hospital, but Dr. Rutledge disagreed. He said the man was a prisoner of his memories. Once the memories of his ordeal were gone, he would be restored to mental health. So I did as Rutledge instructed and transferred the patient to him in the psychiatric ward."

Dr. Brewer fell silent.

"What happened to The Sweeper?" Kerry asked.

"He died. Harrison didn't want to believe it, but it's true. I signed the death certificate myself."

"How did he die?"

"He slipped away during the night. It happens."

Bob frowned. "Why did you sign the death certificate? Why not Dr. Rutledge?"

Dr. Brewer shook his head reprovingly. "You're like Harrison, looking for mysteries where none exist. I was the doctor of record, that's all."

Kerry narrowed her eyes at him. "Did you actually see his dead body?"

He gave a snort of unamused laughter. "Now you sound like my wife. In case you're wondering why I remember him after all these years, it's because my wife and I spent half our married life arguing about him. To answer your question—no, I did not see the body. I did not need to. My boss, a great doctor, a man I respect, told me the patient died and asked me to fill out the death certificate.

"My wife worked for Rutledge as a psychiatric nurse. She never liked him, said he had a habit of touching the nurses inappropriately, so when she claimed The Chameleon didn't die, that Rutledge kept him locked in a special room, I didn't take it seriously."

Kerry sucked in a breath. "Your wife saw him after he had supposedly died?"

Dr. Brewer looked at her in disgust. "No. She said she heard Rutledge talking about a man in a locked room, and somehow she got it into her head it was The Chameleon. Sally, the patient's nurse, told my wife the patient was an amnesiac Dr. Rutledge kept in a drug-induced hypnotic state. Every day, for hours on end, they played tapes of what they knew about his life to help him remember.

"It drove my wife nuts not knowing the truth. She said if I had double-checked to make certain he died, then she would have known for sure."

Kerry lifted her shoulders. "Why did it bother her so much?"

"My wife was a romantic, enamored with the idea of a real-life human chameleon. I tried to explain to her it was physiologically impossible, but she always came back at me with that old adage about all things being possible. Then she'd add that we know so little about the human soul, how could we limit it to what is known." He smiled. "My wife was a delightful woman, a truly inspired nurse, and I loved her dearly, but she had that one tiny loose screw."

"May we talk to her?" Kerry asked.

"She's gone. Died of malaria last year."

"I'm sorry," Bob and Kerry said at the same time.

Dr. Brewer bowed his head. "Yeah, me too. I'd give anything to have one more silly argument with her about the man in the locked room."

After a moment of silence, Bob leaned forward. "Can you give us Sally's name and address?

The doctor leafed through a small book at his desk, wrote on a piece of paper, and handed it to him. *Sally Rutledge*, it said.

Bob snapped his head up to look at him.

Dr. Brewer nodded. "Yep. Married the boss. My wife always claimed Sally blackmailed him into it, that Sally knew where all the bodies were buried, so to speak, and had demanded marriage in exchange for her silence. But that simply is not true. Rutledge fell madly in love with her the first time he laid eyes on her." He rose. "Now, if you'll excuse me, I have paperwork to do."

He ushered them out of the clinic.

To Bob's relief, the cabdriver was waiting.

They spent the night in a hotel not far from the Manila airport. Bob watched the gentle rise and fall of Kerry's chest as she slept. Then he too fell asleep.

He dreamt.

In his dream, he struggled to sit up.

A nurse hurried over to him. "Lie still," she said, smiling. "The doctor will be here any moment."

Bob looked around at the white room and the IV snaking into his arm. "Where am I?"

"You had an accident. You're in a hospital."

"I know, but where?"

"The Philippines."

"Oh, I thought maybe I had been shipped state-side." He closed his eyes. When he opened them again, the doctor, a prematurely bald American with the face of a choirboy, peered down at him.

The doctor smiled, showing large teeth. "Hi, Bob. I'm Dr. Johnson. How are you feeling?"

"Fair."

"Do you know why you've been hospitalized?"

"We hit a mine, I think."

"Very good," Dr. Johnson said with a heartiness that made Bob wince. "You had a concussion, a minor head trauma, but I need to ask you some questions to make sure you're okay. What's your name?"

"Robert Stark."

"Where were you born?"

"Denver. When can I go home?"

"Relax and take it easy. You'll be back in Saigon soon enough."

"No, I mean when can I go back to Denver?" An agonizing pain shot through his skull. He clamped his lips together to keep from emitting a groan.

"What's the hurry?" the doctor asked. "Got a girlfriend waiting for you?"

"No."

"What about family?"

"No family. My father died when I was fifteen, my mother died of cancer three years later, and I haven't seen my brother since her funeral."

"Considering all that, I can't imagine why you want to go back to Denver."

Bob averted his gaze so he wouldn't have to look at the doctor's cheery face. He tried to think of the good things that had happened to him, but the memories surfacing through the pain were all unpleasant. Hadn't there been good times? There must have been, but he couldn't recall any.

"Maybe I won't go back to Denver," he said, suddenly feeling very tired. "But you still haven't answered my question. When can I go back to the United States?"

Dr. Johnson raised his eyebrows. "You mean a medical discharge?"

"Yes."

The doctor grinned. "There's nothing seriously wrong with you."

Bob shook his head slightly, trying to clear away the confusion. A bright white pain stabbed him behind the eyes. He lay still until it dimmed.

"If there's nothing seriously wrong with me," he asked finally, "why am I here?"

"I told you," Dr. Johnson said with exaggerated patience, as if speaking to a small, not very bright child, "you had a minor head trauma."

"I know, but why am I here in the Philippines? We were close to Qui Nhon when the truck got blown up. If I had such a minor injury, why wasn't I taken to the American hospital there?"

"You were, but then they transferred you here. Head injuries can be very complicated, you know."

It still didn't make sense to Bob, but nothing the military did made sense to him.

"You've been unconscious for five days." Dr. Johnson smiled broadly, as if telling joke. "We wondered if you were ever going to wake."

"Five days! I thought you said there was nothing seriously wrong with me."

"There isn't. You sustained no major physical

injuries, but because your brain had been jostled, it shut off your conscious mind to concentrate all its energies on healing itself." Dr. Johnson smiled, looking beatific. "You might sustain minor memory loss, and you will probably be confused for a while, but other than that, you should be okay."

"But you don't know for sure."

Dr. Johnson shrugged.

"And they're still sending me back to active duty?"

"It's not like you're being sent into combat. According to your records, you're a supply clerk."

"But still . . ."

Dr. Johnson's brows drew together. "It's out of my hands." Then his eyes brightened and his voice reverted to its former cheeriness. "However, I did arrange for you to spend a few days at Nha Trang to recuperate before you return to Saigon."

Patting Bob's shoulder, he said in a self-satisfied manner, "You'll do fine."

Bob jerked himself awake. The headache he'd felt in the dream remained with him.

25.

Bob stood in line next to Kerry, ticket in one hand, bag in the other, waiting to board the plane for Denver. His head ached, making it hard for him to figure out what to do. Would their luck hold? Though long and tedious, the flight from Manila to Los Angeles had been without incident.

The line shuffled forward a few feet. He had to decide. Now.

He touched Kerry's arm. "Let's go."

"Go where?"

Seeing the young man in front of them turn around and give him a sharp-eyed look, he said, "I need to make a phone call."

Kerry gave him a penetrating glance, then stepped out of line. Together they walked casually away from the gate.

"What's going on?" she asked. "Another one of your feelings?"

"Not a feeling. I keep remembering that Sam and Ted were at the airport when I landed in Denver before. Luck saved me then, but I can't count on things working out a second time."

She drew in a breath. "Do you think they're going to be waiting for us?"

"No, I don't. I—" Pain stabbed him behind the eyes.

"We should find a place to spend the night," she said briskly. "Or what's left of it, anyway. You need to get some rest."

She led the way outside. They climbed aboard a shuttle bus that took them to a nearby hotel where they got a room.

Lying in Kerry's arms, feeling her fingers gently

massaging his scalp, Bob fell asleep. When he woke in the morning, the pain that had been with him since Manila was but a dull ache.

Kerry took the first turn at the wheel.

"Not bad for a junker," she said as she whipped the 1970 Volkswagen bug past a pickup truck. "But orange? Wouldn't it have been better to buy something less conspicuous? Of course, with all the rust spots it's more of a burnt-orange, but still . . ."

Bob smiled. "It's less conspicuous than that red gas guzzler you picked out. Besides, the bug is the one car I know how to drive."

"Do you still think this is necessary?"

"Not necessary, perhaps, but prudent. The power ISI has is too great for me to want to take any chances. And we have the time. I don't want to proceed with my investigation until I've gone through Harrison's papers, and it will be a few days before we get them."

Kerry chewed on her lower lip. "It looks as if there was a conspiracy between the military and ISI."

"Not a conspiracy. Business as usual. The government, including the military, works for the multinational corporations, and the multinational corporations work for the people who lend them money to stay in business."

"Are you saying ISI is part of the government?"

"It's possible. Ever since the Freedom of Information Act, the most secret members of the intelligence community no longer work directly for the government, but for private corporations like ISI. Private corporations are not required to divulge information about their activities, and they are not subject to the scrutiny or control of the politicians."

Kerry shivered. "My parents raised me to believe the government has our best interest at heart, but I guess it isn't true."

"Governments have no hearts, and our interests are at the bottom of the list of their concerns."

A semi roared up alongside them, rocking the bug. Kerry gripped the steering wheel tightly until it passed.

"I can't stop thinking about the poor guy in the locked room. It must have been horrible for him, being forced to endure who-knows-what." She shuddered. "That Rutledge person is a nasty piece of work."

"He didn't act nasty," Bob said, remembering. "He seemed more like a bluff and hearty Boy Scout leader than a Svengali."

A confused look darted across her face. "What are you talking about? You told me you didn't know him."

"That's what I thought." The dull ache in the back of his head throbbed with an insistent beat.

She laid a hand on his knee. Her warmth seeped into him, and the beat slowed to a more manageable cadence.

"What happened to you in Manila? You were fine when we checked into the hotel, but ever since then you've been a bit distant."

"I had a dream that night."

"The jungle?"

"No. The hospital after the incident with the mine. Every detail was so clear, it seemed real, and I recognized the doctor. I knew him as Dr. Johnson, but he's the man pictured in the newspaper article Dr. Willet showed me in Omaha. Dr. Jeremy Rutledge."

"Rutledge? Oh, no!" After a moment she said, "It was a dream. Maybe your subconscious was playing a trick on you. Or maybe your headache muddled you."

"I wish that were true, but the fact is, Dr. Johnson and Dr. Rutledge are the same man."

She stared at him a fraction of a second too long; the VW strayed into the next lane. She yanked it back into place and focused her eyes on the road for several miles.

When she spoke, her voice was almost inaudible. "What do you think he wanted with you?"

"My memories, of course."

"Oh, right. I forgot about your other self. I don't get it. How could he steal your memories and give them to someone else?"

"Drugs, I imagine, and hypnosis. Technically, he didn't steal my memories since I still have them. He borrowed them."

"You act so blasé about it. Aren't you angry? I sure am." She pounded the steering wheel. "What right did he have to do that to you? Who made him God?"

Bob stared out the window at the barren hills. "I suppose I should be angry, but I don't remember any of it. Besides, this headache is sapping all my energy."

"He probably did that, too," Kerry said darkly. "I bet he gave you a post-hypnotic suggestion or aversion therapy or something to make you sick whenever you thought of going home and to make you horribly sick if you went."

"You could be right." Bob massaged his temples. "Now that I think about it, I started getting headaches even before I left Thailand, but the headaches I got in Denver were debilitating at times. I've never in my life had headaches that bad, not even after the mine incident."

She drew a long, sobbing breath. "He stole your family from you."

Trying to elicit a smile, he said, "Maybe he did me a favor."

She narrowed her eyes. "Are you defending him?"

"You have to admit my family isn't worth much."

"But they're still your family."

"Actually, Jackson is all the family I have left. Lorena, Robert, and their children aren't related to me."

"True, but—" She slammed on the brakes and barely avoided rear-ending a Mustang that cut in front of them.

Leaning back, he closed his eyes against the pain. When he opened them again, it was dark, and he realized he had slept the day away.

He took over the driving while Kerry dozed. The miles slipped mindlessly by.

In the grayness of the pre-dawn world, Kerry awoke. She glanced around with an unfocused look in her eyes, then her gaze met his.

The first smile of the morning broke across her face, and he felt as though the sun had risen.

Bob raised his head and rubbed the sleep out of his eyes.

"Did you have a nice nap?" Kerry asked.

"It was okay. I didn't dream." He stared out the window at the narrow mountain road. "Where are we? This isn't the interstate, is it?"

"I turned off the highway past Grand Junction. I thought we could spend the night at my uncle's cabin. He's not using it right now, so we'll be alone."

The road wound higher into the hills. The right shoulder ended in a sheer drop. Feeling a sickening lurch in his midsection, Bob quickly shifted his gaze from the view to Kerry.

"Maybe I should drive for a while."

She chuckled, sounding not at all offended. "What's wrong? Don't you like my driving?"

"Let's just say if it was me at the wheel, we'd be going slower."

The Volkswagen shuddered as she hurtled around a tight S-shaped curve.

He sucked in a breath. "A lot slower."

She tossed him a laughing glance. "Don't worry, I've driven this road a thousand times and never had an accident. Anyway, we're almost there."

She spun the wheel sharply to the left and veered onto a graveled lane snaking through the woods. The car rattled and bounced, and pebbles smacked against the undercarriage. After about a quarter of a mile, she parked in front of a weathered log cabin in a small clearing.

Bob climbed out of the car. Stretching out his arms, he inhaled deeply.

"Oh, come on," Kerry said. "I'm not that bad a driver. Next thing I know, you'll be kissing the ground."

He smiled at her. "Can't you smell it?"

She sniffed. "I don't smell anything."

He tilted his head back, closed his eyes, and inhaled again. A faint metallic odor rising from an outcrop of sun-warmed boulders mingled with the scent of pine, dry leaves, and melting snow. He felt a heaviness inside of him loosen. All at once a sense of exhilaration percolated to the surface.

"Is something wrong?" Kerry asked, giving him a strange look.

"No. Something is very right."

He turned around slowly. The bright yellow

aspen leaves shimmering against the lapis lazuli sky seemed to cherish him and nourish him with their energy. The air he breathed seemed to become a part of him, and he a part of it.

When Kerry gazed at him, shaking her head, he noticed how her hair gleamed in the alpenlight.

"You're acting as if this is the first time you've been here," she said.

"It is."

"I don't mean here at my uncle's cabin." She made a sweeping gesture. "I mean here in the Rockies."

"I know."

She put her hands on her hips. "You're from Denver, and you've never been in the mountains before?"

"Not that I remember. It's all so different, the way the air smells and tastes and feels. And the sounds."

"What sounds? It's absolutely still. For once there's not even any noise from a chainsaw."

He smiled at her. "Sound is everywhere. I can hear the meadow mice and the deer moving in the thicket over there."

She fixed her gaze on him. "You're making that up."

"If you listen you will hear them, too." He took a breath, released it. "I lived so long in Southeast Asia where it's steamy and overpeopled that I got used to it, but I feel as if I belong here." He lowered his voice. "A raccoon in the pine tree is staring at us."

She flicked back a strand of hair that had fallen into her face. "I thought I knew you, but I don't. I've never seen you like this."

He held out his palms, wanting her to see he had nothing to hide. "I'm the same."

"No, you're not. I sense a . . . a change."

"Is that a problem?"

"Of course not. It's just not what I've gotten used to. Should we see about getting something to eat? It won't be anything fancy, but I'm sure we can find cans of chili and stew in the cupboard."

He flexed his fingers. "If you don't mind, I'd like to paint first, try to capture this light before it fades."

"I don't mind." She smiled at him, but reserve tinged her voice. "I'm not very hungry."

Bob rolled over and reached for Kerry in the dark, but her side of the bed was empty.

He grabbed the patchwork quilt, which was so old it felt as soft as flannel, and padded through the deserted cabin to the front door. He stepped outside. Kerry sat on the stoop, knees pulled to her chest, head tilted back. Wearing the over-sized tee shirt she'd slept in, she shivered in the cold mountain air.

Bob wrapped the quilt around her shoulders and sat next to her. She rearranged the quilt to envelop both of them.

She glanced at him, then quickly averted her gaze.

He held her hand. "You're not afraid of the change in me, are you?"

"No." Her grip on his hand tightened. "I'm afraid you're going to grow away from me. I mean, I'm a waitress, but you're rich, you had a book written about you, and one day you're going to be a famous painter."

"I'm not there yet. Besides, as I recall, you're not a waitress anymore. You're my agent."

"That was a joke."

"Not to me it wasn't. And I'm not going to grow away from you. If anything, this lightness of being I feel is making me more attuned to you."

Her tone sounded almost breezy, but not enough to hide the note of apprehension in her voice. "That's what's scary."

"I know."

She leaned away and looked at him. "You do?"

"The first time I visited the Mulligans, Scott told me he didn't know what was worse, being understood or being misunderstood."

"He's right. I thought that's what I wanted, someone who'd be attuned to me and to notice things like me being cold, but it's . . . I don't know . . . intimidating, I guess."

"It might be a temporary change because of being here in the mountains."

"I don't think so." She relaxed against him. "I forgot how many stars there are. When I was a kid, I'd go outside at night and moonbathe—lie under the stars, looking up. If I watched long enough, I felt as if I were looking down on the stars, then I'd get dizzy, thinking I would fall off the earth. Sometimes I feel the same way when I'm with you."

"Is that good or bad?"

"Good. Definitely good. I love the stars. I love being out at night. Maybe that's why I liked working graveyard. Living in the city, though, I didn't get to see many stars."

Bob stared at the sky. Mesmerized by the white swathe of the Milky Way, he felt a sudden touch of vertigo.

"I see what you mean," he said.

"My family ranch is about three miles from here, so this is the sky I'm used to. You'll have to meet everyone when you get ISI off your back."

Not wanting to think about meeting her folks, he searched about for a change of subject. "How did you know the cabin would be empty?"

"My cousins are away at college, and my uncle's gone." She paused. "A hunting accident. He ran into a renegade band of deer, and they blasted his chest with a shotgun. We found his body but not his head. We're pretty sure it's hanging on the deers' trophy wall, but we haven't found their hideout yet."

An unexpected feeling of love welled in Bob's chest. "You're teasing me."

She laughed. "A little."

"I'm going to have my hands full with you, aren't I?"

"You have no idea."

She pulled his head down and planted a kiss on his forehead. Then, eyes closing, she touched his lips with hers.

Later, much later, he asked, "What did happen to your uncle?"

"Nothing. He and my aunt go on vacation to Las Vegas this time every year."

Bob turned onto Kerry's street and drove slowly, searching for a place to park.

Kerry frowned. "Crossing and recrossing the date line has got me confused. I thought it was Monday, but look at all these cars—it must still be the weekend."

"It is Monday."

"So why aren't people at—oh, I know. Columbus day."

A polo-shirted man came out of a brick house and swaggered to a white BMW.

Bob stopped to wait for the soon-to-be-vacant

parking space.

"My roommate is supposed to be gone this
week," Kerry said, climbing out of the Volkswagen,
"but I better go check, make sure the coast is clear."

Before Bob could speak, she slammed the door
and dashed toward her friend's house.

He watched her run up the stairs. *This isn't
right. We shouldn't be separating now that we're back
in the city.* Glancing at the man by the BMW, he
noticed him patting his pockets as if looking for keys.

Without turning off the ignition, Bob got out of
the car and let the door swing shut. He hesitated,
wondering if he should go after Kerry.

At that moment he heard her scream.

26.

Bob bounded up the porch steps, taking them two at a time.

Kerry came crashing out of the house, swinging an upside-down brass lamp, and yelling. As she hurdled the stairs, she sideswiped him.

He reeled. Before he could regain his balance, Ted barreled through the door after Kerry. He collided with Bob, righted himself, and kept on going.

"Get that bitch," Sam shouted. "Don't let her get away." He staggered out of the house, one hand clamped to his scalp. Blood trickled from beneath the fingers into his eyes. Shaking his head, he let out a roar and bolted past Bob, knocking him into the forsythia.

Bob pulled himself to his feet. Heart thudding, body tensed, he snapped his head toward the sound of Kerry's voice.

She stood in the middle of the street, swinging the lamp and yelling. The man by the BMW shouted at a woman in the doorway of the brick house to call 911. Several other people had come out of their homes to gawk.

Sam and Ted slowly circled Kerry, keeping out of the lamp's range. Bob caught a glimpse of metal and realized Ted held a gun by his side.

Sam moved behind Kerry, facing in Bob's direction. Bob felt a change in the atmosphere like the first subtle shift in barometric pressure that foretells a storm, and he knew Sam had seen him.

Sam bellowed, "There he is."

Arms outstretched, pointing his weapon, Ted spun around. "Where? Where? I don't see him."

"He was by the bushes but he's not there now," Sam said, pulling a portable phone out of his pocket.

"Shit." Ted ran toward the bushes. "We were right there."

Bob waited a second until Sam also headed his way, then he skirted the porch and went around to the back of the house. He listened to make certain the two men were still coming after him.

Sam called for backup, barking instructions into his phone as he ran.

Ted's mutterings kept time with his footfalls. "We had him. It was all over. Then we lost him."

Zigzagging through alleys and backyards, Bob felt adrenaline flooding his veins and charging every sense, every inch of skin, every neuron in his body with an acute awareness. Somewhere in the back of his mind, he remembered this same feeling of being totally alive, but as he tried to capture the memory, it slipped beyond his grasp.

Then all mental chatter died. All sense of time, of place, of self fell from him.

He ran.

A neighborhood park came into view, and a tall clump of bushes seemed to beckon. He stepped into its embrace. The leaves felt cool against his cheeks.

Gnats buzzed in his ears. Crickets chirped. Crows squawked. A small brown dog trailing a leash raised a leg and urinated on his shoe.

The sun slowly dipped toward the horizon.

Long after he realized the hunt must been called off, he remained hidden. Finally, he returned to the house.

The Volkswagen was gone. So was Kerry.

Scott Mulligan answered his knock.

Bob felt a fleeting ache at the sight of the man's calm expression, remembering that once he too had felt serene. He allowed himself a fraction of a second to wonder if serenity would ever be his again, then he stiffened his spine.

"Can I leave a message for Kerry in case she contacts you?"

Scott smiled. "No need. She's out back with the children, inspecting the greenhouse."

Bob let out a breath he hadn't known he'd been holding.

Scott ushered him into the living room. "You're obviously in some kind of trouble. I'd like to help."

"Believe me, I'd welcome your help, but I don't know what you can do. I don't know yet what *I* can do."

"Do you need a place to spend the night?"

Bob shook his head. "We'll be okay."

"At least stay for dinner."

"We better not."

Scott held out a hand. "I'm glad you and Kerry considered my home a haven. When you get everything worked out, be sure to come back."

Grasping the outstretched hand, Bob nodded, not trusting himself to speak. In the silence, he heard the children's excited voices growing louder. A few seconds later they burst into the room, Kerry in tow.

She launched herself into his arms. "You got away. I was so worried."

He held her tightly. The briny scent of her hair reminded him of all she had been through, and he felt something catch in his throat.

Becoming aware of Scott's shrewd gaze focused on them, he loosened his grip and took a step back.

"We have to go."

"Mom's going to be home soon," Beth said.

"And we're having spaghetti for dinner," Jimmy

added.

Kerry hugged both of them at the same time. "There'll be other days."

After a flurry of goodbyes, Bob and Kerry left.

He scanned the cars parked along the curb. "Where's the VW?"

"Around the corner and down the block. I didn't want to get too close to the Mulligan's place in case somebody followed me."

A chill feathered the back of his neck, but he managed to keep his voice steady. "Did anyone follow you?"

"I don't think so." She rubbed her arms as if to get warm. "When I went in the house, I dropped my purse on the table like I always do. I turned around, and this guy came toward me. I hit him with the lamp. It knocked him over, but he got up right away, then the other guy came out of my bedroom. I didn't know what else to do, so I screamed and ran. I didn't hurt you, did I?"

"No."

"I saw you, but I couldn't keep from running into you."

"Don't worry about it. Your flight hormones took over is all."

She shuddered. "Who were those guys?"

"The one you hit is Sam, the other is Ted."

"That's what I figured. Somehow it seemed like a game—hiding out in motel rooms, dashing halfway across the world, but after today . . ."

"I know," Bob said softly. "I am sorry."

"What are you sorry about? You didn't do anything."

"I got you involved."

She planted a fist on her hip. "We already had

this discussion."

He considered pointing out that the stakes were higher for her now, but realized it wouldn't change the way she felt.

"You handled yourself well this afternoon."

"I acted like a dippy girl, screaming and running."

"But you're alive. At the end of the day, that's all that counts."

"I guess."

"There's no guessing. What's that saying, 'when the going gets tough, the tough get going'? Well, you got going."

He was pleased to see her lips curve into a slight smile.

"That's not what it means, and you know it." She paused by the car. "Maybe you better drive since my license is in my purse back at the house." She handed him the keys, then snatched them back. "Wait a minute. You don't have a license either."

She scooted around the car, slid into the driver's seat, and turned the key in the ignition.

"Where to?"

"A motel."

She peeled away from the curb. "After the guys started chasing you, I ran for the car, threw the lamp in the back seat, and drove around. When I couldn't find you, I went back to the house to wait, but a green Ford was parked down the block with two adults in it, and a white Buick with two more adults cruised the neighborhood. I didn't know what to do. Then I remembered the Mulligans. Since they're the only people we both know, I thought that was the best place to go. I've been there for hours. Where were you? I'm babbling, aren't I? Jeez, I'm so tired I feel as if I could sleep for a month."

"It's the adrenaline washing out of your system. That day when I found Sam and Ted in my room, I hid out in a porno theater and fell asleep."

"You fell asleep watching porn?" She laughed, the mischievous glint back in her eyes.

27.

Kerry drove around the block twice while Bob studied the pedestrians and the people in the parked cars. Not seeing anything suspicious, he directed Kerry to park down the street from Copy and Send, the storefront business where she had rented a mailbox.

He laid a hand on her knee. "I'll go in first, check the place to make sure it isn't staked out inside. If I don't come out, or if I'm with anyone when I do, I want you to leave. Go see Scott. He knows people who can protect you."

Her brows drew together. "You want me to drive away?"

"I can endure anything if I know you're safe."

"All right, if that's what you want, but you better take care of yourself."

"I intend to. If everything seems okay, I'll come out and watch from across the street while you go in to see if the package has arrived. After you've returned to the car, I'll wait a few more minutes to see if anyone follows you or if any cars start up. If I don't see anything suspicious, I'll come back to the car. If I don't come back—"

"I know. Go see Scott."

An obese woman with big hair and mean eyes stared at Bob from her position behind the long counter as he looked around.

There wasn't much to see: rows of mailboxes, several copy machines, racks of packing materials and greeting cards. A leather-jacketed man in his twenties, who had six earrings in one ear, pulled envelopes from a mailbox, and an old woman with heavily rouged cheeks made copies.

When Bob saw nothing that struck him as being out of the ordinary, he sauntered outside and crossed the street. Leaning against a pole, he took note of the activity. Vehicles slowing, pulling away from the curb, angling into parking spaces. People scurrying. Kerry walking into the store and coming out a minute later with a box about eighteen inches tall, two feet long, and a foot thick.

A few men glanced at her as she carried the box to the car, but no one showed more than a passing interest. She shoved the box into the back seat, climbed into the driver's seat, and drummed her fingers on the steering wheel.

Bob waited. One minute. Two minutes. Finally, he returned to the car, and Kerry drove off. No one followed.

They were on Highway 6, heading west. Denver lay behind them; housing tracts and office complexes stretched out on either side of them.

Kerry bounced in her seat as she drove, radiating excitement. "I wonder what Harrison left you. Maybe we should stop at one of the motels around here. Whose idea was it to spend the night in the mountains, anyway?"

Bob smiled at her. "Yours."

"Oh, right. Well, how was I to know you weren't going to open the box till we got to the motel? If it was my box, I'd have opened it already."

"We'll be there soon enough."

"If I live that long," she grumbled.

An hour later, they pulled onto an unobtrusive dirt road and descended into a barren bowl dotted with tiny cabins.

"How did you hear about this place?" Bob

asked.

"A woman I waited on a couple of months ago. The way she raved about it, I expected something more than these shacks. Should we go somewhere else?"

"No. It's perfect. We'll be able to keep track of the cars on the road."

They found the office in the largest building, which also housed a snack bar. A watery-eyed man leaning on two canes gave them a form to fill out, then directed them to their cabin.

It felt as chilly inside as outside, but a plump down comforter covered the bed, and logs lay ready in a stone fireplace that took up half of one wall.

"Their insurance must be astronomical," Kerry commented, putting a match to the logs. When the fire took hold, she peeked into the bathroom. "I can do without the rust-stained fixtures, but otherwise it's not a bad place." All at once she let out a strangled cry. "What are you doing?"

Startled, Bob dropped the brush he had picked up. "I'm getting ready to paint. Why?"

"Why? Why? The package, that's why."

He grabbed the brush and continued to lay his painting supplies on the scuffed wooden desk, unable to explain his reluctance to paw through Harrison's papers.

She stared at him. "Every time I think I'm getting to understand you, I learn something that reminds me I don't know you at all."

He met her gaze. "We don't have to know everything about each other right away. Since we're going to be together, we have the whole rest of our lives to get to know each other."

"Are we going to be together?"

"I'm planning on it."

An impish look appeared in her eyes. "Is this a proposal?"

"If you want it to be."

The breath rushed out of her, and she dropped into a chair. When she finally spoke, her voice sounded subdued.

"My whole life I've looked forward to having a wedding and being married, but after what I've learned about the government and their intrusions, I couldn't bear to have to ask their permission, to get their sanction, to let them have any part of our life together."

"I feel the same way."

He placed beads of phthalo blue, napthol red, and titanium white on his palette and mixed the color of the Colorado sky.

"Where are we going to live?" Kerry asked.

"Your choice. Where you go, I go."

She didn't hesitate. "I want to go back home to Chalcedony. I realize it's still a quiet backwater, set apart from the rest of the world by mountains, but with you there with me, I'll have all the challenge I need. We can get a nice place in the mountains. I'll garden, maybe even build a greenhouse like the Mulligan's."

As she continued to describe the future, Bob could see them walking hand in hand along the garden paths, and he could smell the flower-scented air. He could see the years passing. Kerry grew more beautiful and more settled without ever losing her boldness or the glint of laughter in her eyes. Despite their continued closeness, some of their differences were never reconciled. She always opened her mail on the walk back from the mailbox on the highway, and it drove her nuts that he set his aside unopened until he had time to deal with it.

"Bob?"

He pulled himself back to the present. "Yes?"

"You've been painting a long time. Are you ready to eat?"

He glanced at the canvas, surprised to see he'd finished the painting.

Kerry came to stand beside him as he studied the scene. In the distance were the mountains, stark against the sky. In the foreground grew an exuberantly chaotic mix of flowers and vegetables. Off to the side stood the figure of a woman, radiant and serene, one hand raised as if in welcome.

"That's me," Kerry exclaimed. "I thought you never painted people."

"When it comes to you, I'm not afraid of what my fingers will see."

"The garden is exactly as I imagined." She gave him an oblique glance. "It's lovely, but the flaw, as you call it, is still there."

He put an arm around her and drew her close. "I know."

"Are you okay with that?"

"It's a small shadow. I now realize some darkness will always appear in my paintings, and that's fitting. Without shadow there is no perspective."

She laid her head on his shoulder. "You never answered my question. Are you ready to eat?"

"I can wait a little longer. While I clean my mess, why don't you open Harrison's package."

Kerry ripped open the box, shoved aside layers of bubble packing material, and pulled out a battered brown leather valise.

Bob recognized it instantly. Harrison's valise, the one he had dragged all over Vietnam, having found that a briefcase could not hold all of his writing paraphernalia. Bob imagined he could feel Harrison's presence, as if, once again, his friend had left the case in his safekeeping while he went in search of another beer.

It seemed impossible that Harrison was dead, that he himself was leading this chaotic life where he was both hunter and prey.

What about Hsiang-li? Had he at least found what he sought? Bob pictured Hsiang-li living peacefully amid the ruins of the ancient monastery, with ageless Buddhas and the spirits of his long-dead wife and son to keep him company. Bob clung to the image, hoping it was true. He could not bear to think of his mentor still wandering the jungle, alone and hopelessly lost.

Kerry snapped open the latches of the valise, withdrew a handful of papers, and looked through them.

"These are all transcripts of interviews with ex-soldiers concerning The Sweeper. They must be research for the book Harrison planned on writing about him, but it doesn't seem as if anyone knows much. One guy swears The Sweeper simply faded into the jungle one day and no one ever saw him again. An ex-corporal says he knows for a fact The Sweeper was a Russian spy who returned to Moscow after the war."

She set the papers aside and pulled a few more from the valise. "Here's an interview with someone named Todd who says he served with him. According to Todd, The Sweeper didn't fit in. He kept to himself, and he didn't smoke or drink or take drugs because those things dulled his senses, clouded his mind, distorted his perceptions, and interfered with his ability to blend into the jungle. Todd says they kept telling him that was the whole point, but the guy never listened to them."

She laughed. "Here's a note in what I assume is Harrison's handwriting. It says, 'Sounds like Todd used more than his share of the drugs. He can't remember what The Sweeper looked like, what his name was, where he came from. Quite a commentary on modern life, wouldn't you say? For months, Todd lived with a soldier with an incredible gift, yet all he can remember is the man was a loner who didn't take drugs. He couldn't even tell me if the man kept to himself by his own choice or because no one would have anything to do with him.' What do you think?"

It took Bob a moment to realize that Kerry directed the final question at him.

"Probably a bit of both," he said. "If in fact The Sweeper did have an unusual talent, he'd feel a need to nurture that talent, particularly since it would help him survive. He wouldn't be able to do that if he was just one of the boys. Nor would the boys want to have anything to do with him. Being different, truly different, is a failing few people can tolerate in others."

Kerry nodded. "I can see that." She held out a batch of papers. "Do you want to go through these?"

"Not now. I feel a headache coming on, but you might as well continue."

She sorted through the papers in silence for a few minutes, then let out an excited cry she quickly stifled.

"Here's Harrison's interview with Dr. Brewer." Her head bobbed as she turned the pages, then she tossed it on a stack of papers she'd already skimmed. "Nothing new. At least we know Brewer told us the same story he told Harrison."

Bob massaged his temples. "That means the doctor had plenty of time to get the story straight in his mind, not that he told us the truth."

Kerry continued to examine the contents of the valise. When she finished, she frowned at the piles of paper littering the floor.

"Most of the interviews are with people who rambled on without saying anything. I don't understand why Harrison insisted you have these papers. I thought they would be notes about the war, but most of this is research into the mind and memory, nothing so controversial that it needed to be locked in a safe."

"Harrison had brain cancer. Sometimes paranoia is a side effect."

"Even if someone gave the cancer to him?"

"*Especially* if someone gave it to him."

They sat on a braided rug in front of the fireplace and ate a picnic supper. A buried memory kept niggling at Bob as he listened to Kerry speculating about what it must have been like to be a war correspondent, and then all of a sudden he had it.

"The valise has a false bottom where Harrison kept extra cash and important papers. That's why he never left the case unattended."

Kerry jumped up. "A false bottom. Of course." She brought the valise to Bob and sat back down.

He pulled the tab that opened the hidden compartment and drew out a fat manila envelope with his name written on it in wobbly block letters. He handed it to Kerry.

"Are you sure? Don't you want to read it in private?"

He shook his head, ignoring the pain. A feeling of dread crept over him, and he didn't want to be alone when Harrison revealed the secret he had died protecting.

Kerry opened the envelope, removed the sheaf

of papers, and read aloud.

"'Dear Bob. There's something I haven't told you, something you need to know. A couple of months ago we met in O'Riley's for a farewell drink before I took off for New York. After you left, a man slipped into the seat you vacated. He introduced himself as Ed Keaton, then said Robert Stark walked pretty good for a gimp. As you can imagine, that caught my attention.

"'Keaton proceeded to tell me that you and he had both been supply clerks in Vietnam, and that one day, inexplicably, the two of you had been ordered to accompany a truck convoy. The entire story coincided with what you once told me. Until the punch line, that is. The Robert Stark he knew got a foot blown off and a medical discharge. You got your head jostled and a flight back to Vietnam.

"'I thought the coincidence remarkable and kept questioning Keaton. His story never wavered. He said he knew about the foot because he had found it. He had been in the rear of the convoy. Unscathed by the explosion, he went running to help. He stumbled over a boot with your foot still inside, then found you ten feet away from it.

"'He said he was hurt that you hadn't recognized him, but he admitted that, despite being stationed together, you two had never been buddies. He also said, somewhat sheepishly, that he'd changed a lot—lost his hair, gained weight, grown old. He recognized you immediately. Said you looked the same except that you were in much better condition than when you were in the army. He thought it incredible, considering your foot and all.

"'I couldn't get the bizarre coincidence of two Robert Starks with such similar histories out of my head. When I arrived in the states, I called a source in the Pentagon—a file clerk in the records department. I had him check the service records for both Robert Starks, but he could find only one—the one belonging to the Robert Stark with the missing foot.

"'My source told me a flag attached to the file demanded that ISI be notified immediately if anyone requested the records. He'd never heard of ISI, but he assumed it was one of the super-secret intelligence agencies, and he wanted nothing more to do with the file. He did say he had taken a quick look at it and saw nothing of note. Even the injury was not uncommon.

"'I tried to tell you this when I got back to Thailand, but I didn't know how, and then I had to leave on my book tour. After we said goodbye, I turned back, determined to tell you what I had discovered. Looking into your clear, calm eyes, however, I could not find it in me to mess with your serenity.

"'I've spent the entire plane trip working on this letter. Now, if something happens to me before I can find the proper time to tell you what I discovered, at least you will know what I know. The problem is, I don't know what it means. Maybe nothing. In that case, I can tear up this letter and we can have a good laugh.'"

The memory of Harrison was so strong, Bob could feel a disturbance in the air, as if the writer were actually in the room with him and Kerry. He remembered how agitated Harrison had been the last time they'd been together. He opened his mouth to tell his friend not to worry, that it was okay, then he snapped it shut. It was not okay. Harrison was dead, possibly because of him.

Kerry took a long drink of water. "Do you want me to keep going?"

Bob closed his eyes against a stab of pain.

Maybe it would be better not to know what the rest of the letter said. Finally, he opened his eyes and nodded for her to continue. If these were Harrison's last words, the least he could do was listen to them.

28.

Kerry hesitated a moment as if waiting for Bob to change his mind, then read aloud once more.

"'As you can see, I haven't torn up this letter. During the course of my research into The Sweeper, I found out that a doctor named Jeremy Rutledge might have treated him. I went to see Rutledge at the Rosewood Research Institute in Boston and, to my surprise, the doctor agreed to talk to me.

"'Forgive me if I ramble, but I'm having trouble concentrating. I woke with the flu this morning, and besides all the usual symptoms, including a splitting headache, I am so weak it feels as if my bones are dissolving. When I'm finished writing, I'll go to bed and stay there until I get better.

"'Although I have every intention of telling you this in person when I return to Bangkok, I still feel compelled to write it. If I don't get well, it's the only way you'll have of learning the truth, but of course I'll get well.

"'I'm rambling again, aren't I?'"

Kerry looked at Bob, her eyes reflecting the horror he felt. "My God, he's writing this while he's dying, isn't he?"

Bob put his arms around his middle and rocked himself, trying to still a sudden nausea. He felt as if he should be doing something to help his friend, but nothing he could do would change the fact that Harrison had already died.

Kerry began to read again. Her eyes were bright with unshed tears, and her voice shook.

"'Rutledge told me about a soldier who had been brought to his attention, one so mentally exhausted he was catatonic. Rutledge felt sure the soldier continuously relived a traumatic experience. The doctor decided to help the soldier by getting rid of the memory of that experience.

"'There is a chance the soldier would have recovered on his own, but Rutledge didn't want to wait. He had heard that the soldier had a tremendous gift, a supernatural ability to blend into his environment, rendering him practically invisible. Rutledge saw the soldier as his ticket to fame and fortune, but as long as the man remained non-responsive, the doctor could not study him.

"'To make a long story short, when Rutledge zapped the neurons to sever the soldier's connection with his terrible memories, the laser pulsed, destroying the links to his entire memory bank.'"

Kerry's voice still shook as she continued to read, but Bob could tell that anger had displaced the sorrow.

"'As often happens with amnesiacs, the soldier remembered how to speak and to read, but he could not access his past, his sense of self, everything that made him unique.

"'Rutledge found him as non-responsive with no memories as he had been with too many. To rectify the situation, the doctor decided to give him a new memory.

"'He searched the hospital for someone who looked like his patient and found a couple of men who were also average-looking with an average build. He chose a man from Denver, but he didn't mention if it was a coincidence, or if he wanted someone ISI could easily keep an eye on.

"'Did I tell you about ISI? I don't remember. They're a multi-national corporation based in Broomfield, Colorado that funded a private hospital in the

Philippines during the Vietnam War where all sorts of mind control experiments were done, and they fund Rutledge's research institute in Boston.

"'The doctor had the man from Denver transferred to the psychiatric ward and proceeded to borrow the man's memory.'" Kerry stopped and stared at Bob. "My God, he's talking about you, isn't he? You're the man from Denver. That must mean the other Robert Stark is The Sweeper."

Pain exploded behind Bob's eyes. He put his hands on his head to keep the top from blowing off.

Kerry gave him a concerned look. "Maybe you should go to bed. We can finish this another time."

"Keep reading," he said. The words came out sounding like a croak.

"Where was I?"

The rattling of the papers and the crackling of the fire hammered in Bob's ears, but her voice soothed him.

"'Under drug-induced hypnosis, the man poured out everything he could remember about his life, even the most trivial things, like the mole on his fourth grade teacher's chin. After weeks of such sessions, after hundreds of hours of recordings, Rutledge sent the ringer home, but kept the ringer's wallet containing all of his ID and a picture of his college girlfriend.'" Kerry stopped. "That's not right. You still have your wallet."

She looked at Bob as if waiting for an explanation, but he found no words.

"It happened a long time ago. Maybe Rutledge got confused," she said, then continued reading. "'The tapes were almost perfect for his project, but Rutledge felt the need to make a few minor changes. First, he erased all mention of the other man's missing foot. Then, to explain the massive scarring on his patient's chest, he turned an insignificant childhood hunting accident into a major event. Next, to take away any desire for his patient to return to his supposed home, he created a memory of the mother's death. He also forged a Dear John letter from the girlfriend and stuck it in the wallet.

"'He kept the man in a drug-induced hypnotic state for weeks, maybe months, playing those tapes over and over and over again while showing him pictures of Denver and snapshots of his new family. One of ISI's operatives had stolen the ringer's family album for this very purpose.

"'I keep calling the other man a ringer, but he wasn't really. The two men bore a superficial resemblance to each other. Plastic surgery enhanced the likeness.

"'When Rutledge felt certain his patient's new memories would hold, he woke him and told him he'd been unconscious for five days with a minor head trauma, though in reality he had been unconscious for many months.

"'And so a new Robert Stark was born.'"

Kerry put a hand to her mouth. "Oh, Bob. That's even worse than having your memory stolen. Do you remember any of it?"

"I remember I'm Robert Stark, I'm from Denver, and I have both my feet."

She paced the scuffed wooden floor. "How could they do something like that to you? How could they think they had the right?"

She stopped, bent down, and peered into his face. "You can't remember anything beyond Robert Stark?"

He gazed back at her. His legs were crossed, and his hands lay palms up on his thighs. He felt no trace of a headache.

She jerked herself erect. "How can you sit there like nothing happened?"

"Nothing has happened," he answered calmly. "I'm the same person I was a minute ago."

The floorboards squeaked as she resumed her pacing. "They stole your life from you."

"Perhaps they gave me life."

"What are you talking about?"

"Remember me telling you about the little girl who was catatonic because she couldn't face the memories of her abuse? Rutledge thought he could save her by removing those memories. Maybe he did for The Sweeper what he couldn't do for her."

Kerry's voice rose. "Are you defending him?"

He rubbed his chest and felt the scar tissue through the thin material of his shirt. "All I'm saying is that memories cause their own torment. The worst thing about a bad experience often is not the experience itself, but the endless loop of memories that come after."

"I feel like going to Boston and smashing that doctor's arrogant face, and you're talking philosophy?"

"Look at it this way. Many people spend their whole lives trying to deal with, and possibly eradicate the memories of their youth. I no longer have to be concerned with mine since they're false."

She stamped a foot. "Don't you dare try to make light of the situation. They stole your identity from you. You don't even know who you are."

"I'm the man who loves you and who is going to be with you always. That's who I am."

"But what if you were supposed to be a different person?"

"Then maybe I wouldn't have met you and, for me, that's unthinkable. Besides, you always become a different person when you choose to be with someone. My new life is what matters, not some mythical past." He paused. "Maybe I was someone I wouldn't like to know."

Her pacing slowed. "You make it all sound so normal."

"It is. Do any of us know who we are? Deep inside your bones and soul, do you know who you are?"

"It's not the same thing. I didn't have my past stolen from me. I know who my parents are, who my brothers are. I know my name." Her eyes widened. "Your family! How are we going to find your family without a name?"

"We're not. I've been dead to them for seventeen years, plenty of time for them to come to terms with my demise."

"But we have to look for them."

"Why? After the first excitement of finding out I'm alive, the truth—that the son they had known no longer exists—could bring them nothing but more grief."

"The military would still have your fingerprints on file, wouldn't they? We could find out who you are by contacting them."

"If the army discovered that I hadn't died in the war but am still alive, they would want to know why. The thought of being back in the army's clutches is every bit as repugnant as being under Rutledge's control."

She peered at him. "You can live without knowing what your name is?"

"Yes. We define our names. Our names don't define us."

She sat next to him. "We haven't finished the letter. Maybe Harrison found out who you are." She read aloud. "'I know I sound cold and distant as if I'm talking about a stranger and not you, Bob, but if I let my emotions get the better of me, I would never be able to continue writing, and you need to know the truth. Or maybe not. Did the truth ever set anyone free? At the very least, it comes with a price.

"'I seem to be rambling again.

"'Though I kept questioning the doctor, he couldn't, or wouldn't, reveal your true identity. He told me, quite condescendingly, that since you were officially dead, you no longer existed as a real person. You were merely his lab rat and, as such, merited no name.'"

Kerry let out a heavy sigh.

"Is it going to be a problem for you not knowing my birth name?" Bob asked.

She was silent for several seconds, then she smiled at him. "No. You're right. What's important is our life together. At least I won't have to worry about your parents liking me."

He returned her smile. "Now who's making light of the situation?"

"I guess it's no more bizarre than thinking you had another self running around or that your mother died twice."

He yawned. "Let's finish the letter and go to bed. I'm exhausted."

"All right. Harrison continues, 'Despite the memory transplant, as Rutledge called it, the new Robert Stark showed no signs of being a chameleon, but Rutledge was certain the ability would eventually resurface.

"'Around this time, the State Department asked ISI to lend them someone completely unknown to the intelligence community to help with a special project.

Rutledge volunteered the new Robert Stark. He thought such an assignment would be the perfect thing to help you regain your powers.

"'To the doctor's disappointment, it didn't happen. You still had the ability to blend, but it was more of a meek man's tendency to fade into the background than a true chameleon-like ability.

"'Rutledge hoped that one day you would become a chameleon again. To that end, he had someone from ISI keeping track of you all these years. He is no longer interested in waiting, however. He thinks he knows a way of inducing the return of your abilities so he can find out if your talent for near invisibility is physiological or if it's a form of mass hypnosis where you don't in fact disappear but somehow make people think you do. He went on at great length about how much you were going to contribute to the field of psychology. He wants to find out how the imposed memories shaped your life and personality. Have you, in truth, become Robert Stark or have you retained a vestige of the person you once were?

"'After a while, Rutledge's enthusiasm for his experiments, both past and future, made me sick, and I could not bear to spend even one more minute in his presence. Pleading illness—no lie. I really did feel sick—I staggered to my feet and somehow managed to drag myself out to my rental car.

"'Rutledge followed me, urging me to stay. He said he had an empty hospital bed I could use. I got the impression he wanted to physically detain me, but in the end, he stood and watched me leave.

"'I have a very bad feeling about all this. I'm sure it's a symptom of my flu, but I am consumed with a feeling of impending doom. For you? For me? For a world that harbors such men as the good Dr. Rutledge? I don't know.

"'If I were able to concentrate, maybe I could figure out what we could do, but I'm losing focus.

"'So very, very tired.

"'Have to finish this letter.

"'Put it away where they can't find it . . .

"'I nodded off for a minute there, but I'm trying to hold myself together long enough to finish this.

"'I honestly don't know what to say, Bob. That I'm sorry? That if I could undo what they did to you, even if it took everything I have, I would?

"'Words. Just words.

"'Keep in mind that however phony those other memories are, you have forged new memories, ones that are true.

"'Hsiang-li loves you like a father.

"'I love you like a brother.

"'We are your real family, as you are ours.'"

Tears were trickling down Kerry's cheeks when she set the letter aside. "It must have pained him deeply to find out what Rutledge did to you."

Bob took her in his arms and kissed the tears away. He understood her grief and Harrison's, but felt only silence within himself.

"Where are we going?" Kerry asked the next morning as they got dressed to leave.

"Chalcedony."

"So that's it? Rutledge and the people at ISI are going to get away with what they did to you and Harrison and all those others?"

"I might not be emotional about what they did, but I never said I wouldn't do something about it." He flexed his fingers and a feeling he couldn't identify stirred deep within him.

"Then why are we going to Chalcedony?"

"I'm going to drop you off, make sure you're safe, then I have some things I need to do."

"You don't have to go all the way to Chalcedony. I can call one of my brothers to come pick me up." An uncertain look crossed her face. "What about Sam and Ted? Won't they be able to track me there?"

Bob's jaw tightened. "They won't bother you. I promise."

She took off the money-belt encircling her waist. "You should probably have this."

"You keep it." He handed her two envelopes. "You'll need these also. One is a letter to Harrison's lawyer naming you beneficiary in my will, and the other is a letter to my bank in Thailand giving you access to my account. If anything goes wrong, I need to know you're taken care of."

"I'd rather have you."

"I know. I'll do everything in my power to come back to you."

She hugged him tightly. "I'll be waiting."

Epilogue

Alex Evans surveyed his surroundings with deep satisfaction.

The day was perfect, as only an October day in Colorado could be. Newly fallen snow powdered the mountains, but not a single flake had visited the lower elevations. The skies were clear, and the sun shone brightly on the beautiful people gathered on the broad lawn.

Evans breathed deeply, savoring the bouquet of expensive perfumes and after-shaves wafting toward him on a cool breeze. He smiled to himself. Everything he had ever dreamed of lay within his grasp.

He had a lovely home set on five lushly land-scaped acres halfway between Broomfield and Boulder.

His children had been a disappointment, but they were grown now, with families of their own. He smiled fondly at the thought of his grandchildren. De-lightful tots, all of them.

Catching sight of his still stunningly beautiful wife, he congratulated himself for having won her even though, back then, he'd been able to offer nothing but an overweening ambition. She had been the perfect helpmate, never complaining about his long days at the office or his frequent business trips. Ever the diplomat, she had made friends with the husbands of important women as easily as she had made friends with the wives of important men.

This party celebrated her triumph as well as his.

He looked around, pleased to see the governor standing at the buffet table talking to a state senator and a United States congresswoman. At the bar, some of Denver's old money socialites condescended to drink with a group of recently rich.

This is merely the beginning, Evans gloated.

Berquist's prostate cancer, which had been so slow-growing it had been practically benign, had suddenly taken on a life of its own, courtesy of Dr. Reed. In a very few days Berquist would be dead.

Evans grinned. As new Director of Research and Development, he would be a very powerful man. And rich.

His grin spread as he thought of all the money he had tucked away in a bank in the Cayman Islands. He also knew Berquist's Cayman account number. He should; he set it up. As soon as his boss died, he would be doubly rich.

Blood rushed to his head as he thought of the single thorn marring the perfection of his rosy future.

It seemed inconceivable he was being bested by that lab rat, that skinny nothing, that freak with the secondhand memory.

Until Stark had come to Denver, Ted Kowalski had been the man Evans most relied on to get things done, the man he had chosen to take over his job when he took over Berquist's. Ted had been a natural born leader, whose charm and utter ruthlessness had given him an aura of great power. Then Ted had started acting like a raving lunatic, spewing hatred and vowing vengeance.

Ted's partner, Sam Jacobson had once been the voice of reason, keeping the more volatile Ted in check; then Sam too had gone off the deep end.

Evans banged his fists against his thighs. *Damn that Stark!*

It should have been a simple, mindless courier task.

When he had received word from the computer department that the target was on the move, on his way to Denver, no less, he had sent Ted and Sam to the airport to pick up Stark and escort him to Boston where an eager Dr. Rutledge waited. They were also to have relieved Stark of William Harrison's papers, which were still unaccounted for.

Normally, he would not have sent Ted and Sam on such a trivial assignment, but he had chosen his best men so nothing would go wrong.

That was ten weeks ago.

Stark was still at large.

And Ted and Sam were dead.

Somehow, someone had managed to snap both Ted's and Sam's necks in sight of hundreds of ISI's employees, on ISI's own grounds.

Not one person had seen it happen. Unless, of course, you counted the two obviously demented individuals who had insisted a bush reached out and killed them. According to both witnesses, the bush had first killed Sam while Ted, sitting next to him, had obliviously munched a sandwich. Then the bush had killed Ted. All in a matter of seconds.

Evans made a mental note to send both witnesses to Boston for an attitude adjustment. He blew out a breath when he remembered Rutledge was also dead. The doctor had been found in his backyard with a broken neck. No witnesses.

Dr. Reed and a voluptuous young lab assistant had been found dead in a sleezy motel room, still entwined in a macabre parody of the sex act. Both their necks had been broken, too.

Evans gritted his teeth. All three deserved it. If he hadn't needed them, he would have killed them himself when he found out about William Harrison's death.

Why hadn't they followed the plan? It had been

foolproof. His operatives in New York had been waiting for the right moment to give Harrison the cancer. Later, posing as emergency medical technicians, they would have taken him to Boston for "treatment."

Instead, when Harrison had visited the Rosewood Research Institute, those idiots had taken it upon themselves to do the job. The lab assistant had shot Harrison with the bio-innoculator, while Reed had readied his lab for his guinea pig. It had been Rutledge's job to keep Harrison occupied until the super-fast-acting cancer could render him helpless.

A pained expression tightened Evans's face. Rutledge had not bothered with such benign topics as weather and sports. Oh, no. He had entertained Harrison with stories of his own exploits. Even worse, the doctor had let him walk away, giving Harrison plenty of time to commit the confession to paper before he died.

When Harrison landed in a New York hospital, Reed had finally told Evans what they had done and demanded that Evans retrieve his guinea pig. They had tried, but Evans's men had been unable to wrest Harrison from the hospital.

A genteel burst of laughter by the buffet table reminded Evans he was neglecting his guests.

Looking around, he noticed his wife Lucille coming toward him with a young man in tow. Lucy chattered animatedly, a look of fatuous adoration on her face. The young man stared at Evans.

Evans winced in distaste.

Lucy had recently decided she had the soul of an artist. Instead of taking up painting, however, she had taken up painters. A steady stream of impoverished and sexually ambiguous young men, such as this one, had been parading through the house for weeks now, delighting Lucy, but making him uneasy.

He felt proud he kept in such good shape for a man of fifty. He had a small roll of fat around his middle no amount of exercise could melt, but otherwise he was as lean and trim as he had always been. He even liked the sprinkling of silver in his full head of thick brown hair and the faint crinkling around his gray eyes, thinking they made him look distinguished.

What he did not like was the way some of Lucy's young men ogled him with unconcealed desire.

As Evans watched Lucy and her new protégé approach, he noticed no lust or even admiration in the young man's gaze. Just a bland, almost cold regard.

Though unimposing, the young man moved with the suppressed power and fluid grace of a panther padding silently through the jungle. He had none of the languid affectations that usually characterized Lucy's artist friends, but carried himself with the easy manner of a man at peace with himself and in tune with his environment.

"This is Mr. Noone," Lucy announced. "He says he's been looking for you. He knows you."

Evans studied Noone. The man did look familiar, but he could not place him.

Lucy giggled, sounding like a lovesick adolescent. "He says his name is pronounced like noon but is spelled with an *e* like no one."

"Mrs. Evans!" One of the caterer's assistants hurried toward them. "Mrs. Evans," he called out again.

Lucy sighed. "Excuse me, Mr. Noone. I must go see what he wants. Promise me you won't leave without saying goodbye?"

Noone held out a hand. When Lucy placed her fingers on his, he lifted her hand and kissed it lightly.

"Oh, puh-leese," Evans said, rolling his eyes. He couldn't believe Lucy actually had fallen for the man's phony act.

After one last lingering look into Noone's eyes, Lucy left to deal with the latest catering catastrophe.

"She's a lovely lady," Noone said.

"You keep your mitts off her." Evans glared at him. "What do you want? Come on, come on. I don't have all day."

"I've come for that golf game you always wanted."

"What golf game? As you can see, I'm busy right now."

"We're a long way from Thailand, but I hear Denver has some nice golf courses, too."

"I have no idea what you're talking about," Evans snapped. "Who the hell are you anyway?"

Noone gazed steadily at him. "That is the question, isn't it? Who the hell am I anyway?"

Evans frowned at Noone for a moment, then his face lit with a triumphant smile. Robert Stark! The very man he wanted to see.

He cocked his head to study his elusive prey.

No wonder he hadn't recognized him. This confident, sleekly muscled, youthful man with the burnished copper highlights in his brown hair and the flash of amber in his brown eyes bore little resemblance to the humble, middle-aged man he had known in Bangkok.

"I can see why some of my men think you're a chameleon," Evans said.

"You don't agree?"

Evans hooted derisively. "You're kidding, right? Despite what that idiot Rutledge claimed, there is no such thing as a human chameleon. I admit, when you lived in Thailand you did look Asian, but that doesn't mean you're a chameleon. There are such things as hair dyes and dark contact lenses and makeup, though why you'd go through all that trouble to look like a slant-eye is beyond me."

When Bob remained silent, Evans added, "It was probably a pathetic attempt to fit in, but someone like you will never fit in anywhere."

"Someone like me?" Bob questioned, sounding more amused than affronted.

"A loser."

Bob's smile sent chills up Evans's spine. He shifted his feet, reassured by the feel of the pistol nestled in his ankle holster.

"A loser," he repeated. "The problem is you have no ambition, no goals. You're content to drift through life doing as little as possible."

"You think I should be more like you and Dr. Rutledge?"

"At least we have goals. We're making something of our lives. Doing something worthwhile."

"Like using mind control to turn people with personality quirks into ideal employees?"

"It's for the greater good. But that's not all we do."

"You also commit murder. Why did you have to kill Harrison? He didn't pose any threat to you."

Evans shrugged. "He got too close to the truth. It's a shame. I liked the guy."

"What about Doug Roybal?"

"My, my. You have been busy, haven't you? Little Dougie poked around in things that were none of his business, just like your friend Harrison."

"And Dr. Albion?"

"Who's Dr. Albion?"

"The doctor at the VA hospital who requested Stark's service record."

"Oh, him. We couldn't have him putting two and two together, now, could we?" Evans stared at Bob through slitted eyes. "I thought we were friends—I sure wasted enough time on you—yet you didn't call when you returned to Denver after The Lotus Room closed. And how did you find me? I never told you my real name, and the phone number on the business cards I gave you was for an answering service that cannot be connected to me in any way."

"I saw you at ISI and followed you home. Since the letters in your mailbox were addressed to Mr. and Mrs. Alexander Evans, it wasn't too hard to figure out who you are."

"What were you doing at ISI?"

Evans bent over to tie a shoelace that didn't need tying. When he stood, gun in hand, he saw Lucy, accompanied by the senator's wife, headed his way. But he didn't see Bob.

"Where's that nice young man?" Lucy asked. "Janet wants to meet him." Her eyes widened. "Alex! What are you doing with that gun? Put it away before someone sees it."

Evans spoke through clenched teeth. "Shut up, Lucy. Shut up. There's an emergency. Go to the front gate, find Grimes and Clayton and whoever else is around, and tell them to get their asses over here immediately."

"But—"

"Now!" Evans barked. "Do it now."

Lucy trotted off, trailed by Janet. Evans edged around a lilac bush that had yet to lose its leaves. Since it was the one large plant in the vicinity, he was certain that's where he would find Stark.

Chameleon, my ass. He had recognized the man's clothes—the brown pants and the mottled green, gold, and brown sweater—for makeshift camouflage.

If the man wanted to play games, that was okay with him. He had the home-court advantage, and back-up was on the way. Stark or Noone or whatever he called himself would not escape this time.

He rounded the bush with his arms outstretched, pointing his pistol.

"Freeze, asshole!"

Even as he screamed the words, he realized he had made the unforgivable, fatal mistake of under-estimating his opponent. Then the bush's cold steely fingers tightened around his neck.

By the time his men arrived on the scene, Alex Evans was dead. They found no trace of the perpetrator.